ROLL
WITH IT
A CRIME NOVEL

AND MODERN WESTERN

ALSO BY JAY STRINGER

The Eoin Miller Trilogy

Old Gold

Runaway Town

Lost City

The Sam Ireland Mysteries

Ways to Die in Glasgow

How to Kill Friend and Implicate People

The Marah Chase Adventures

World War Zero

The End of Eden

A SWAG TALES PAPERBACK

First published in the United Kingdom and United States in 2022.

This edition published by Swag Tales, Glasgow, G40 4TR.

Cover design by Jay Stringer.
Book formatted in Affinity Publisher.

Standard Paperback Edition ISBN: 9781916892354
Ebook Edition ISBN: 9781916892330

ROLL WITH IT
A CRIME NOVEL

AND MODERN WESTERN

JAY STRINGER

For Lis.

ONE

"You really think you can get me all the way there by yourself?" Ben Nichol paused. "I mean, no offence, but..."

Chloe Medina didn't smile. Didn't take her eyes off the road. "You keep talking, I'll get you all the way there in the trunk."

One hand steady on the wheel of the Shelby, the other near the gun strapped to her thigh. The line about the trunk was mostly a bluff, but it sounded good. Medina had two shotguns, three suitcases and two Kevlar vests stowed back there. A box full of batons, handcuffs and stun-guns. Not room enough for a wanted felon.

Right now, she had two problems.

The same set of headlights had been in the mirror for five minutes. A black van. Outlines of two people visible through the windscreen. Only two vehicles on this stretch of road at night, both heading towards the border. Most likely it was nothing. But the driver was hanging back, keeping a steady distance.

Nichol was twitchy. The tightening of his shoulders and neck. Tattoos moved as he coiled. Even with his hands cuffed to the door handle, Medina could read the signs. He was gearing up for a second go.

He'd reacted the same way when she first caught up with him, sitting at the bar of Eddie's Safari. A roadside joint on 602, just off Bronco Road and before the Zuni reservation. The place served burgers, burritos and frybread, while women danced around a pole on a stage decked out in a faded jungle theme. Nichol seemed to sense Medina was there for him the minute she walked in, and his body had tensed up right before he bolted into the men's room. Medina followed him, and they fought a bit. Her shoulder smashed into the mirror. It still stung like hell, but he'd never know. Nichol's face flushed bright red as she led him out of the place in cuffs.

An ego like that could be dangerous. He'd want to go again, make himself feel less of a wimp.

Medina watched the lights. The quickest way back to Phoenix was to stay on the 53, straight through the Zuni reservation to the Arizona border. Problem was, she hadn't applied for permission to track a fugitive onto tribal land. Even though she'd caught him before crossing the border, technicalities like that didn't go down so well with the Rez cops.

They passed a dirt road on the left. A small gateway with a cattle guard, and nothing but the evening darkness beyond.

The van took the turn.

That left only one problem.

"You don't remember me, do you?" Medina said. "We've met before."

"If I'd met you, I'd remember. Hey, these cuffs are real tight."

"Deal with it. The trial for your brother's gang. What was left of them."

"The bank job?" Nichol grunted. In her peripheral, Medina could see him reappraising her. "That was so dumb. Those masks, firing guns into the air. They'd seen it in a movie the night before, eating edibles like candy. I'd said to Jimmy, don't do banks like that, you'll get hurt. Truth be told, I'd said don't do banks at all. There's no money in it. Not these days. But he never listened. Comes running out and, right there in the street, there's this U.S. Marshal. Blonde. Total coincidence. Just having a coffee. Jimmy comes out, and she's standing there in the road, all on her own, and..." Nichol grunted a second time. "Shit. You look different."

"I used to dye it. And it was ice cream, not coffee. Still had it in my hand when I walked across the street, told them to freeze. I warned your brother to stop, right there."

"They said at the trial."

"Three times." More like two and a half, Medina thought. "I told all of them. Put your weapons down, drop the bags, in that order. Then put your hands over your heads where I can see them. Your brother started to raise his gun. Semi-auto, I already had reason enough to shoot, but I gave him two more warnings."

"See what I mean?" Nichol said. "Told you he never listened."

"I wanted it to go another way. But he was going to shoot."

"Don't worry about it. He was an asshole."

"When the ambulance arrived, the cops, I walked back across the street, bought another ice cream. That's the one I'm holding in the news pictures. The TV crew got a kick out of that, tried to make out like it was the same one I'd had to start, shot three guys without dropping it."

"Was the other thing true, the bit you said to the reporters?"

"They asked me why I'd joined the Marshal Service. I said I liked catching the bad guys."

"That was a good line."

"I mention this, your brother, because there were three of them, and one of me. I put all three down before they fired their weapons. And I figure whatever you're planning in the next ten seconds doesn't beat that math."

Nichol laughed. Caught out. His muscles started to relax. He eased off slowly, his pride still in control.

"I like you," he said. Trying to make it sound like his choice to stay in custody. "So how long you been tailing me?"

"Since you ran."

"*I* mention this, because, maybe you don't know why I ran."

Medina looked over at him now. The threat had passed. He was going for the laid-back charm that probably worked more often than not. His smile. The shock of Jack Nicholson crazy hair.

"You ran. I caught you. That's all I need to know."

Nichol leaned forward to rub his bruised jaw. Medina was glad the fight had gone out of him. She didn't think her shoulder was up to much. She was good at playing tough, but it took a lot out of her.

"I'm just saying, if you knew the reason, we could maybe cut a deal."

"I meant what I said about riding in the trunk. You start telling me how none of this is your fault, I'll pull over and change the seating situation."

They drove in silence for a couple more miles.

Nichol said, "If you like catching bad guys so much, why'd you leave the Marshals?"

"Better pay."

Medina heard the van before she saw it. The roar of an engine. No lights. Tyres crossing a cattle guard. The large black shape moved at them from the left. The impact spun the Shelby, taking them off the road.

TWO

A second later and the van would have hit the door next to Medina. As it was, the hood took the impact.

Nichol grunted.

His head hit the window, then he shouted: "Fuck."

Medina gripped the wheel with both hands, trying to bring the Shelby back under control as they spun. She bounced against the seatbelt, catching her sore shoulder. The van continued to push them across into the dirt, towards a ditch. The driver revving the engine over the sound of bending metal.

The tires skidded, searching for purchase. The axel hadn't broken. Medina gunned the engine, and the roar said the car was still with her. She dropped into reverse and accelerated before pulling hard on the wheel, taking them into a sharp spin. They were back up on the road now, but facing the wrong way.

Medina watched the van in the mirror, glowing red in her taillights as it blocked the way to Arizona. There was a white stripe down the side. It looked like something out of the A-Team.

Medina revved the engine but didn't move.

"Friends of yours?"

"No way." Nichol made a point of trying to turn in his seat to look behind them. He could see in the mirror easy enough. He pulled on the cuffs. They rattled against the handle. "What now?"

"I want to get a look at them. If you recognise them, maybe I can scare them off. If they're locals, they'll get more protection from the Rez cops than we will. And if they're bounty hunters, well, they're not looking to leave any evidence behind."

"Which option we want?"

"They're all bad. I want to know what kind of bad."

The trick with the side road suggested they were local. They knew the area well enough to have outflanked her in the dark. Outrunning them wouldn't be a problem in a flat race.

As long as the Shelby could move, it could go faster than the van. But Medina didn't want to head back deeper onto the reservation. There would be a turn a couple miles ahead, leading off tribal land, but it would take them north to Gallup. That would be a frying pan, fire situation.

There was movement through the van's passenger side window. The engine turned over and the high beams came on, lighting up the bushes at the side of the road. They sat there, watching. Waiting for Medina to make the first move.

Fine by her.

Medina popped the trunk and unfastened her seatbelt. She could hear Nichol shouting after her as she slammed the door. She walked the length of the Shelby to the trunk, never taking her eyes off the shadows in the van. Medina glanced at the trunk. It had opened a couple inches. She had some serious firepower in there, but didn't want to reach for it yet.

She smiled, just a little. Enough to let whoever was watching see she wasn't worried, then she stepped past the end of the car, out into the open. Her right hand hovering near the holstered gun.

The van rocked slightly, then the large door on the side slid back, taking the A-Team stripe with it.

A teenager stepped out. She looked Zuni, with a buzz cut, wearing what looked like a band t-shirt. She held a shotgun pointed straight at Medina, but the end shook a little. The front passenger door opened, and a kid with paler skin, curly auburn hair and a bad attitude slid down. As he took a couple steps forward, he brought with him the smell of weed and cheap beer. He raised a small revolver. Medina was willing to bet he'd never fired it. Probably stolen off a family member, from a drawer or forgotten shelf.

"What do you guys want?" she said, calm and slow.

The Zuni kid started to speak, but the redhead wanted to take charge. "You on our land."

"Guess I missed the sign with your name on it, in all the dark."

"Gotta pay a tax," redhead said. He took a step forward. "We'll take a look through that car, see what we like."

Medina didn't move. "That easy?"

"That easy."

Medina looked at the girl.

The shotgun still wobbled.

Her eyes gave her away. She wasn't as committed to this whole idea as her wannabe-gangster friend. Had they tried this before? Or maybe talked about it, idly, but now only trying it out for the first time.

"What, you saw me leaving the diner?"

Redhead nodded. "Watched you come out of Eddie's. That guy you got there in handcuffs."

"And that wasn't the first sign to you that maybe this was something you didn't want part of? You know who I've got back there? He's wanted in seven states for murder, and two for terrorism. I'm bringing him in on my own, and you think I'm going to stop because two kids got drunk and stupid?"

Medina's shoulder ached, just to remind her it was there.

"We're not stupid," the redhead said.

The defensive tone creeping into his voice.

Medina switched her attention to the girl. "I'm guessing you're the one who's going to be smart here."

The girl faltered. The gun lowered a few inches as she glanced across at her partner. Medina took the chance to draw, putting the redhead in her sights. He coughed and followed it with the high-pitched laugh of a mellow high.

"Shit, that was fast."

"Wait till you see how fast a bullet moves," Medina said. She kept the gun on the redhead but looked back at the girl. "Or are you going to do the other thing?"

The girl nodded and pointed the shotgun down at the ground. The nerve went out of both of them after that. Medina kept her own weapon raised as they backed up to the van. She nodded for them to get inside, then lowered her gun as they drove past, back towards Black Rock.

Medina pushed the trunk closed and went back round to the driver's side. She slid down into the seat in silence, watching the taillights disappear. Beside her, Nichol was eased back in his seat, looking comfortable.

"Murder? Terrorism?"

Medina smiled as she keyed the ignition.

"It worked, didn't it?"

THREE

Nichol broke the silence. "How old you think they were?"

South of Flagstaff. Tall pines just visible on both sides of the road, no other headlights in sight. Medina took a second to check both mirrors again, making sure they were alone before she gave Nichol some of her attention.

"The kids back there?"

"Yeah"

"The girl, I think maybe sixteen. Fifteen. She had a bit more to her, seemed older, but girls grow up faster. The redhead? Maybe fifteen. Or seventeen-going-on-fifteen. Not old enough to do anything. Couldn't see from where you were, doesn't even shave yet. Peach fuzz on his chin."

Nichol grunted an agreement. "Kids, yeah. So you wouldn't've shot them. If they hadn't backed down, I mean."

Medina didn't let any doubt into her voice. Clear and straight. "Old enough to point a gun at me, old enough to get shot."

"You wouldn't, come on. What would you have done?"

"This is you, the guy handcuffed to a car after jumping bail, trying to take the moral high ground?"

"I just pass off fake currency, that's all. And most people do that, they don't even know it. I do it, it's a crime. But I never shot anybody. Have you? Wait, I already know. You drew pretty fast. Was it like that with my brother?"

"Told you, I warned him. Those kids just had more brains, that's all."

"That the only time you've shot someone? Pulling on my brother's crew?"

Medina didn't answer. She let the silence sit there, no interest in giving her life story. She looked out at the hood, the crumpled driver's side. The car was running fine, but the damage itched at her.

The Shelby was important. Tied to a moment in her past. She'd get it fixed once she'd dropped Nichol off.

After another twenty miles, Medina said, "How's your head? You hit it when we crashed."

"Yeah, well I'd rub it and see if you didn't have me cuffed. Jaw hurts, too, where you hit me. Hey, that's going to be a problem, right? I heard the jail won't take us anymore if you hand us over with marks. Bruises, cuts."

"That what people are saying?"

"Yeah, hear it like they're worried we'll sue, say the injuries were caused in their custody, a guard or an accident, like we walked into a door, and sue the state."

Medina smiled. She nodded slow a couple times. Let him think she was agreeing.

"You think it would be that easy? Every fugitive in the state just starts hitting themselves in the head, get a good bruise going, and then none of us will take you in? When we get there, they'll take pictures, any injuries you have when I hand you over, they'll be on me. "

"So how bout I sue you? Get this head checked, maybe say it's concussion. Could be from your punch, could be from the van, who's to say? And I was in your charge when the van hit, so..."

"Remember that form you signed when Don fixed your bail?"

"Like buying a house."

"Yeah, and waiving a whole bunch of rights. Anything I've done to bring you in, you gave me permission when you signed that form." Medina paused, let that settle in. She had something else eating at her. "How'd you know I was there for you? Back at the bar? You made me the minute I walked in, but you didn't remember who I was."

Nichol shrugged. Or tried to, as much as he could move, with the cuffs. "I don't know. Maybe I did? Remember, I mean. Maybe it was down there, somewhere, and I just didn't know it. But there's this other thing. Like a sense? Always had it, like Spider-Man. Tells me when to run, when to hide."

"Doesn't tell you anything about a van coming to hit you in the dark."

"No."

"Didn't stop you getting arrested."

"Yeah. I guess it's not really fine-tuned."

"So you got lucky, is what we're saying. You got lucky when I walked in."

Nichol rattled the chain against the handle. "I wouldn't say lucky."

"Why'd you pick that place? Figure nobody would come look for you that close to the reservation?"

Nichol's voice was tired. He didn't want to talk anymore. "I like the burgers."

An hour later they pulled up outside the Fourth Avenue jail in Phoenix. Medina could have pulled in one block over, on Third, and taken Nichol in the back way. Even at this late hour, there would be a full complement of staff in there. But Medina liked to do it the old way. Have a little fun. March the bad guy in through the front door. The second time she'd made the news, after the shooting at the bank, had been when she was filmed walking a drug lord in through the front. She still had the picture from the story at home, looking cool behind sunglasses, leading him in by the arm.

Nichol was processed in under thirty minutes. Pictures taken of the bruising to his temple and chin. Signatures from both Nichol and Medina confirming the injuries had happened before he got to the jail. Medina signed to confirm she'd returned him on behalf of the bail agent, Don Price. Don would get the notification when he woke up, start the payment process. She'd be making her mortgage payment by the end of the week. She never had any problems with Don.

The guy on the desk used the same joke as the last time. "This is the third one you've bought back in less than a month. I bet Superman wears Chloe Medina underwear."

Medina smiled and walked out in the dry heat of the early morning. This time of day was always good for perspective. Standing in a city in the middle of a desert. The sidewalk cracked like a cooling oven, and the air carried sounds and smells that reminded her of the vast emptiness that lay a few miles in each direction.

Deputy U.S. Marshal Treat Tyler was kneeling beside the Shelby. He held a coffee in one hand. The other was running across the damage to the side of the car. He straightened up when he saw Medina, and the pants of his suit dropped smoothly back into place, no creases. Tyler always liked to look good. Expensive clothes. Hair combed just right, to look slightly ruffled. The exact amount of stubble to suggest he had a slight edge. Tyler was never a man in a hurry, and Medina knew that counted double in front of the mirror.

They'd worked together when Medina was still in the Marshals Service. Each of them nursing an unspoken competitive grudge against the other.

He gave her his laid back smile. "Good to see you're still catching the bad guys."

"Good to see you're still a bad guy."

"Picking up, or dropping off?"

"Ben Nicol."

"Good catch."

"You?"

Tyler bobbed his head, something like a shrug. "Waiting for a source to get off shift." He looked down at the car again. "Who did this?"

"Couple of kids. On Zuni land."

"Deal with them?"

"They were kids, Treat. I'm not shooting kids."

FOUR

"Those moving walkways at airports?" Tyler sipped at his fresh mug of coffee. "Why do people get on them and stop, like it's a ride? This coffee is good."

"Yeah." Medina nodded. "Maybe they're disabled."

The Welcome Diner was set to close at 2 A.M. But they could always be talked into bending the rules if someone put money into the register. Especially if the money came with a badge. Tyler enjoyed flashing his around.

Medina liked to stop here after a drop-off. It had become a ritual. The transition point between the hard face she put on at work, and the person she was at home. A way to keep them separate.

She looked out at the parking lot in front. The Shelby parked on the opposite side to Tyler's pristine Charger. It gleamed under the streetlamp. Medina knew Tyler was waiting to get in another shot about getting the Shelby banged up.

He was biding his time, focusing on his favourite subject. Himself.

"Sure, okay," he continued. "But we both know I'm not talking about them. I mean the fat guy who gets off the plane ahead of you, walks slow, then stops the minute he gets on that thing. Like he's at Disney. I expect him to get out a guidebook, look at the sights on the way past."

"There's a lot to take in."

"The whole point is to go faster. I've been on a plane for six hours, I want to get the hell out of the airport. Don't they want to do that? They want to be in this new place so bad they flew through the air to get there, but then they want to stop and take a break before getting on with their business?"

"You've thought a lot about this."

Medina finished her slice of pie. She looked over at the counter, thinking about a second one.

It had been a long time since she'd eaten, but a further slice would keep her from home that little bit longer.

Tyler held up his mug for a refill "Well I have plenty of time, stuck behind them and their seven bags."

"You don't need to use it. You could go round, walk the normal way."

"But the whole point is to get out of there fast."

Medina asked for the second slice, then turned back to Tyler. "You pull into a gas station to cut a corner, too."

"Every time. The light goes red, I want to turn right, and there's a gas station? I'm cutting through."

"Only on red?"

"Well," Tyler smiled. "If there's cars ahead, too."

"What's the over-under? How many cars in front, for you to take the turn?"

"Two, maybe? Definitely at four, no way I'm waiting. So two or three. Come on, don't give me that look, you do it too."

The fresh plate was set down in front of Medina.

Tyler put a hand out before the waitress could turn away. She was tired, but polite. "What other food you got on?"

"Kitchen's closed, but I could probably fix you something?"

"No, that's okay. I like the look of the pie there, you got more of that? Maybe some ice cream on the side?"

As the waitress walked away, Tyler pulled out a hip-flask and topped up his coffee with amber liquid. He offered it to Medina, though he knew she didn't drink.

Medina shook her head. "I've done it," she said. "My dad does it all the time. Growing up, if I was in the car, he'd do this thing, pretend we were pulling in for gas. Saying, 'I'm just gonna pull in here and let's see where...' Then he's like, 'Oh wait, I don't need gas. My bad.' Pulls off into the next street. Like it was the first time he'd ever done it."

"How's he doing? Still teaching?"

"Part-time. He wants more time at home to write his book."

"And your mom?"

"Arizona went blue, and she went down to Florida. Enjoys fooling around with the pool boys and wrestlers."

"Bet your old man pretends he's going to buy food if he wants to use the men's room at a place, right? Walks around a bit, look at sandwiches or the coffee, then walk right into the men's room?"

"Oh yeah, we all do that."

"Don't do any of that. Know what I do?"

"You don't."

"I do." Tyler slipped out his wallet, flashed his shield. "Tell 'em 'marshal's business'. Then I go do my business."

"Why don't you do that on those moving walkways?"

"Look, I'm saying, it does cross my mind that I'm armed."

"What kind of marshal's business could you have in the men's room?"

Tyler leaned back, looked out at the cars. "Maybe a fugitive has run back there. Or there's some stolen property under the sink, I don't know."

"My guy tonight, Nichol? He ran into the men's room."

"What did you do?"

Medina shrugged. Took the coffee away from her mouth, where she'd been about to sip. "Followed him in. Cuffed him, led him out."

"Nice." Tyler's smile was easy, slow. "Course, that means you let him get away in the first place. Losing your touch, Chloe."

Medina let that go. She'd seen it coming. Every conversation with Tyler was a competition. He always needed to show he was best. They'd played the same game over and over when she was a marshal. They had the same fugitive recovery rates, the same test scores at Glynco. On the shooting range, they were evenly matched at both single shots and moving targets.

"Got this app." Tyler laid his cell on the table, tapped the screen. "Shot timer, measures how fast I can draw."

Medina caught a hint of movement in the darkness of the parking lot. She turned to look, but couldn't make anything out. Maybe a passing car, or someone walking by.

Tyler was still going. "You and me could finally have a go. Just dry fire. Maybe you've slowed down a bit. I hear that happens, after people get shot. The muscles don't heal up right. It's like a runner coming back from an injury, you lose a few seconds."

Medina touched her side. Two shots, near the end of her time in the Marshal Service. Tyler had been the one to put the fugitive down after that, while Medina was in an ambulance. He never let her forget.

"I haven't lost anything," she said.

Straight away, Medina knew she'd let herself get sucked into his game. Tyler managing to find the raw nerve.

"That wasn't the Glock on your hip."

Medina had noticed him eying the weapon as she'd taken it off, locking it in the glove compartment of the Shelby.

"Kimber 1911. Less recoil."

He nodded, appreciating the choice. "Sure. I like it. But with the Glock, you're always ready to shoot, anytime."

Medina said, "I'm always ready." Her voice calm. Letting him know she meant it.

But she couldn't help think. She *had* felt slow when she drew on the kids. Along with Nichol making her so fast at the strip joint. She'd been getting good at talking her way out of trouble lately, but was it just cover, compensating for that lost edge?

No. Change the subject. "Why are you working this late?"

Tyler's mouth twitched. It was his tell. Medina had found a nerve for herself. Evening the score.

"Working a parole jump."

"Reed's got you working a parole? What did you do to get on his shit list?"

Tyler ignored the question. "Just some nobody. Out early after serving a couple years. Get this, she went away for ten. Bank robbery. Cut some deal so they let her out after two. Only had a few rules to follow, but breaks them straight away."

"Got a name?"

"There's nothing in it for you, so don't even."

Medina's turn to smile. "You're worried I might get her first."

"Never gonna happen. The best bit? She's a comedian. I'm being sent after a stand-up comedian. Feel like I'm the set-up for a joke every time I talk about it. Dancer, too. Double whammy. I let her get away, I'll never hear the end of it."

"Emily Scott?"

"You know her?"

Medina gave her best poker face. "I know the case. There aren't that many stand-ups who also strip and rob banks."

"I bet I could do it," Tyler said. "Stand-up, not stripping."

Medina was willing to bet he couldn't, and counted down the seconds before he mentioned Bill Hicks or George Carlin.

"Like Hicks, you know? Tell it like it is." Tyler checked his phone. "My guy will be finishing now, gotta go."

Tyler made the token gesture of reaching for his wallet. Medina leaned back and smiled. "Marshal Service can get this."

Tyler cracked a grin and continued on for his wallet. He touched a finger to his forehead, like the brim of a hat, then paid the check and left. Medina sat in silence, finishing up the coffee. In spite of the caffeine, she could feel the tiredness in her joints. Tracking Nicol had been a long job, and she was ready for a couple days off.

Emily Scott was interesting, though.

Medina had held back from Tyler. She knew Scott. Or had known her, a long time ago. Might be able to get to her first, if there was money in it.

Let Tyler measure *that* in an app.

Medina stood up from the table and waved to the server on the way out. In the parking lot, she paused to take in the early morning sounds again. This time they felt different, the mix of caffeine and exhaustion giving them an unnatural edge.

No. Medina realised too late, it wasn't the caffeine. Something was off.

Reaching the door of the Shelby, she saw a large shape moving behind her in the window's dark reflection.

"Turn around." A man's voice, low, quiet. "Hands where we can see them."

Medina turned, keeping her hands low out of habit, ready to draw a gun that wasn't there.

A man in a sharp suit stepped forward. He'd been out of sight in the shadow of a van, Medina presuming it belonged to the cook. The man looked young. Mid twenties, maybe. He was holding a Glock. No expertise needed. Just like Tyler had said, always ready to shoot.

"Hands."

Medina cursed herself for locking her own gun in the car. Thinking at the time, how much trouble can I get in eating a slice of pie.

She raised her hands.

FIVE

Coyote Coady took a long pull on the medicinal herb. Held it in a while before coughing. "I mean, look, we had to let her go. There was that other guy in the car. We shoot her, we need to shoot him."

Drey Bowekaty said nothing. She took the joint and sank into the old cushions they'd piled into the back of the beat up Vandura.

"I didn't want to have to shoot them both, you know?" Coyote said.

Like it had been his choice to make.

This from a kid who'd never even held a gun until the night before, when they found the pistol and shotgun in the back of the van. To listen to Coyote now, they were two seasoned outlaws. Stars of some crime movie. All based off one idea. A joke, really. More drugs than genius. Drey finding the Vandura, left behind by MAB, her Mom's Asshole Boyfriend, and wanting to burn it. Coyote smoking and saying, Hey, let's be bad guys.

"She was a guest on our land," Coyote said now, running a hand through his red hair. "We call this one a test. For next time."

Drey still said nothing.

Not even at Coyote calling it *our land*. With his red hair and freckles. Now he was rewriting the whole plan. The idea had been simple enough. Sit and wait. Spot a white driver passing through the Rez. Pull them over and act gangsta. Play into their fears. Tell them, *'you want to come on our land, you got to pay the tax.'* See how fast they panicked and handed money over, while not being racist.

Coyote had explained all of this with a grin. Drey had said, *but they're not being racist, are they? They're not assuming all Indians are criminals, they're actually being robbed.* Coyote said, *sure, okay, but they're still thinking it, that's the point.*

Drey kept thinking about the woman's eyes. How sure she was. Shoulders set. Not tense. Calm. Just *being*. And how fast she'd drawn her gun. Held it there, staring them down like now she was the star of the movie. Drey wanted to be that cool. It was real life goal stuff. Was it a natural thing, or could she learn it? Did it come with practice?

"We need to come at it different," Coyote said. "I mean, how do we know who has money and who doesn't? It's not like they're going to tell us up front. This one, she had a cool car, but what's that mean, really? She could be borrowing it. Could've stolen it. Should've gone after the other guy. The Ford. He looked easy. Didn't have nobody handcuffed, neither. In a hurry, like he was already scared of something."

Coyote making out like he hadn't been the one to make the choice. They'd sat there all night. Letting people go by. Coming up with a different excuse each time. Finally, sitting across from the burger place, they'd said, next one, we have to do it. Then three people come out around the same time. The first, the skinny guy. He'd looked spooked. Nervous. Drey thought he was already halfway to handing over the cash. But Coyote spotted the other two. The woman, coming out with a man in cuffs. Leading him calmly over to the cool car. A car that looked like money.

Drey thought again of the woman's eyes. She had to be some kind of bounty hunter, did shit like this for a living. And that meant, to Drey's thinking, they'd messed up. The guy in cuffs? He was a bounty. That was the real trick they'd missed. Grab him, find out how much he was worth.

Drey was thinking that, but didn't say it. The best way with Coyote was to sneak up on the idea. Plant the seed, and let him be the one to put it together. Make him feel like it was all his own work.

"What you think," she said, "She was some bounty hunter or something?"

Coyote nodded. "Totally, yeah. I was just thinking that. You believe that story she told? Made him sound like a real badass."

Blue lights filled the window. The tinted glow bounced around the inside of the van. The double squawk of a police siren was followed by a car door opening and slamming shut. Footsteps led towards them, and the van's side door rattled as someone knocked.

"We're not in," Coyote said, following it with a stoned laugh.

The handle clicked and the door slid to one side, squeaking on its rusty track. Officer Alva Bobelu looked in at them. Drey had known Alva her whole life. She'd been a teacher back in the day, when Drey was five or six. Started working for the Rez police part time on weekends. Making extra money after the world went to shit. She'd been good at it, switched to full time. Now waiting to see if she could transfer to State Police. Half the kids in the area still called her *Miss* Bobelu.

Alva looked from Drey to Coyote. "Audrey. Aidan. You kids having a party?"

Drey saw Coyote's face flush red. He hated to hear his first name. Like he managed to forget about it until reminded. Aidan Coyote Coady. His parents both burned out white folks who settled on the Rez with some idea of going 'off grid' before going fully 'off world' when they got super into opiates.

Coyote blew out smoke into the air in front of his face and said, "I have a card for this."

He looked defiant, but Drey was thinking, why even mention it? Alva hadn't said a word about the herb. But if she'd noticed the front of the van was smashed up, now she would have a choice to make.

"Late for you to be out here on your own," Alva said. "I'm driving by, see this van parked at the side of the road, miles from anywhere." Drey felt Alva focus in on her, the same way the bounty hunter had. "How much you smoked?"

Drey gave her best smile. "We just having fun. Drove out to the reservoir, took a walk out there. But you know, I figured we're not fit to be driving, so we pulled over here."

"Want me to run you home?"

"No, thanks. I called my mom. She's working late, but going to drive by after, pick us up."

Alva paused. Looked at each of them again. Her smile said, well done. The lie was obvious, but the effort was good enough. It gave everybody an out. "How's she doing? I haven't seen her in a while."

"She's got a second job now, out most of the time. Doctor says she's a diabetes risk, so she's freaking out about insurance."

"Yeah, that'll do it. Listen, the Sheriff's Department are doing sobriety checks out here tomorrow morning. Stopping every car that passes. They need to make up their stats for the quarter, and I don't want you kids to be one of them, okay? I'll stop by your house tomorrow," Alva said. "Make sure you got home."

Alva slid the door shut. Drey listened as the footsteps headed back to the car. A door opened and closed, and the engine revved. Alva let the siren sound out again as a goodbye.

"Why she need to be like that?" Coyote said. "Giving me all that shit."

"She was okay. Could've been worse, she saw the front of the van, then it's an issue, looks like we got stoned and crashed."

"I told you, I have a card for this. Anyway. You know what I was thinking? I was thinking, we got it wrong. That woman, with the car? She's some kind of bounty hunter. That means the guy in the cuffs was probably worth something. We should've grabbed him."

SIX

Sitting in cuffs in the passenger seat of the Shelby, Medina couldn't help but smile. They were heading back up through the pines towards New Mexico, on the reverse of the same route she'd just taken with Ben Nichol. The guy with the gun and the sharp suit behind the wheel. The dark shape with the shotgun following them in a black Toyota.

"What's so funny?" the driver said.

"You have to explain a joke, it doesn't work."

Medina left it there. A chance to see what the guy was made of. He looked over. Up close he was maybe twenty-five. Styled hair. Working hard to pull off a look. He cared what people thought about him, just like he cared why she was smiling.

"What?"

"I did this same trip a few hours ago, sitting where you are, with a guy right here." Medina held up her cuffed wrists. "Like this."

Not *exactly* like this, though.

She'd cuffed Nichol's hands to the door handle. It was modified, reinforced to take restraints. Medina's hands were in front, sitting in her lap. She only needed a few seconds to get to the gun hidden beneath the dash. If it was still there.

Keep the guy talking. Play with him. Try to get his distracted, relaxed.

The driver nodded. "You spent the whole time trying to figure his thoughts. Look into his head and see what he was planning."

"See? Right there. Funny."

"What did you do, tell him some story about another time a guy tried to escape? Like, listen up, I'm threatening you without threatening you?"

"Told him about how I killed his brother while eating an ice cream."

"What flavor?"

Medina looked at him again. "I've been telling that story five years, nobody ever asked me that."

"Most important part." He smiled. Easy. Letting her see he wasn't looking for drama. "I mean, vanilla, shit, just drop it and get on with the shooting. Go back buy another. It'll taste exactly the same. But a nice raspberry, or something with some cinnamon in it? Each one of those is a precious flower. You want the other guy to wait, come back later."

"Think that would work? 'Wait right there, I gotta finish this.'"

"'I'll murder you momentarily,' yeah." He laughed.

Medina could like this guy under different circumstances. He had a good calm about him.

"There's an art to vanilla," she said. "Most of it is garbage, I agree. But if you get one done right, it's got depth to it. Like a flavour that can keep going down." She waited a beat, letting him see her look in the mirror. "The guys back there, what flavours do they like?"

The driver grinned. "I like how you did that. There's only one guy. Bosco. Bit crazy, but he works for my uncle, so I'm stuck with him."

"Good cop, bad cop?"

"Either of us look like cops to you? No. The shotgun was Bosco's idea. That was overkill, I'm sorry about that." He slowed down while a state trooper passed by. "So now that you know how many of us there are, I should tell you I found the gun under the dash. Swept the car before we put you in, figured you'd have something hidden away like that. I'm Leyton, by the way."

"I just was beginning to like you, Leyton." Medina relaxed into the seat. "Who's your uncle?"

"Eddie Wray."

Two pieces fell into place. She'd heard the name Eddie Wray a few times back in the Marshal Service. A low-level bookie who'd turned informant a couple times to keep himself out of trouble. That was information she might be able to use.

And the second piece...

"I'm guessing he's the Eddie in Eddie's Safari?"

"Best bit," Leyton said, "he isn't even the Eddie in the name. Been called that for years, before he bought it. The guy who opened it wasn't called Eddie either. Just thought it sounded like the right name for the bar."

Medina ran the name around her head a couple more times, more information coming loose. "He's the guy been trying to get a racino built out by Gallup?"

"Given up on that. Too much politics. The Zuni don't want it so close to their land, the names in Gallup don't want anything they don't have a piece of."

"And why does he want to see me?"

No answer.

After a couple of miles in silence, Leyton gunned the engine. "I love this car. It's just waiting to go, isn't it? Any time I want. But I need to focus. I relax on the steering for even a second, it's changing lanes."

"Takes a while to get used to."

"How long have you had it?"

"*Her*. We've been together little under four years."

"One year less than you've been telling the ice cream story?"

Medina thinking it over before answering.

Telling the story was a good way to show him a few cards, let it be known she knew the world he and his uncle worked in.

"You ever hear of Clarence Durville? He was a name, in all the newss. Clarence was an accountant. Everyone knew he was dirty, laundering for criminals. We all called him the Milk Man, his family had been in dairy farming. Every agency was watching, all of us. It was kind of a race. The FBI, ATF, DEA, everyone wanted to be the ones to get him. Roll him over, play six degrees of Kevin Bacon and get information on everyone he'd worked for." Leaving that hanging for a second. Heavy on the *everyone*. "But he wasn't an idiot, never stepped out of line, none of us could touch him."

"So what happened?"

"Turned out, he *was* an idiot, stepped out of line. A plane ticket, I think it was. He got the date wrong when he filed his expenses. The Treasury used it, jumped the queue. Once Clarence knew the gig was up, he ran. And it was our job, my job, to bring him in."

"You were a cop?"

"Deputy U.S. Marshal. So, Clarence's other thing was cars. Loved cars. Old ones, he said he liked it before cars were computers. Wanted to hear real engines, see grease and oil. The thing I'd heard, he had a big collection. Kept it in a garage somewhere, under a fake name so it had never shown up linked to him. I stopped looking for Clarence, started looking for cars. Found him hiding out in Scottsdale, in this big warehouse full of them."

"I'd kill to see that."

"When I get in there, first thing I see is this Shelby. Just sitting there, talking to me."

"You stole her?"

Chloe, not for the first time, thinking *is it really stealing if the system is built to let you do it?*

"Everything Clarence owned was property of the Marshal Service after that. We held onto them for a while, then put them on auction. I got a good deal before the public got a look."

"She have a name?"

"She decides whether you can know her name."

"You want me to talk to a car?" Leyton grinned. Playing along. He stroked the steering wheel, put on a smooth voice. "What's your name, baby?"

Medina closed her eyes and smiled, thinking, I got him to talk to a car. When she opened them again, Leyton was looking right at her.

"Nice try," he said. "I still want to know, what flavor was the ice cream?"

Medina held the cuffs up again. "Maybe after you tell me what this is about."

SEVEN

"Shit man." The first thing Jimmy Garza said when Treat Tyler popped the trunk. "It's smaller than you think here." He stretched his neck, adding, "Where are we?"

"They say it's average, for its class."

"I don't know. I mean, my neck's all cricked. I was bent up the whole way."

Jimmy climbed out, making more of a show of rubbing his neck, his lower back and knees. Stretching out in the mini mall parking lot. They were standing in a corner, away from the lights.

"Why'd you have to shove me all in there like that, I told you, I don't..." Jimmy stopped talking as he read the signs outside the mall. "Come on, where are we, man?"

Tyler smiled. "Blythe."

"Holy shit. Dude, we're in *California*?"

Tyler pointed. "Joshua Tree that way, if you want to go visit. Take some pictures."

"But that's, I mean, we crossed the state line?"

"Looks like you have, Jimmy. No respect for your parole. I gotta say, it's a dick move. Just when we were starting to trust you. Weird that you'd break the rules like this."

"But I didn't do it, man. It was *you*. Made me cross the line."

"And who they going to believe, the ex-con on parole, or the guy with the badge?"

"Oh hell, man. That's not fair."

"If you start talking, maybe this problem fixes itself. You get back in the trunk, I drop you home. You keep on saying you don't know anything, well, there's a whole bunch of cameras around here. Sun'll be up soon. Enough for me to prove I chased you down for crossing the line."

"Why you doing me like this?" Jimmy already sounding defeated. "I thought you were cool, man."

"I have a badge and you don't. That means we both made choices, Jimmy."

"You know it wasn't me, I was set up."

"The dye pack exploded in your face. They caught you three blocks over, in the Starbucks, trying to wash it off. The way the report's written, the cops went in, and the barista says, 'You looking for the guy with the blue face?'."

"What I mean is, I was just the driver. I didn't rob the place. They set me up. Handed me a bag in the car, told me to check it, they were using me to test for the packs, is what it was. I didn't know that until it was all over me. One minute I'm sat at the wheel, next thing, I'm walking down the street, paint in my eyes. You know, I still don't see right out of this one." Leaning forward, pointing to his left eye. "It messed with my, what they say, my depth perception. I can't play pool no more."

"You should sue the bank."

"You think?"

"No, Jimmy. You robbed the place."

"But why me? Say that. Why just me? I'm here, you're messing with me. I pee into a cup, prove I'm sober. I get hassle from a probation officer, but the other guys, they used me and ran away clean. Nobody ever caught them."

"They deserved to do time right along with you."

"Yeah, man. What I'm saying."

"But you never told anyone who they were. Kept quiet all the way through. Right up to now. As far as I know, that part of the case is still open any time you want to talk."

"No way. Not my style."

"But you want them to do the time?"

"If they're caught, yeah. But I'm not rolling them. This is America."

Tyler opened the back door and bent down, pulling out two cans of beer. He popped one and stood there for a moment, letting Jimmy stare at it, before taking a sip.

"I don't care about a bank robbery," Tyler said. Smiling as Jimmy stared at the second can. "They get caught, maybe I get to transport them, or hunt them down. Until then, not my problem." Tyler held the second beer out. He pulled it back when Jimmy tried to take it, then held it out again. "You know what I want. Talk to me about Emily Scott."

"I don't know anything. I swear."

"Spoke to three guys so far. They all say the same thing. You and Scott were tight at Douglas. Hung out together after they started letting the men and women mix more in the education programs. I talked to your landlady while you were at work, you know what she said?"

"What?"

"Told me a woman fitting Scott's description was staying at your place. I guess there's no law against fucking someone while you're on parole, unless they're an escaped con."

"We weren't..." Jimmy started to speak, then clammed up, shaking his head.

Tyler turned on his heels, starting back towards the car. "I'll give you a head start," he said. "Only fair. Five minutes, run in any direction you want. I'll wait the full five before I come get you."

"Treat."

"Deputy. And I'm already counting."

"You can't do this. How you going to make it work, man? You're going to say you just happened to be in town? Those cameras, they're going to show you here, too. It won't work."

"How hard do you think it will be? Four minutes."

"I can't, Deputy. They'll kill me."

Tyler turned back. "Who will?"

Jimmy did a little jig on the spot. To Tyler, he looked like a child who was about to wet himself in public, seconds away from crying. Tyler held out the beer again, let Jimmy take it.

"You know I'll fail my piss test if I drink this. It's, what they say, entrapment. You're tricking me again."

"I can fix the test for you. Come on. Who'll kill you, Jimmy?"

"I don't know."

Tyler breathed in. Held it. Stared at Jimmy.

"No, really, I don't. Emi didn't tell me who it was, just said they were after her. That's why she ran."

"Start back at the beginning."

"Well, so these guys, I'd known them like, three years? No, five. They came to me and said... No I think it was three. They came to me with this idea, said all they needed me to do was drive the car, and they'd-"

"Is this the bank robbery?"

"You said the beginning."

"Tell me about Emily Scott, and what she told you."

"All right. So, okay, yeah. Me and Emi were pretty tight in Douglas."

"She set up this performance class in there. Acting, comedy. Workshops, lessons. She wanted to do dancing too, but the prison said no. I signed up more for the acting. The comedy part got old. There's only so many times you can hear somebody say 'how's about that prison food,' you know? Anyway, I got out before her. Then she shows up at my door."

"You weren't expecting her?"

"No. No way. I swear. She says she's on the run. See... hang on, don't you already know all of this?"

"I want to know what you know."

"Well, she said she'd got some dirt after I left. Something big. Really big. Like, there's a big secret, she said it would make the papers, bring someone down."

"Did she say who?"

"I didn't want her to. I'm not an idiot."

Tyler smiled. Let that one go.

"So then she shows up at my door, and what am I going to do, turn her away?"

"You like her."

"Nah man, not like that, we're just friends."

"So she's not interested in you."

"Well, she's gay. Like, all the way."

"Turning her away would have been smart for your parole, Jimmy. Taking her in. You'd been caught, you'd be back inside. Hell, you still might, now I know about it. I'm ethically bound, you know that? I should report you."

Jimmy started doing his shuffle again.

Tyler waved away the panic. "Look, all I need to do, I need to find Emily and bring her back in. Like you say, she's got a deal on the table. Had a legal way out, no need to run. If I can get to her before anyone else, I can put her back at the table with the DA. She stays out on the run, with you saying she's got people want her dead? That doesn't go so well."

"I guess not."

Jimmy finished the beer. Tyler ducked back into the car to grab another, tossed it over.

"When was the last time you saw her?"

Jimmy popped the can. Beer fizzed all over him, dripping down onto the warm concrete. "Ah shit." He sipped through the foam. "I guess, I think, two days ago? She said she was going to hit the road, travel, and when I get back from work, she's gone."

"And you don't know where?"

"No, I swear. Really."

"I got you on three violations now, Jimmy. Not the time to hold back."

"I swear. I mean, okay, look. Maybe I know a few people. Like, friends of hers, people she told me about when we were inside. Maybe she's talked to them?"

"You know them?"

"A couple, yeah."

Tyler popped the trunk again. "We're going for a ride." Tyler watched Jimmy take a step back. "You want to do it up front, risk being seen in the car this side of the state line? Jump on in, we're going to see these friends of yours."

Jimmy climbed in. Tyler tossed the rest of the six-pack in after him and shut the lid. He walked round to the door and slipped into the seat.

EIGHT

Eddie's Safari was still open. There were four cars parked out front before Leyton added the Shelby to the list. The Toyota pulled in a minute or so later. Bosco stayed inside with the engine running. The sun was rising to the east, and the glare caught the Toyota full-on, keeping Bosco hidden.

"Twenty-four hours," Leyton said. "Used to be up there in lights. *'Eddie's Safari: Burgers 'N' Tits, 24/7'*. People complained about that last part."

"You get customers this late? Early?"

"The food's good. I'm serious. We do a cheap breakfast. The guys coming onto the Rez to work the airfield? They stop here on the way in and out, get full. The ones from the Pueblo or Black Rock, heading to the city, they roll in around six, seven."

Leyton got out and opened the passenger door. He knelt down, holding up the key to the handcuffs. "Bosco wants to march you back in cuffs. You pissed him off, walking out with the guy like that. He's security here, took it personal." Leyton paused, looked back towards the Toyota. "Now, the way I want to do it, I let you loose, and we walk in like friends. No drama."

"That what we are?" Medina said. "Friends?"

"Like I said, this is just a business meeting. My uncle wants to meet you."

"And after that?"

"Nothing. You're free to go. That's why we brought your car. I'll give you the keys back, you do what you want."

Medina held her wrists out towards Leyton. He turned the key and pulled the cuffs loose, handing them back to Medina. She threw them onto the driver's seat and climbed out.

"Car keys?"

"After you meet him."

Medina waited a beat. Thinking it over.

Her size against his. Unarmed. But Bosco was still back there. A total unknown. She hadn't gotten a good look at him. Only a large shape in the shadows. She didn't want to make a move without knowing her chances. She nodded and motioned for Leyton to lead the way. At the top of the steps, he held the door open. To the right, the bar looked clean and modern, with booths lined up at each end. Medina saw Native men and women, dressed in overalls, eating breakfast in silence. She looked to the sunken dance floor. A stage against the far wall had fake jungle trees on the sides. The walls were painted with bushes, trees and animals. A circular platform stood in the middle of the room, a gleaming metal pole in center. Pleather sofas and chairs faced the action.

A young white woman was clinging to the pole with her thighs, showing too much energy for this time in the morning. She was moving in silence, with no music backing her up. The sofas nearest to her were occupied by white guys around the same age.

"Students," Leyton said. "They drive in from NAU. It's all a game to them, come here with friends, treat it like a workout. One time, one of the girls came in with these guys, and we saw them handing her Monopoly money when she was up there. Probably what they all do, brag about it later. Look cool that way."

"What do the real dancers think about it?"

Leyton shrugged. "Never asked. We get all kinds on the night shift. Office workers. Nurses. They drive in from Gallup or Albuquerque. Some of the older dancers have families now, they're soccer moms during the day, come here at night. We put other acts on, too. Musicians. Comedians. But they're part of a package, like buy a pizza meal for two, get a free comedian. Folks don't come in for them, like they do for the dancers. Can I get you a drink?"

"Black coffee," Medina said, not wanting to show any nerves.

Leyton shouted the order to the woman behind the bar. He called her by name, Rose. A white twenty-something with sleeve tattoos. She had a zebra on her apron, and looked ready to punch the next guy who asked what time she'd be dancing.

After getting two coffees, handing one to Medina, Leyton pointed back towards the toilets where Nichol had bolted a few hours before. "This way."

Through a door marked *Private* and down a few steps to a lower level at the back, he led the way down a small hallway to a closed door. He knocked, then opened it without waiting.

"Eddie, she's here."

He motioned for Medina to squeeze in past him.

The room was small, barely large enough for the desk wedged into the center of the room. The walls were hidden behind piles of boxes, packs of napkins and rolls of toilet paper. The man standing behind the desk looked like a smaller, more weathered version of Leyton. His forehead was higher, hair thinner. He even wore the same kind of suit, with less style and more creases.

"Oh, hey, how are you? Come on in. Give us a minute, kid, will you?" He waited until Leyton stepped back out and shut the door, before giving her a smile that showed tobacco-stained teeth. "I'm sorry about this. Miss Medina, right? I was reading about you online, the news stories." He held up a smartphone. "Did you really do the thing in Florida, the way they said it in the story?"

He held out a hand, but Medina didn't take it.

"I was driven here in cuffs, Mr. Wray."

"Eddie."

"Eddie. My car was stolen, and I was kidnapped. They took me across a state line. You know how much shit you're in?"

His face developed a couple more creases, and he said, waving at the empty seat in front of the desk: "Aw, shit. I'm sorry. Really. I didn't ask them to do all that. See, Leyton, he means well. I ask him to do a thing, he does it. But he's got some strange ideas about *how*." He waved again at the seat. "Please."

Medina thought it over and sat down. Not buying his plausible deniability act. "Well, it was your idea to send Bosco."

Eddie's eyebrow's pressed together, lines showed up around his nose. "Bosco? He took Bosco? Gina's gonna kill me."

"Gina?"

"His mom. Bosco's. He's just a kid who comes in after school to work the kitchen. Does the dishes, breaks down the boxes, takes out the trash. I thought he'd gone home hours ago. I'm really sorry about all this. I should've called you myself. I asked Leyton to do it, but you know. He has ideas. It's the army, he was never the same."

"Where did he serve?"

Eddie shook his head. "He didn't. Failed the medical on account of the asthma. Really messed him up. Now he gets weird fixations, likes to try be different people, like out of movies."

"Mr. Wray. Let's pretend I don't have a clue what's going on here. Why don't you fill me in. From the beginning."

"See, I saw the way you handled that guy. Nichol. We all saw. And then when I found I had this problem, I thought, I need someone like that chick who was just here. Sorry, that woman who was just here. What's her deal? And Leyton says he'll go talk to you. And, well."

"From the beginning, Eddie. What's the problem?"

Eddie sighed. Rocked back in his seat. He turned to point at the wall behind him, where a large architect's diagram was held up with pins. It looked like a large building, vaguely art deco, with neon hoardings out front.

"That was the dream," he said. "Casino. Right here. Across the road, with buttes all lit up behind it. I own the land over there, too. Bought it the same time I got this place. Then the Zuni Tribal Council starts negotiating with the state about a gaming compact, and I'm thinking, this is it. I have the best spot. I own the land, I know all the right people. Racinos are legal in New Mexico, I'm not on tribal land so some of the red tape will be easier, but I can maybe cut a deal with the tribe to endorse me."

"Leyton told me they blocked it."

"Yeah. Straight up. No debate. Like I'm nobody. I tell you," he paused, looking at the design again. "It's always been there, under the surface. See, I was born here, but I grew up out of state in Florida. My family moved when I was young. I came back with some money under me, I had a good run of luck in Florida, car sales, property, that kind of thing. I come back here and try to show I'm home. I buy the laundrette next junction up, a convenience store. I helped with some restoration work at the pueblo. I bring in money. I bring in jobs. Everyone wants to know me, talk to me. Then I buy this place, make a few changes." He pressed his fingers together then mimed an explosion. "Everything changes. Like that. I'm part of the problem now."

"They don't like the dancing."

"Now it don't matter how much money I raised. Don't matter what promises I make about the name, or the number of people I'll employ. They say no. The Zuni say it will hurt them. The big names up in Gallup say it will hurt them."

"I'm not seeing where I come in."

"Are we covered by, you know, confidentiality?"

"Not in any way, Eddie."

"But if I hire you?"

"I'm not a lawyer or a doctor, so, no."

Eddie sucked on his lower lip. Medina could see him trying to read her. "You know the best part? The land isn't worth a thing now. Everyone knows it won't be used for the racino, and it's not like there's demand for more houses here. I sell it now, I might as well be giving it away. Can you keep a secret, at least?"

"Only one way to tell."

"I'm on my ass here. Forgive me for saying so. But I am. I overextended to try and make all of this work. These bills, you can't pay them and stay honest. When the credit was due, I was done."

"You took a bailout."

"Some guys I used to know. Big rollers in Arizona and Gallup. In my old life I wasn't as honest as I try to be now."

"I know about your old life."

He smiled, perking up at the idea of being infamous. "Oh yeah? You heard of me?"

"I know how high you didn't go."

The air let out of his tyres, his got back to the story. "I put Leyton in charge of it. Figured it would give him a start into something he could build on. Make connections, build something for himself. And keep me out of it enough, give me some deniability."

"Take away your temptation to snitch?"

He eyed her for a second, saying so you know about that without saying it. "The deal was, they paid off my debts but hold them over me, like running a book. Saying they didn't pay them off so much as take them on. They made big promises too, said if I played nice for them, they had the pull to help me get the racino. But I know that's not happening."

"And what is the deal?"

"We're neutral territory between all the big groups. We're not Gallup, not Arizona, not Albuquerque, not Canon City.

They use this place for meetings, clear the whole place out for hours at a time so their big shots can come in and hold conferences. Treat us almost like another country, like we're actually on the Rez. But this close, we might as well be, the law never looks here."

"Never?"

"Only people who know to care about us are the Sheriff's Department, and we pay them not to."

Medina nodded for Eddie to continue. "How does it work?"

"My part is, there's two safes here, one for my stuff, one for theirs." He turned and pointed at two metal safes, next to each other on the floor, buried beneath packs of toilet paper. "People come and make drop-offs, then every few weeks someone comes to pick it all up. Sometimes the money is going out, sometimes it's coming in."

"And you don't know that the money is for?"

"I don't think about it too much."

"They have the combination?"

"I do. I always have to be here when they come."

"They trust you?"

Eddie smiled. "I don't think *trust* has anything to do with it. They own me. But I messed up, I looked inside last week. Three bags, full of money. Cash. I started to count and stopped, what was the point? Seeing all that money I'd never have? There had to be over a million in there. I reckon two."

"You really don't know whose money it was?"

"I don't. Leyton says that deal was from some big guy in Arizona, nobody knows who he is, or if they do, they get killed."

Medina flinched. For a second she could feel her old gunshot wounds. She put her hand to the spot. "Big Wheel."

"Eh?"

"Nothing."

Big Wheel was a codename.

Informal at first, around the Marshals' Office, then later committed to paperwork. It was the handle given to an unknown criminal. A figure who was believed to have a cut of all organised crime in Phoenix, maybe Arizona. Big Wheel had been the real target when they brought down the accountant, Clarence Durville. The hope had been to roll him, get him to flip on his boss. It hadn't worked out that way, and Medina had been shot in the chase. Took shelter behind the Shelby in the garage, while Tyler went after Durville and gunned him down.

Medina knew where this was all leading. "The money is gone."

"One of our acts stole it, a comedian."

Everything was lining up. Medina wanted to smile, but Eddie would read it wrong. She let him keep going.

"See upstairs, it's not just dancers. We put on other acts too. Bands, comedians. I tried a magician, but he was disrespectful, making out like he was using Navajo magic. So, there's this one girl, comedian." Pausing there. Medina knew he'd been about to launch into something about women comedians but thought about it in time. "Leyton knew her from somewhere, said she was struggling, couldn't get gigs anywhere else because of a criminal record. And that she was a dancer, too. A good one. So if we comped her stage rental as part of the fee, she'd do a set of comedy and a set of dancing, and we'd get two for the price of one."

"And then she robbed you."

"I still don't really know how. I think she was talking to Leyton after her set, and found out about the money. See, I said I messed up? So much money in there, I *had* to tell someone. You see two million in cash, you need to talk about it. So I told Leyton, made him swear, this is just between us. But Leyton is Leyton. Next thing I know" - he waved at the safe - "this comedian is off with the whole lot, and the pickup is due in three days."

"What's the comedian's name?"

Medina asking the question even though she knew the answer, so not to tip Eddie off.

"Emily Scott."

Medina smiled. Putting him at ease. On home ground now, even in someone else's office. She knew how to play this. The universe was throwing her a bone. Big Wheel owned Eddie, in his own words. Working with Eddie now would put in her in that chain. She could use it to get a second chance at Big Wheel, and compete with Tyler in the bargain. Beat him to Emily Scott.

"You need the money back in the next three days."

"Right. Or, I don't know." He tried to match her smile, but the worry was writ large. "I just don't. These guys, not having their money isn't an option."

"My standard fee is twenty percent," Medina said, doubling her usual rate. "That going to cause problems?"

"But it's not my money, I can't give you a cut of something that's not mine."

"Maybe I should talk to these guys, make the deal with them?"

Eddie looked up at the ceiling, bobbing his head side to side, counting. "I've got fifty K in my safe. Money I've been saving. You bring their money back, you can have mine. It'd be tight, but I could go that. It's not a cut of two million, but it's fifty more than you had walking in. And Leyton can go with you to help, so you won't need to hire anyone else."

"I work alone. And fifty? Eddie, I don't know. I'd be getting mixed up in some pretty big business, these guys find out I was helping you after you lost their money..."

"Okay, wait. Leyton tells me you got a nice car, a Shelby, got all banged up out on the road? I got a guy, my cousin, I own his garage. I can get him to fix it up for you, free of charge. Throw that in."

Medina waited, making it look like she was thinking it over. "Okay. But only the damage from the crash. There's two bullet holes on the right, by the gas tank? It was a miracle they hit where they did. I like to keep those."

"Sure," Eddie grinned. "And you can use my car next couple days. I think you'll like it."

NINE

The way the night had gone, Drey was starting to worry about Coyote. He had these deep moods, days when anger or sadness rolled in like a cloud. Most times, the bud or edibles would take the edge off. The fog would bury whatever he was feeling. But sometimes, it went the other way.

He had nobody looking out for him. Sure, his aunt. He stayed with her, and with his grandparents sometimes. But nobody much seemed to really be keeping an eye on him. Drey took it as her job, but that sometimes led to nights like this.

They hadn't gone home after the run in with Alva Bobelu. Instead, they'd sat in the van, talking about nothing. They drove around the edge of the village for a while. Then out to the small airport, to see if they could watch anything coming in to land. They both liked the way the planes would come down in the dark, lights looking like a UFO. Drey read somewhere that's what most UFO sightings are. Planes are lit from the top, so from the ground at night you don't see the whole thing, just a weird shape with a triangle of lights. And if it's flying towards you, with the way perspective works, it'll look stationary for a long time. Science was cool like that.

Now they were heading up the 602 toward Gallup. Somehow, driving around felt like less effort than going home. They'd known to get off the reservation thanks to Alva, so the 602 was the best bet. But also, Drey was trying to look out for Coyote. Hoping time would cool him off or he'd fall asleep, wake up later wanting beans or a burrito. Drey led the way, making up games, trashing movies. She didn't like to talk much. Silence was more her way. But around his moods, she got nervous and chatty. Filled in silences, looked for laughs. But Coyote wasn't smiling. He had this way of letting things simmer. He'd never been any good at confrontation, but couldn't help finding it.

He'd back down, or stay quiet. His face flushing red. Then later on, once the problem was over, he'd keep talking about it. Retelling the story, changing how things went down.

"See, I could've shot her," he said.

Drey thinking he was talking about the bounty hunter, changed the subject. "You remember that rich guy, fired a car into space in a rocket?" No answer, she continued. "I saw it on TV, you remember? Put a space suit in this red car, sent it up in a rocket. I mean, Melika with that much money, why not? But now I'm thinking, say you're that rich, and you want to kill somebody. How you get rid of the body? Fire it into space. That'll do it. Did anybody check the suit before they loaded the car into the rocket? Whole world looking at the proof of what you did, but not knowing it. That'd be a trip."

She trailed off after that. Talking drained her, it felt like giving her energy to someone else.

"I could've shown her," Coyote said. "Just because she's got a badge now."

"Miss Bobelu?"

"You not paying attention? Yeah, Bobelu. Like, you know I could've done it, right? She gets all up in my face, trying to make me scared, see if I'll back down."

Drey remembering it different. Miss Bobelu being nice. Doing them a favour and overlooking all the reasons she had to drag them in. Coyote sitting there, not doing anything until she'd gone. No drama in the moment, but now, in Coyote's mind, it was a scene.

"She was just looking out for us," Drey said. "Didn't mean anything."

Coyote's hands were tight on the wheel. "Looking out for you, maybe."

"Both of us. You were the one she saw smoking. She didn't say anything."

"She was thinking it though. I could see. The way she looked at me. Did that nose thing, the way she twitches it. She's only ever seen me as Anglo."

Drey had long ago let that one go. Coyote taking the idea of being white coded. Of being Zuni who looked white, got the shit from both sides. Whatever. Okay, so he was from a white family. He'd been born on the Rez, grown up here, looked after by locals.

He was Zuni to anyone who cared, but he couldn't let the idea go. Always something for him to get angry about.

This one time, after he'd got in a fight at school over it, Drey had said to him, "Why you try so hard? The way you look, you could be anything you want. Go anywhere. They'd see what you tell them to see."

"I want to be here," he'd said.

And that was it. The end of it, as far as Drey saw. He wanted to be here, he was here. But he looked past the acceptance, only having eyes for rejections.

And now, sitting in the front seat of the van as they headed up the 602, he was shifting in his seat. Rocking a little. Drey knew the sign. Anger was crawling in his guts. They were just the right kind of tired, where it sounded like a good idea to stay up all of the next day, too. With the plan to head to whichever movie place opened first, buy a million years' worth of popcorn and soda, and sit at the back. Maybe they'd get the giggles, and Coyote would calm down. Best option, Drey would get some sleep. Any of those was a win.

Staying on the 602 as it turned left, Coyote pulled into the parking lot of a small 7/11, next to a burger place that wouldn't be open for hours.

"I like this one," Coyote said. "Bananna Yoohoo. They don't have it anywhere on the Rez." He smiled. "We can look for a space suit."

Drey relaxed. He was snapping out of it. She followed him into the store. A middle-aged man stood behind the counter, and Drey could feel his eyes on them the whole time. Coyote picked up four of the drinks, a few bags of chips, and seven candy bars.

"Go on out," he said, nodding to the door. "I'll get this."

Drey was back at the van, her hand reaching out to open it, when she remembered Coyote didn't have any money on him. She'd been the one paying for things all day.

That's when she heard the gunshots.

TEN

Tyler parked behind the coffee shop on the corner of West Marshall. Getting out, he felt both knees crack. How many hours had he been awake? He wasn't sure, but now the question was better asked in days.

Banging on the trunk, he said, "How you doing in there?"

Jimmy's snoring had filled the car for the last thirty minutes. It came in bursts, even through the back seat's padding. Stop start, stop start.

"I need a piss," Jimmy said, voice muffled.

"Hold it another ten minutes."

"Come on man, let me out."

Tyler looked around. They were in an alley behind the row of storefronts. On the other side was a low wall, with a house beyond. He looked at the windows, scanning for any sign of movement. Was anybody watching? What the hell, they could watch his badge, it came to it. Tyler popped the trunk. Jimmy was surrounded by empty beer cans. Both hands over his crotch like he was holding back the dam. He climbed out and shuffled away down the alley, towards the metal bins behind the Mexican place on the end.

"We're back home, right?" Jimmy paused to look round on his way back to the car. "Yeah. I can walk home from here."

"We're not done yet."

"I'm sick of this, man. I'm leaving. You can't stop me."

"Look, Jimmy. I'm playing fair with you. Really. You're drinking. You've been harbouring a fugitive. Then there's that whole thing with you going to California. All I'm saying is, you give me one solid lead, and I let you walk on all of it. But so far..."

Tyler shrugged, like, what can I do?

They'd made two stops so far, acting on Jimmy's tips, and both had been busts.

At Lichfield Park they spoke to Shaun, and ex-con who'd been in Emily Scott's classes at Douglas. Shaun was bald and white, but spoke like a Jamaican. He offered Tyler drugs even after he'd seen the badge.

In Glendale they dragged another friend out of bed, an exotic dancer and part-time yoga instructor who went by the name of Twitch. It didn't take more than ten seconds to see why she'd earned the name. Both of them said the same thing. As far as they knew, Scott was still in prison. Neither of them heard from her since she broke out.

Jimmy begged for another stop in Glendale, long enough to pick up another pack of beer and a bottle of liquor. Tyler was starting to question the wisdom of pushing him off the wagon. Both times, Jimmy had gone in with Tyler to make the introduction. Looking around at the morning traffic, Tyler was going to play it different.

"Back in the trunk."

"No way," Jimmy pulled a face. "There's no air conditioning back there. I don't got to hide, we're home. Come on, let me sit up front, get some air."

Truth was, Tyler had been enjoying the game of playing with Jimmy. Seeing how long, and how far, he could be pushed around before he stood up for himself. If this was his one small stand, well, good for him.

"Tell you what," Tyler said, handing over his keys. "Sit up front. Maybe listen to some music, just don't mess with my settings, all right?"

Jimmy bobbed on the spot, proud at the promotion.

Tyler headed round front to the coffee shop. The ground was already warming up beneath his feet. Even this early in the day, he was glad of the shade at the front of the of the building, where a large green awning covered the walkway. It was going to be a hot one. Some days were like an oven, some were like a grill.

The glass door was covered with a large, painted coffee cup. There was a face, with large eyes and a smile, and a speech bubble giving the hours. Tyler pushed through, feeling the eyes on him as he moved. Inside, a queue of morning commuters stretched nearly to the door. Two baristas were working flat-out behind the counter. The smells and sounds woke something up in Tyler. The promise of caffeine.

He stepped around the queue. People tutted, groaned, someone said, can you believe that? Nobody stopped him. The nearest barista looked up from the cash register, while handing change to the customer at the front. Her hair was iron-straight, and her ear was lined all the way around with earrings. Tyler couldn't stop staring at them.

"Hey," she nodded at the people in front of her. "There's a line here."

Tyler flashed his I.D. "Looking for Lisa Afobe."

"Yeah," she said.

"That you?"

She stopped what she was doing. Her shoulders set square. "What I done this time?"

"Just a couple questions, that's all." He smiled at the customers now, acknowledging them for the first time. "Sorry, this won't take long."

Lisa called for someone to come out from the back and serve, and led Tyler out front. She lit up a cigarette and leaned against the wall, round the side, next to a seating area that was already too hot to use. In the daylight, Tyler revised his impression of her age. At first glance he'd said early twenties. Maybe twenty-five. Out here, he could see a few more years, maybe early thirties. There was something about the way she stood, the attitude she gave off, reminded him of his ex, Jasmine.

"Sounds like you get this a lot."

"What you think? Always something. I don't get one week's peace without some kind of badge in my face."

"I can imagine." He smiled. "I'm not really here for you. Truth is, Lisa, I call you that? Thing is, Lisa, I'm looking for someone else. Emily Scott."

She stepped back and laughed. It was hollow, just for show. "I knew where she was, I'd draw you a map."

"I heard you were friends."

"Who told you that? Friends? I guess that's one way to say it."

"You were together?"

"Years ago, yeah. After high school. She was always trying to get something going. Comedy. Acting. Whatever it was that week. I swear, she couldn't hold down any job more than a week. She'd come home, be like, 'I had to quit baby.' Go into this big whole story, like it was a stand against *the man*. It'd come down to something like they changed her shift for the weekend, or wanted her to wear a uniform or something."

"Looking for excuses."

"Then, just when she's starting to get somewhere with the comedy, getting the good shows? Suddenly she's all, 'Baby, I think we've grown apart'."

"Wanted to see other people."

"Wanted to screw the college girls who laughed at her jokes."

"You broke up before she went down?"

"Who you think dimed her out?"

"You tipped them off?"

"Like I said, I knew where she was, I'd draw you a map."

Tyler let the silence stretch out for a minute while she smoked. "The thing is, Lisa. Twice you've told me you don't know where she is. Not once have you asked me why I'm looking. But I would think, the last you heard, she was in prison, right?"

He watched her brown eyes change, giving up the truth. "Shit."

"Someone told you she was out. I'm betting it was Emily herself."

Lisa stared away from him, across the road to Starbucks.

"She's in trouble. Got the wrong kind of people after her." He flashed the badge again. "It's best for Emi that I get there first."

Lisa, blowing smoke up into the air, said something he couldn't make out, under her breath, then, "Fine. Look, she came to me yesterday morning. Said she was broke, needed help. She's always had this...I hate her, you know, but she's always had this way. Makes you feel like...anyway, she asked to borrow my car."

"You give it her?"

"No way. Need my car."

"She say where she was going?"

"Mentioned some friend of hers, Leyton Wray."

Tyler knew the name.

"That the last you heard from Emily?"

Lisa nodded, dropped the cigarette and rubbed it out. "Last I want to."

Tyler handed over a business card. "Call me, you hear anything." Turning to leave, he paused. Remembered the feeling inside the shop. "Hey, can I get the biggest coffee you got, and something to eat?"

ELEVEN

If Medina had been asked to guess, she would have said Eddie Wray owned a '77 Firebird. In black. With the T top panels removed, and gold hubcaps. Living out the Burt Reynolds fantasy every time he got behind the wheel. She could see it in the way he smiled, saying she'd like it.

She was one year out.

"I wanted the one from the movie," he said. "A '78 was the closest I could find." Handing over the keys as they walked around the car. "Panels are in the back. They're different from the movie. They changed the grill after '77, so that's not quite right, either. Got more power, though. Not as much as your Shelby, but it's a different ride."

He wasn't kidding. Medina opened the Firebird up out on the asphalt, and left a strip of rubber behind. She pushed it up to 110, feeling through her hands and feet when the car didn't want to go higher. The Shelby could go faster, and handled better, but there was something fun about the Pontiac. It had no subtlety or grace, like a high-powered shopping cart, but it wanted you to enjoy the ride.

She slowed down to keep an eye on the bars of her cell reception. The signal had been weak on the reservation, and wasn't much better on the 191. She got enough to make a call on the outskirts of Holbrook and pulled over to the side of the road just after the river.

Reed Palmer answered. "You know what time it is?"

Medina smiled.

Her old boss Palmer would have been up for two hours already. In all the years she'd known him, he never stayed in past six. Right now he'd be sat in his kitchen, getting ready to leave for work.

"On your third coffee by now," she said.

"Well." He paused. "Only two. But okay. What can I do for you?"

"That's it? Straight to business? No, '*Hi, Chloe, how you doing*?'"

"Hi, Chloe, how you doing?"

Medina could picture his scowl. The way he would've just breathed out and hung his head to the side before delivering the line, but all for show, enjoying it really.

They went back nearly ten years. As close to a living legend as you could get in the Marshal Service, he'd bought in three of America's Top Ten at different times. Though he was cheating with that line, because two of them had been the same person - a repeat fugitive.

Palmer was from Buffalo originally. Not that you could hear it in his voice. A deep cocktail of every state he'd worked in. He'd been Chief Deputy in the Miami office when Medina was just starting out down there, and had been the main reason she'd transferred back home to Arizona after he'd taken over the Phoenix team.

"Some kids busted up my car," she said.

"You ruined the Shelby?"

"Some kids, I said. It's fixable, but I'm without it for a couple days. Feels like I'm missing a limb."

"These kids, what they do?"

"Rammed me, in a van. A foot or so further back, I'd be dead."

"They rammed you, just like that, huh? I guess you didn't tell 'em who you are."

"Didn't get a chance."

"Couldn't tell 'em your ice cream story, either. That would've done the trick."

Medina shook her head, trying not to let the smile into her voice. "I miss talking to you, boss."

"You know you could stop by the office anytime."

Medina didn't answer. She hadn't been back since the day she handed him her shield.

"I got a few problems," Palmer said into the silence. "I'm getting worried."

Medina pushed off from the car. "What?"

"I think my grandson is turning into an asshole."

"Oh sure. That's a problem."

"I'm serious. He just grabs at things. Screams if he doesn't get it. You try and get him to talk to visitors, say hello, goodbye, even please or thank you. He won't do it."

"How old is he?"

"Two and a half."

"Maybe a bit soon to be worrying about him joining ISIS, there, Boss."

"Start out like that in this world, it's nothing but trouble."

"Or he gets to be President. But sure, you don't want him getting bad habits. If only there was something you, as his grandparent, could do about teaching him manners."

"Oh, the chance would be fine. It's my daughter-in-law. She who must be obeyed. Won't let me anywhere near the kid for more than five minutes. Says I fill him full of candy, get him all worked up."

Medina smiled again, loving the idea of the legendary U.S. Marshal unable to control a child.

"So, what's the real reason, Chloe?"

"I was thinking the candy."

"For the call."

"What's Treat done to deserve parole duty?"

There was another pause on the line. This time Medina didn't fill it with an image of Palmer enjoying himself. They were getting to it. "He tell you that?"

"Spoke to him this morning."

Another pause.

Medina, already having an idea how everything fit together, tried another way. "Tell me about Emily Scott."

"Ah, hell." His voice dropped, talking to himself. "Maybe this is better away from the office. This a business request?"

"She's stolen something. I've been asked to get it back."

"What did Tyler tell you?"

"Told me Scott cut some kind of deal, out after only two years. Rabbited on her parole, and you've got Treat tracking her down."

A third pause.

This one long enough that Medina almost checked to see if he was still there.

Then she heard something that sounded like a whispered curse, followed by: "Scott knows who Big Wheel is."

Medina felt the old gunshot again.

Palmer kept on talking. "She got lucky. Or unlucky. However you want it. Some guy she knew in Douglas got shanked. Scott went to the warden, said the guy was killed because he knew the name of some big criminal. The DA gets wind of it, and Scott says she was told the name before it all went down. Says she knows who it is. And says the only reason she hadn't been done the same time was because she was in the women's facility, and whoever did the shanking couldn't get to her. But she would only have until they could get to the right person in her wing."

"And they let Scott out?"

"Well, not quite. She cut a deal to reduce her sentence, but it was taking time. Two attempts on her life while she's waiting. So now she knows how serious this is, and the deal changes. We need to offer her WITSEC, immunity from future prosecution. All kinds of things. So, okay, she gets that. And we agree to a safe house, little bungalow here in town, where we'll guard her before the deposition, and then she goes off to a new life."

"So what happened?"

"I sent my best guy to go get her. Well, my second best. Because my best has been pretending she doesn't want to be a marshal for the past four years."

"Couldn't get one of Sheriff Jed's deputies to handle it?"

"We could. But the DA wanted us, Scott specified nobody from the Sheriff's Office. So Tyler goes to get her, transport her to the safe house. They're waiting there, playing cards, watching TV, somehow Scott gets spooked and runs."

"Treat's trying to find her before..."

"Well, Treat's trying to find her before his ego gets hurt. But he's suspended. Not my decision, the DA's office exploded when they found out, said I suspend him pending an investigation, or fire him outright."

"You sent him home."

"Told him, look at it like a vacation, take a week off, let me fix this. And I am, I have everyone on this, trying to find this little Emily before Big Wheel does."

"But Treat's trying to fix it himself."

Medina touched her side again.

Big Wheel was still out there. The one that got away. The reason she'd taken the bullet. Life was throwing her a second chance, if she could get to Emily Scott first.

And now she knew for sure Tyler had lied to her.
Why?

TWELVE

Out past Queen Creek, south-east of Phoenix, where cotton and nut farms were losing ground to property developers, Redmond Peters had just caught a shoplifter.

Red, standing behind the counter of Reds Grocery &, whatever originally followed the ampersand long-lost, was in serious conversation with the six year old criminal.

"See, Danny. This is how it goes down. Now, I know your daddy's not worked in a while, and you know me, I do what I can. But you think I can let even nice boys like you come in here and steal candy? How you think I make my own living, if I let people do that?"

Red, nearing seventy, had a grandfatherly way about him. He had plenty of practice, his seven kids each producing a minimum of two of their own in the last ten years. And like all good grandfathers, he knew when to scare the hell out of small boys.

Danny, the youngest son of an under-employed family who lived a mile down the road, in a town that used to be called Nut Grove but was now better known by the number of the nearest highway turnoff, emptied the candy out of his pockets and dumped it on the counter in front of Red.

A bell above the shop door jangled as it opened. Red nodded at Treat Tyler, stepping in from the outdoor oven.

"See son," he said to Danny. "Here's the lawman, come to deal with you."

The kid turned to look at Tyler, his eyes wide.

Tyler, getting up to speed on the situation in a hurry, took confident steps forward and put his hand round behind his back, like he was reaching for something. "This the boy you called me about, Mr Peters?"

Red nodded. He looked down at Danny in disappointment.

Danny started to babble, apologising, Red trying to keep track of whether this was the tenth or eleventh time Danny had said sorry.

Tyler placed his hand firmly on the boy's shoulder, squaring off into the full lawman pose. "Jail's kinda full today, to be honest, but I'm sure we can find room." Then to Red. "You remember Bobby Calitri? The guy with the hook? He's been kinda lonely since his last cellmate got stabbed." Turning, talking to himself, but loud. "Shame we never figured out who did him."

Danny didn't say anything.

Red leaned down on the counter, smiled at Danny, that old grandpa twinkle. "You know, officer. I think maybe I was mistaken." He slid a candy bar across the counter for Danny to take. "I'm getting old, I forget things. I think Danny paid for this, and it just plain slipped my mind." As Danny reached out to take the chocolate, Red patted his hand with his own liver-spotted version. "But I'll make sure to pay attention in future."

"Yessir," Danny mumbled. "Thankyousir"

The kid turned and ran from the store. Red cracked up as the bell jangled, patted the counter top and waited out a full laugh and the cough that followed.

"The youth of today," Tyler said.

Red shaking his head again after the cough had gone. "I remember when his daddy was that age, used to try and steal beer. I think the kids now lack ambition. I worry about them. Bobby Calitri?"

"First name popped into my head."

"Never heard of him."

"He was the first person I ever shot. On the job. Already a fugitive by the time I was involved, fresh out of Glynco. Had my star a month, and this guy, insists he's innocent, holds a kid hostage at a gas station, wants a re-trial, a new lawyer, and a pizza."

"What happened?"

"Suicide by Deputy Marshal."

Red cackled, letting the humor last for a moment longer, before saying, in the same tone he'd been using on Danny, "Okay, show me."

Tyler leading the way back out into the heat, round the corner to where his car was parked in the narrow shade of the run-down old bungalow attached to the side of the store.

Tyler popped the trunk, and waved like a bored magician doing the tenth *ta da* of a matinee. Red leaned in for a closer look at the corpse. A skinny guy, maybe half-Mexican, stinking of alcohol and piss. Two neat bullet holes in his chest.

Red took a step back and craned his neck to look up at Tyler, making himself as big as he could at his age. "Did you have to do that?"

"Came a point, he'd been in my trunk so long he was starting to figure out I shouldn't be doing it."

"What was his name?"

"Jimmy."

"This Jimmy, he get us anything?"

"Led me to an ex-girlfriend, says..."

"Girlfriend?"

"Yeah."

"Of this funny bitch. Emily."

"Yeah."

Red shook his head. Weary with the mistakes of his world. "Let's get in out of the heat."

He turned on his heels, walked up through the unlocked front door of the bungalow, not worrying about whether Tyler was following. He would be. The AC was ice cold in here. Faded old furniture arranged in front of a television set, everything in 1970s shades of green and brown. Representing the last time anyone had really lived in here, rather than using it as a prop. Red's real place was up in Paradise Valley, where right now his wife, Gloria, twenty years younger and wearing it like thirty, would be sunning by the pool. Or maybe *doing lunch* in the city with some of her rich friends. She had no interest in living the fiction Red used to pass his days.

He waved for Tyler to settle into one of the seats, then took the other one himself, easing down into the cushions as every joint in his body made a cracking sound.

"My eldest granddaughter. Not even ten yet, she's saying I need to refer to her by gender neutral pronouns, and announcing that she thinks she might like girls. I tell her, nothing wrong with liking girls, I've been liking them my whole life, but could she keep her options open on boys? She tells me I'm being, what was it. *Hetero-normative*. She's nine." Pausing long enough to use the remote to turn the TV on with the sound off. A political rally occupying the news cycle. "So, this funny bitch, Emily, she the options-open type?"

Tyler said: "Far as I know, she's the options closed type."

"Shame, those tits. Anyway. So this dead Jimmy kid led you to a girlfriend."

"Right. And she tells me Emily was working on something with Leyton Wray."

"Our Leyton Wray?"

"I presume so."

Red leaned forward. "You presume so. Give me one good reason I don't just fucking kill you, will you please? Bury you out in the desert the same hole as Jimmy."

"None of this is my fault."

"Seems to me all of it is. You the one let Emily escape."

Tyler leaned forward, defensive, now, almost as panicked as Danny had been. "I would've killed her the first day, you let me, instead I had to sit on her."

"We can't be obvious about these things, Treat. I needed to figure the best way. Funny bitch had already told the DA she didn't want no deputies involved, casting all kinds of doubt on the Sheriff's Office, which Jed was pushing back on. All you had to do, keep her in that safe house for a couple days, cook up delays if the ADA tried to get to her, give Jed or me time to work something out."

Red pushed himself back into the deep cushions of the threadbare chair. Stewing on the mess. Life had been so much easier before Charlie Starr went up to New York and got himself all shot up. Charlie knew how to manage things. Now Red was left dealing with the second string. Deputy US Marshals who drove around with dead half-Mexicans in their trunk.

He turned his attention to the TV to calm down. Footage from Sheriff Jed Bashford's rally. The politician leaning over the podium, his shoulders hunched, as he shouted into the microphone.

Red pointed. "Isn't he great?"

"He's loud."

"Sound like my wife." Smiling, letting Tyler see he was self-aware about his own volume. "She's saying to me all the time, you don't need to shout, Red. They're microphones, they pick up what you say." Red pointed again. "He really is great, though, isn't he? Gets them worked up every time. Can't stick to a script for shit, but give him the bullet points and he'll hit them. The voters just like a showman, you know that? They want someone to love and hate. The words don't matter all that much, just give them some theatre."

"The border stuff has them worked up."

"Good, that's what I say to him, keep that going. All eyes down there, none here. Works for me. Of course, then you go and bring all eyes up here anyway."

"I've been trying to do it on the quiet, not get seen, not let my boss catch any sign. You want the ADA getting wind of me looking for the woman I let escape, right before she's dead, when they're already looking to see if you got people on the payroll?"

Red make a clicking noise with the inside of his mouth. Lifted up his feet to stare at them for a full minute. "All right. Done is done. Let's forget about the whole thing. So, Leyton. Our Leyton. The kid who guards our money. He's friends with this funny bitch who knows my name. And was doing time for stealing money."

"Looks like it."

"You talked to Leyton?"

"Not answering his phone. It all smells wrong. You know what I think?"

"Of course I do. I need that money, Treat."

"I know."

"I'm saying, *this* money, I need. And no drama." He pointed again at the screen. "I got my boy throwing out distractions, I got a meeting with the Water Resources people in three days. I'm saying *this* money and *this* week, I can't be having any problems."

"I know."

Red rested his feet back down, turned to look at Tyler. "I used to love the Milk Man, you know that? Like a brother. His family and my family, we were like family. Then he got stupid, started making mistakes. I'm a reasonable guy, Treat. One mistake, maybe. Two, maybe. But any more than that, I need to start looking at the bench, seeing if someone else needs called up."

Tyler nodded. Red hoped to hell he'd got the message. Tyler earned his own call-up by killing the Milk Man. The next guy in line could earn it by killing Tyler.

"I'm on it."

"You need to be. Get over to the Safari. Put your hands on that money, make sure it's there. Find Leyton, do whatever you need to with him, get him to tell you where the hell funny bitch has run off to."

THIRTEEN

Leyton let out a long sigh. "We getting so good at this, it's scary."

Rose Hudson rolled off him, swung her leg over the edge of the bed, saying nothing.

"I'm serious," Leyton said. "Actual fear. How good we are? I'm worried we might cause some earthquake, maybe."

Leyton waited for a response. Rose fished around in her pile of clothes: jeans, t-shirt, zebra apron. Picking up a pack of cigarettes, she lit up.

"What?" Leyton got up on his elbows, watching Rose as she watched him. "Come on, you don't think that was great?"

"I think you should sleep. You've been up all night."

She pulled on her underwear, wiggling from side to side to work it up. The trailer shook a little with the movement.

"You saying I'm too tired? You didn't have a good time? I'm fine." He threw off the covers. "Come on, let's go again, I'll prove it."

Rose blew smoke up into the air. Gave him one of those looks, mostly attitude, using the cigarette as a prop. Hair flicked just right. Yellow. Not blonde, yellow. "I love messing with you."

She'd always been that way. Since the first time he saw her, a student deciding to stay on the Rez after dropping out, because the cost of living was lower. The cost of getting high, too. She walked into the Safari and demanded a job. Eddie pointed to the pole, Rose pointed to the bar. Looking at Leyton, giving him the same look she was giving him now, she said, "I look like a dancer to you?"

She'd looked like a lot of things.

Still did.

Rose headed out of the room on bare feet, her shoes somewhere out near the door. Leyton leaned back, closed his eyes. She wasn't wrong. He was fried. Tired as hell. The night had been longer than he'd planned.

The stuff with Emily. Getting the bounty hunter. Bringing her back. That was a good detail, he was proud of that. Thinking on his feet.

She'd been good to talk to. Easy, not worried even when she was handcuffed. He'd played it like a movie, a cool one from the 90s, when the good guys and bad guys were basically the same, all getting good lines.

Rose came back in, fully dressed now. Tapped ash out in the cup next to the bed. "You call Bosco, make sure he got home okay?"

"He's fine, doesn't need me checking on him."

"He's a kid. After last night, you should make sure he got in."

"Loaned him my car, he got home okay." Leyton looked up at her. "Okay, alright. I'll call him later. Not now, he'll be asleep, you want me to wake him up? He's a kid, needs his rest. Come on." Leyton threw back the covers. "Let's kill some time."

"You got something in your dick?" Rose patted the sole of his naked foot. "I gotta go."

"Hey."

"No. You might be ready to run a marathon or whatever, but I'm tired and not afraid to admit it. Worked double shift last night."

"Think we just worked a double shift here."

"What are you, twelve? Come on." She waited a beat. The look again. "This was more like triple time. I need to go, where's my bag?"

Leyton blinked, looking up at her. It took him a second to think. "It's in the car, with mine."

"You left it in the car?"

"Had shit to do, you know."

"The car you loaned to Bosco?"

"Everything went nuts. Your friend, that Ben guy, he had the fight with the bounty hunter, then Eddie made me go after her, bring her back, then I had to get her car out to the garage. I got busy, there was no real time for me to move it. It's fine, it's safe. Bosco doesn't know it's there, and why would he go looking through a couple bags in my car anyway? I'll get it when I check on him later."

Rose looked down at him. Was she frowning or squinting? Then took a step forward and pulled the curtain to one side. "There's a big fire out there."

"What?"

"Right out there. That your uncle's land?"

Leyton shuffled up to look out the window. A column of thick smoke was rising up into the sky, alternating grey and black as it moved. "Shit. Yeah, I think it is."

"You sure?"

"No."

Leyton stood up, wrapping the bedsheet around his waist and shuffling to the chair piled with his clothes. The way he walked out into the world was the way the world saw him. Looking down at the pile, he wasn't sure who he wanted to be. The guy in the suit last night had been fun. Smooth, acting calm around the bounty hunter, talking money with Emily like a big shot. But that guy wouldn't wear the same suit twice in a row, and Leyton only had one. He needed it for later, his meeting with the boss. Needed to play that one cool.

"You going to check?"

Leyton said, yeah, settling on jeans and a shirt. Slipping on a pair of Vans without socks.

"Great, we go check the fire, and then we go get your car, grab my bag. We can go over in Eddie's truck."

"You'll need to get his keys."

Rose giving him another look now that said, obviously.

They both stepped down out of the trailer, onto the hot concrete at the back of the Safari. Leyton's trailer was one side of the private parking lot, Eddie's bungalow over on the other. Eddie had promised them both condos in the casino, top floor apartments so they could be on hand 24/7, living it up. In the meantime, they would stay here, waiting for their luck to break.

But now Leyton knew that luck wasn't going to break. Not without a hammer.

He stood by Eddie's pickup truck while Rose let herself into the bungalow. She had a set of keys. Leyton tried not to be jealous about that. She came back out soon after, and mimed throwing the truck keys to Leyton, to get him ready for the real thing. A second later, she tossed them over for real. Leyton missed, and they hit the side of the truck before landing in the dirt. Rose smiled and gave him the finger.

Leyton picked up the keys and took a look at the smoke again. Thinking, in the action movie, this is when the hero rides towards the danger.

He stood up straight, feeling good about himself, and climbed into the truck. Rose came round the other side, got in.

They turned out onto 602 and then across, onto the dirt road cutting through the land Eddie owned, snaking around and up eventually onto the Reservation and coming down near the reservoir. It was hard to tell at this distance, but it looked like the fire was coming from the other side of a rise, which would put it right on the border.

The truck bounced along the track.

"Eddie's suspension is shot," Rose said.

Leyton shrugged. "You should know."

"Screw you." Rose, smiling, slapping his arm with no real force.

The road led up over the rise, and at the top he could see down to the source of the smoke. A van was burning, the metal frame showing occasionally through thick black smoke and red flame.

The fire truck was standing nearby, with the crew leaning against it, just watching.

The car of a Rez cop was closer to Leyton, sitting about half a mile down the hill, with a woman next to it, Officer Bobelu. She'd have no jurisdiction here. If the van was twenty feet further along the road, she'd be in charge. Leyton drove down. Officer Bobelu didn't wave for him to stop, or shout. She just watched him approach, from the middle of the road, knowing he couldn't get around her. As he slowed down, she came round the side.

"Road's closed."

"I saw, yeah. Just checking if it was on my uncle's land."

"Is it?"

"Yeah." Leyton paused, watching the flames for a second. "Hey, why aren't they putting it out?"

"Waste of water, they say. It's as hot as it's going to get. They'll let it burn down, put it out when the fire's smaller."

Rose said, "Anyone hurt?"

"Not here." Bobelu looked back the way they had just come, nodding at something out in the distance. "But the driver shot a store clerk in Gallup."

"Dead?"

"Wouldn't you be?"

Leyton looked at the van again. Impossible to tell now. The paintwork gone, the tires melted.

It looked familiar, the same shape as the one he'd seen hanging around at the Safari all night. Those two kids.

"You catch 'em?"

"Not yet."

...

Drey wasn't having the best of days. She was just going to go ahead and admit it. Out loud, finally. The first thought she'd had in about two hours that didn't involve cussing. The first chance she'd had to say anything out of earshot of Coyote, too, as he'd climbed out of the van after directing Drey to come to a stop on this dirt track.

"Hang on," he'd said.

So now she was alone in the cab. Tapping fingers on the wheel. The blood feeling hot in her neck. Pumping. Her heart, too. Both of them screaming, demanding to know what happened. One minute, two kids who were messing around. Now?

Now she was pretty sure she was an accessory to murder.

If that clerk was dead. She didn't know. Coyote got in the van and they drove away. Didn't stop. Didn't go back to check. What Drey wondered, when did she cross the line? Was she in trouble the minute he pulled the trigger? Or when she started the van? Was it when she didn't go back and try to help?

And what would she do? There's an angry guy with a gun, and now she's maybe scared of him for the first time, and she's supposed to stop him? Argue? Refuse to drive away?

So Drey let the thought out, for the first time. She breathed out, closed her eyes, and said, "fuck."

There was a noise. Carried loud on the still morning.

Like, a match? It was that kind of thing. Something flaring and fading. Then a *whoosh*.

Coyote stepped into view, leaning in to pick up his bag.

"You hear that?" Drey said.

Coyote didn't look at her, just pulled out his gear and turned away. "Yeah, I set fire to the van."

"Wait..."

He gestured with his arm, toward the back. "Rag in the tank."

"Hold..."

Drey only thought about it for a few more seconds before grabbing her coat and jumping out. The whoosh hit the gas, and everything went up. Loud, bright, and hot. Drey was surprised by the heat. The day was already warm, but she was used to it.

This thing though, it was like all of the day's warmth in one go, pressed into her face like a wave. She sat on the ground and watched as the flames picked away at the paint. Dancing: yellow, red, gold.

Coyote, already walking away along the dirt track towards the Rez. "We should go, they'll be here soon."

"Why did you do that?"

"Burn the evidence."

Drey got to her feet. Not worried so much about the gun now, or Coyote's feelings. Enough was enough. "The *evidence*? Like the bullet you left in that guy for no reason? Like the cameras they have at those places?" Coyote flinched as her voice went up a gear. "We been driving around in that thing all night, everyone's seen us, we already committed one crime. You think burning the van, putting a big sign out here that points to where we are, you think that is burning evidence?"

Coyote pulled out the gun. For a second, Drey thought he was planning to use it. Instead, he was just looking at it. Turning it over in his hand.

"Why'd you do it?" Drey said. Giving enough time for him to answer before: "Why'd you shoot him?"

Coyote didn't answer. He shrugged and turned back on his heels, down the path.

She stepped fast to catch up with Coyote but fell in behind, thinking it best to keep him where she could see him for a while, until she figured out the next move. The land around her, as far as she could see, brown and red. Meeting the blue of the sky on the horizon. Drey paused to look back, finding it weird how a bit of land can probably look the same for a thousand years and then someone blows up a truck on it.

She thought of the dam, just over the butte on the Rez. Her mother was into all the history, that kind of stuff. She hated the dam. Said the American government had destroyed a sacred well, like the most important site to their history. Covered it over with dirt while they rearranged the land. MAB, her Mom's Asshole Boyfriend, in one of his few sober moments, had said the dam was a good thing. He said water was going to be real important soon, when all the white folks start to run out, and realize the tribes controlled most of the water in the south. They'll be able to set their own price.

But he also used to say things about some secret group who controlled all the banks, and one time he was talking about lizards dressed as humans.

Now she'd left a burning van on the land. Was she just as bad as the government? They wouldn't just let her pay it off, she knew that much.

Coyote wasn't waiting around for her to stand and think, he'd already opened up a lead. She ran to catch up.

"Where we going to go?" Drey said. "What we do next?"

"He looked really shocked," Coyote said. "They never tell you that."

Drey asked, "who?" Already knowing the answer.

Coyote stopped walking for a moment. "Guy in the shop. He had a few seconds on the way down, looked so shocked. I think his brain was still figuring it out, telling him, *hey, you been shot.* Then he had this other look, like he'd just accepted what was happening."

They walked in silence. Twenty minutes. Forty. An hour. Over the hill, down the other side, the dam in sight now, and the built-up area by the Community Health Center. Old houses, some newer ones.

Coyote came to a stop at the end of a duplex driveway. A black Toyota was badly parked behind a blue Kia. The door wasn't even shut properly.

"Why'd you do it?"

Coyote looked at her. She could read his face. His thoughts. He said, "Didn't have a reason."

FOURTEEN

First thing Medina did when she got back to her apartment overlooking Tempe Town Lake was sleep. Not for long, but enough to take the edge off. It was one of Reed Palmer's golden rules, instilled into his deputies the day they joined his office.

"Staying awake is an amateur move," he'd said, in a speech Medina heard several times over the years. "You're out on the road, or on a stakeout, you're chasing someone down, you always—*always*—make time for sleep. You're no good to me tired. And if you're no good to me, you're no good to this office, you're no good to the country. Tired people make mistakes. Tired people miss clues, or pull triggers, or fail to pull triggers. Tired people damage property. Tired people are shitty to work with."

There was another lesson there, hidden away. In demanding his staff always turned up to work fresh and ready, he was also setting an expectation of how they lived off-duty. No late nights, no parties, no stupid decisions. Palmer's whole thing was: commit to the work, put in the hours to be good at it.

Medina had committed to being *great* at it.

The trick was to enjoy your job. She'd learned that early on, with her first attempt at employment, working behind the bar on the university campus. It lasted one whole afternoon until the manager, a married forty-something, said he wanted her to be his special friend. Medina had said, "God damn it," and walked out. Made sure her next job came with a badge.

And more than following any of Palmer's rules, Medina loved sleeping. Switching her thoughts off, letting things flow wherever they needed to. Her bedroom was the part of the apartment she'd invested the most time and effort in. The first room she'd decorated and furnished. Large bed. Firm mattress. A selection of pillows, cushions and throws, to cover every mood. She could live in this room, and mostly did.

Between that and the Shelby, she had what she needed.

Though one of those things was missing from her life right now, and she felt it.

Same way she was feeling that dulled edge. Avoiding shoot-outs. Leyton getting the drop on her. Ben Nichol seeing her coming. Even the kids, that stunt they pulled with the van, outflanking her in the dark.

And now she was in her own head. Stuck there. Thinking about things more than usual.

The second thing she did, once she was showered and fresh, was get straight back to work.

Emily Scott.

A ghost from her past. A specific time in her life. Another invitation to spend time stuck in her own head.

Emily Scott, the cool girl. Most of her friends boys. Always vaguely suspicious of the girls. Emily Scott with the Avril hair. The boys thinking she put no work into it. The boys pretending just to be friends. Emily Scott with the goofy voices, the jokes, the impressions.

Emily Scott with the broken nose.

Medina didn't have any social media accounts in her own name. Another one of Palmer's old rules. But she had a few dummy accounts set up to use when she was tracking people down. She spent the best part of an hour diving through the friends and follow lists of people she'd been to school with. Opening up memories she hadn't thought about in over a decade. Seeing which of them had gained weight, had cosmetic surgery, gone bald, gotten married. She found out that the first boy she'd kissed, Ricky Freidburg, was dead now. That caught her cold for a couple minutes. A gut reaction. None of their lives had been what they'd wanted. She hadn't looked back after graduation, hadn't kept contact with people or wasted any time reliving 'glory days'. The invite for the ten-year reunion had been ignored. It would be fifteen soon enough, and she'd been planning to ignore that too. Nothing she saw made her rethink the choices she'd made along the way.

Emily Scott had a page called Emily Scott Official on Facebook. Nothing had been posted to it in three years. There was a Twitter account that went cold around the same time. There was nothing to show who she'd been close to, and

Medina couldn't quite remember. All those boys blurred into one mass image of skater pants and streaked hair. She wasn't even really sure she'd been in her year, only that they'd been at school the same time. Maybe a little older, maybe a little younger.

She headed to her spare bedroom.

Her Marshals Service income would have allowed her to get a mortgage on something closer to the office. She'd looked at a few, considering the idea for half a second when she moved back from Florida. But buying this condo off a developer's plan had been cheaper. If she'd known what was coming, quitting her job and going freelance, she would never have committed to the mortgage. But she'd learned to go with the flow. Some months were tight, some months were easy. She'd never missed a payment, but the doubt was always there. The whole area was an ongoing failure. Every ten years they redeveloped a new part, tried giving it a fancy new name, and then nobody moved there or used the name, and the prices dropped. Vacant lots turned into vacant buildings.

"Second bedroom, too," she remembering the polished blonde realtor saying with a smile, "in case you want to start a family."

Or in case your family want to dump a load of shit on you, Medina thought, looking at the pile of boxes and bags in the corner of the room. Most of it hers, from her parents' garage when they split. Some of it belonged to her younger brother, Sammy, who got a notion to travel the world but settled down in the first place he visited. She had a box of postcards from him. All the same one, over and over. A joke between them, his world tour of Seattle.

At the bottom of the pile, in a cardboard box covered in faded stickers, was Medina's high school yearbook. She opened the book, ignoring every attempt the smell made to drag her back in time, and flicked through the pages. Bad jokes. Teachers. Sports clubs. Pages of faces and names. She found Sammy, grinning out at the camera with frosted hair. Her older brother Gabe, more serious, looking slightly off to the side like his focus was on something else. And then she found herself, between the two. What was she trying with her hair? Why did she ever leave the house like that? Had she been worried that, if she didn't wear all of her eyeliner in one go, someone would come and steal it? And why did she look so serious?

No sign of Emily Scott.

Medina flicked back through. No comedy clubs, she wasn't in the drama group. Had she gone past her? Maybe in Sammy or Gabe's years? No, she wasn't in the book.

She called Gabe.

"Chloe. Hey, listen." She could hear him walking away from a conversation as he talked. Somebody in his office. "I have a bet with Melissa, something we disagreed on the other day. Maybe you can settle it for us."

Melissa, Medina's sister-in-law, a big shot at one of the local tv stations.

"Sure."

"Okay. The thing we need to know, do I have a sister?"

"Funny." Chloe, holding back a smile.

"Don't roll your eyes at me."

"You can't see my eyes."

"I don't need to." He was playing around, but with truth on his side. "I know you."

"Alright, I know it's been a while since I came over."

"Just too busy catching bad guys."

"I say that one time, you're never going to let me forget it."

"You said it to the press, Chlo. That's your thing now. Arnie has 'I'll be back', Bruce Willis has 'Yipee Ki-Yay'. This is yours."

"You're just jealous, you want a catchphrase, like *Better Call Saul*."

"You know, I was thinking about that. Like Gotta Get Gabe? Something. Use the same font. I don't think a TV company's going to sue a lawyer, and if they did, free publicity."

"I think you should probably run that by another lawyer."

"Whole reason I went to law school was so I wouldn't need to run anything by lawyers."

"How's it going?"

"It's tough, you know? Some days it feels like starting from scratch, trying to build up new clients. But then other days, I remember why I did it. You know, yesterday, I was on my way back from a meeting, and it was so hot, I just wanted a drink. So I stopped off, bought a Coke, and just sat there by the side of the road, drinking Coke and doing nothing."

"And that's why you set up your own law firm?"

"That and other perks. You know how it is."

She knew exactly how it was.

One of the first things she'd done after going into business for herself was throw out all her old suits. Her own rules, on her own time.

"So, what do you say? Do I have a sister? Is she going to some see us?"

Chloe let the smile spread now. Rolled her eyes for real. "Sure, let's work out a dinner or something."

"We can get Sammy in by Zoom."

"You remember Emily Scott?"

Gabe's tone changed. "She's *not* coming to dinner."

There was something there. Still joking, but with an edge.

"You do remember her, then?"

"Think I'd forget the girl whose nose my sister turned to pulp?"

"It wasn't that bad."

"They had to reconstruct it, Chlo. Her parents tried to get our parents to pay for it."

Emily Scott, the first girl Medina kissed.

Emily Scott, the cool girl with the breasts and the Avril hair, the first time Medina really took out her interest in girls as well as boys for a test drive. Emily Scott, the first girl to kiss Medina, and to do it maybe five minutes before Medina was ready to admit she was down for it.

Medina remembered exactly how it happened. For real now, not the way she'd told herself it happened at the time. Emily Scott the cool girl hanging back from the group on a mall trip one Saturday, talking to Medina. But not talking. Flirting. The two of them maybe both testing an idea out. Emily Scott the cool girl brushing Medina's hand, casually. Then touching her shoulder and arm a few times. Then wiping something from her face. Then kissing her.

Then the boys turning. Then the laughing and whistling.

Then the punch.

"In fairness, it was a good punch."

"Oh yeah," Gabe said. "From what I was told, it was a great punch. She went into comedy, right? I remember seeing her name on club posters. Then she got arrested, I think?"

"Armed robbery. She went down."

Medina could almost hear the exact moment Gabe figured it all out. "She's out, and you're after her?"

"That's pretty close."

"What's the rest?"

"Well, okay you're exactly right. She's out and I'm after her. I was looking in the yearbook to try and find a lead that the Marshals might not have, something personal."

"She's not in the book."

"Well, I know that now."

"Yeah, missed getting her picture done because she'd just had surgery on her nose. Huge plaster thing sitting on her face, swollen cheeks, black eyes."

"When you say it like that, I sound bad."

"Her ex is still around, I think. Lisa Afobe, you remember her?"

Another half memory. A pretty black girl, with a smile like she'd just cracked a wise-ass joke. She flipped through the pages of the yearbook, recognizing the face before she read the name.

FIFTEEN

Lisa Afobe was smoking outside the coffee shop as Medina pulled up, standing under the cover of the awning, her feet only inches away from where the shade gave way to the bright heat of the sun.

Lisa smiled. "Chloe Medina," stretching the words out.

Medina nodded. "You remember me."

"Never had chance to forget, you were all she talked about when we first started going together."

"You know why I'm here, then."

Lisa's smile widened. "Already had another Marshal come round askin'."

Medina let that pass by, choosing silence rather than either truth or a lie. Clearly, Lisa knew Medina had been in the Marshal Service. Maybe from gossip, or from one of the news stories. If she didn't know Medina was a recovery agent now, there was no harm in keeping that omission going a little longer.

"You on a break?"

Lisa snorted. "Guess you can call it that. End of my first shift, starting a second one soon as this is finished." Holding up the cigarette. "Then I go home, sleep, do it all again tomorrow."

"It's good to see you."

Lisa shook her head a couple times, like, don't even try. "You going to pretend we were friends at school now, play catch up?"

"Thought I might try that approach, yeah."

They both laughed. Just a little. Enough.

"Saw you on the news a bunch of times." Lisa stubbed out her cigarette, took a look through the shop window, and lit another. "Always looking cool. What was that line you said?"

"I don't remember."

"Yeah, you do. I bet you said it a bunch of times, that was the only time it caught on, got on the TV. Now you can't ever say it again, because everyone'll think you're faking it."

Medina was growing to like Lisa Afobe. Out of nowhere, not talking to each other in over ten years, Lisa had a way of seeing right through her.

"You'd make a good marshal."

"I don't like catching bad guys."

"So you and Emily stayed together after school?"

"Yeah, I told all this to the other guy."

"Treat Tyler?"

Lisa squinted. "Don't think he told me his name. Showed me ID, but I didn't read it. Just looked at the star. I guess it's fun carrying one of those?"

More than you know, Medina thought, but said: "Taller than me, but not much. Acts like he owns the world."

"That's him, yeah."

Medina decided to go all in. Thinking Lisa would see it for the truth and trust her more for it. "I'm not in the Marshals anymore. I work for myself."

"No shit, like a detective or something?"

"Bail recovery agent. But bounty hunter sounds cooler."

"You track people down, like that guy on TV?"

"I think I have better hair, but yeah. Someone skips bail, I go get them."

"So that's why you're after Emi."

"I don't really like Tyler much. The way you talk about him, I don't think you did, either. I want to get to her before he does."

"Either way, I give you information, you're using it to bring her in."

"I think she's in trouble, Lisa. I think she's mixed up over her head with the wrong people, and if they get to her first, they're not bringing her in, they're heading out into the desert."

Lisa stared at her for a second, looking from one eye to the next, reading her face. Then she turned to look out into the sun. "Shit." The tone said she knew it was all true.

"Tell you what, why don't you just start with what you already told Tyler?"

Lisa sucked on her cigarette, blew out smoke. "So, I said how we was together for years after school. Emi was always trying to get this comedy thing going, and I was saving for college. I swear, she couldn't hold down any job more than a week. You know how they are."

"Anything that's not one hundred percent of what they want, it's something to rebel against."

"Right. Truth. And I'd cover her lazy ass, every week, or end of the month, whenever she needed. I'd buy all the food, pay the bills. She'd keep borrowing, add it to some list we both pretended she kept, like she was ever going to pay me back."

"You know the figure?"

"Probably to the nearest dollar. But I didn't care about that."

"Sure."

"So then one day, after her comedy is taking off, she's on the road for three weeks. Comes back different. You can just tell, you know? She was changed. Looks at me different. She took me out for dinner, said, 'Baby, I think we grown apart.'"

"In a public place, so you wouldn't shout."

"Yeah, she was wrong about that."

"You shouted?"

"Shouted. Threw things. Straight at her head, then at the people on the next table who complained, the waiter who asked me to calm down. The manager. I'm saying, I caused a *scene*. Looking back, wish I'd set fire to something."

"Did you stay in touch after that?"

Lisa took a long drag on the cigarette. "Yeah. Long enough to turn her in, get my revenge."

Medina grinned.

She flat-out liked Lisa now. This attitude, these miles on the clock. Another time, different circumstances, they could be friends.

"And you knew she was out?"

"She came to me. Yesterday. Saying she needed my car, had a line on a job and some money, and she would add the car to what she owed me. Tried giving me that look, like I'd fall for it just because we used to have a thing."

"You said no."

"I said *hell* no."

"Not right away, though. You thought about it."

Lisa squinted, then grinned. "I see why she was so crazy about you. Yeah. I thought about it. You know. She has this thing. You just want to like her. Doesn't matter how much she owes you, somehow you come out feeling like you owe her."

See why she was crazy about you.

New information, right there.

"You told all of this to Tyler?"

"Not that last part. But yeah. And he asked if I knew anything else, like where she was going. I told him I'd heard a name, one of her friends, Leyton."

Medina looked down at her feet for a second to hide her own smile. Of course, Leyton would come up. How many different versions of him were there?

"And what didn't you tell Tyler?"

Lisa pushed off from the wall, checking the time on her phone. "I need to get back."

"Come on, Lisa. Help me to help Emily. You knew her better than anyone, and after all that time it was you she came to for help. You know more, even if you don't think you do, you'll know something I can use."

"You're the one broke her nose, you want to help now?"

"I want to get paid. You know that. Tyler's getting paid. The criminals who're after her will be getting paid. We're all doing this because it's our job. But some of us are better for Emily than others. The wrong people get her, she's dead. Tyler gets her, she's back in the system. I get her? Maybe she still has choices."

Lisa nodded, once, twice, okay, okay. "She said this thing with Leyton, it wasn't on the level, but she'd be getting a load of cash. She didn't say how much, but said she'd send me some of it to pay for the car. I need my car, so I told her to try Chuck."

Medina remembered the name. "Thane."

"Yeah. He was her best friend, years back. but they fell out after what she did to me."

"Where could I find him?"

"KUPD, he's a DJ. He's on air right now, I think."

"And Emily said she was going to send you money, did she say where from? Any idea where she'd be heading after the job?"

"No, but she always used to say, 'baby, when I make it, we're moving to LA.' She was obsessed with it. So, if she got money...." She shrugged. "I don't know."

"Thanks, Lisa."

Medina headed over to the Pontiac, feeling the burn as soon as she stepped out from the shade.

Lisa called out, "You didn't remember me, really, did you?"

Medina paused. Thought it over and chose the truth again. "No, sorry."

"So you don't remember the hundred bucks I lent you?"

Medina smiled as she slipped into the seat. "Nice try."

SIXTEEN

"You believe that?" Leyton slammed his hands on the steering wheel. "You believe that? I'm saying, can you even-"

"Don't matter if I believe it." Rose, in the front passenger seat, leaning across to touch his arm, calm him down. "It happened."

"One thing. All he had to do. One. Thing. Drive my car to his house. Park it up. Drive it back to me a few hours later. Just *one thing.*"

They were sitting outside Bosco's house, in the subdivision behind the Community Health Center. Bosco, sleepy eyed and smelling of reefer, answered the door, not really understanding why Leyton kept asking where the Toyota was.

"It's right there," Bosco said, pointing at the empty spot behind his mom's Kia, before seeing the problem and saying, "Oh."

Leyton exploded at him. Rose was calmer, touching Leyton's arm to take control of the conversation and saying, "When was the last time you saw it?" With a smile, nice like. Rose had a power over Bosco, he turned into a shy child around her.

"Drove home like you said," Bosco to Leyton, before smiling again at Rose. "Came right here."

"Were you lit up?" Leyton talking softer, following Rose's lead. "Smoke one on the way?"

Bosco grinned. "I was smoking all the way back from Phoenix, dude. Following you and that lady we grabbed. Getting a nice buzz on, you know? Then a stronger one while I was waiting at the Safari, I knew I didn't need to do another long drive so I could get nice and gone for a while. Then you let me borrow the car to come home." He cracked a snort of laughter. "Car was smelling pretty ripe by the time I got here, figured you want me to air out so..."

His words trailed off. There was a realisation setting in.

"So what?" Leyton already knew the answer, but asked anyway.

"Left the door open. Just a little. Give it some air."

"Didn't think maybe crack the window an inch?"

Bosco didn't have a reply. He stood there, nodding slowly.

Rose waited to make eye contact with him again before asking, "And the keys?"

Bosco went through the motions of searching. He patted his pockets, despite already wearing a different pair of cargo shorts, so then he went and checked the others. Walked round the house, came back to the door to say what they'd already know, he'd left them in the car.

Leyton, back in the truck now, beating the shit out of the steering wheel and swearing loud. Rose lit a cigarette and took a long drag. Eased back into her seat. Leyton couldn't understand how she wasn't freaking out.

"You get what this means?" He said, looking at her. "Both our bags were in that Toyota."

"Still are, I hope."

How the hell was she so calm? "I'm saying, you get what this means though, don't you? We don't have them. Whoever stole the car has them." He hit the wheel again. "This whole thing's been a mess since it started. Since the very first minute."

"Complications." Rose blew out a line of smoke, gave him one of her special looks. "That's all. Last night was a complication. This is a complication. We can figure it all out."

"How? How we going to do that? How we going to find..."

Rose smiled, nodding. Leyton could see her reading his expression, watching in real time as the answer came to him. The trackers. After a bunch of cars got stolen from in front of the Safari, Eddie had paid for GPS trackers to be fitted to both his Pontiac and Leyton's Toyota, with a subscription to a security service, a company that can track the signal across country, let you see where your car is any given moment.

Leyton had thought of the one in Eddie's car last night, when his uncle insisted on hiring the bounty hunter. Chloe Medina hadn't been part of the plan, but once Leyton suggested to Eddie he should loan her his car, everything got easier again. His new plan, use the tracker to let Medina lead him right to Emily.

See the job got done right. But he'd not been thinking about the one in the Toyota.

"We go get my laptop," he said. "Log in to the security system, follow the little blue dot all the way to the Toyota."

Rose nodded, well done. "And our bags."

Leyton's brow furrowed. Yeah, that worked. But created another problem. "How can we go after both? We can't follow the bounty hunter to Emily if we're following my Toyota."

Rose placed her hand on his thigh, focusing his mind real fast on her words. "Which one you care about the most?"

•••

"You believe that?" Coyote was grinning, almost howling. More animated and excited now than Drey had seen him in months. "How cool was that?"

"Pretty cool."

"I just walk up, open the door, the keys are there. I don't even think we stole this, you know? A car sitting on the drive with the keys? That's an invitation. It's like they just loaned it to us."

He was talking differently now, he was riffing, like he was in a movie scene. His accent was different too, and Drey wasn't even sure he noticed it.

Drey trying to figure out now exactly how much trouble she was in. Why was she even here? She hadn't shot anybody. Only thing she'd done wrong, this whole time, was pointing the gun at that bounty hunter. But she'd lowered it, hadn't she? Backed down, let her go. No, all she'd done was hang out with her best friend, tolerate his weird mood, and been too scared to stand up to him when he shot somebody. Was that a crime? Except now, she was sure, she'd helped steal this car.

Had she, though? Sure, she was there when it got stolen, and she was in it now. She'd seen it happening. Got in, knowing the score. But it was Coyote who did it, just like it was Coyote who shot that guy, and Coyote who torched the van.

She'd seen enough news, watched enough TV. What she was was an accessory.

But looking at Coyote now, seeing him smile, holler, seeing him happy, everything started to feel like a dream. They were back to sitting in the garage, or in MAB's van, smoking herb and planning crazy heists they'd never get round to doing. Having fun, playing roles, dreaming big.

"I think this is Leyton's car," Coyote said, flooring the pedal now, heading west along the 53. "The guy from the Safari, you know, the one likes to play gangsta."

Drey knew Leyton. Everyone in the area knew Leyton. But she focused more on his girlfriend, the white girl, Rose. She was interesting. Always watching you, like she was always thinking, figuring things out. Drey liked to watch people's eyes. Not say anything, just watch their eyes as they talked, she felt like you saw what they were really saying if you watched. Sometimes, she felt like she knew what they were going to say even before they said it. Like when she'd looked into Coyote's eyes and heard, even before he said anything, that he didn't know why he'd shot that guy. He'd been a different person then, for a few seconds. A version of him she'd never seen before.

"This thing can move," Coyote said as they picked up speed. "Doesn't look like it can, but it really does." Then he looked over at the glovebox. "Hey, he likes to play gangsta, let's see what he's got."

Drey opened it up. Something small and black fell out, landing between her legs. A Taser. She also found a gun, a small one, neither of them knew what make it was, and a couple bags of weed. There was another bag. Drey held it up. A powder. Off white, more like a pale brown.

Coyote slammed the wheel in celebration. "You believe that?"

They passed a road sign. Drey said, "MAB lives in Tucson. We could go there, get a chance to sit and think, figure things out."

"We can't go there," he laughed. "They'll expect that. We can't do anything the feds will expect. We gotta change our thinking now, we're outlaws."

Feds.

Outlaws.

Drey looked into Coyote's eyes as he turned to smile at her. She started to think, he's not understanding any of this. He's not really here.

For the first time in forever, Drey wanted her mom.

SEVENTEEN

Medina found Chuck Thane's voice on the Pontiac's radio. Recognized it straight away, now that high school memories were coming back. People she hadn't thought about in ten years, starting to take up space in her head.

"See the thing about these movies," Thane said. "is they want us to believe people will get sick of dinosaurs. They say after a few years, after people have been paying to see the T-Rex, that we'll all get bored and they'll need to start designing new ones."

He was sounding rehearsed. This was a bit, a speech he'd made before, now just a lifeless repeat. Medina could picture him, as he used to be, a class clown. Always talking in different voices, pulling faces. Putting '*hello*' on the end of a line and waiting for the laugh.

On the radio, a woman replied, "Sure," humoring him.

"But what I'm saying is, numbers at Disneyland never go down, do they?"

"I don't think so?'

"And that's just immigrants in suits, women dressed up like princesses. If we'll keep going there, why would we get sick of being able to see dinosaurs?"

"Well, I think, when the Pirates of the Caribbean breaks down..."

Medina killed the engine, taking the voices with it. She was sitting in the parking lot outside the radio station. KUPD was on north Fifty-Second, sharing a two story building with a gym and a dentist. Through the windows, Medina could see men and women working out on stationary bikes and treadmills, working up a sweat indoors, away from the sun.

She headed in through the front door and up a flight of stairs, to the radio station's first floor reception. There was nobody on the desk, so she walked straight in, down the hallway

that ran alongside the studio. Through the glass she could see
Thane. He was older, but not different. Still too much product
in his hair, still with a chain around his neck. His face was a little
wider, and even from a distance, Medina could see the line
around the edges where the fake tan gave way to the real one.

Medina pushed in through the door to the next room,
finding a young woman with purple bangs manning the control
desk. She had a headset and held up a finger to ask Medina to
wait.

"Yeah, sure Chuck," she said.

Medina realised this was the other voice off the radio, the
bored sidekick.

From a speaker on the desk, Chuck said, "And now, from
one thing that makes no sense, to another, as we play into the
news with 'Drops of Jupiter'."

The song started to play and the studio door opened. Chuck
stuck his head out and said, "Oh, hi Chloe," like they'd seen each
other recently. Then, to his sidekick he said, "Come on, Gina,
what was that bit with the Jurassic Park quote?"

"I thought it was funny." Her tone didn't suggest she ever
found anything funny.

"You're killing me here," Chuck said. "You're the straight
man, I do the jokes. You gotta set me up for fun shit like that, not
steal it." Then, to Chloe, "Haven't seen you in..."

"Thirteen years."

"Thirteen? Wow, yeah. So," he switched into his DJ mode,
high-beam smile. "How you doing?"

"I'm looking for Emily Scott."

Medina watched his reaction. It wasn't surprise. He didn't
say, 'well, that's easy, she's in prison.' He blinked. The smile
going down a notch, for just a second, before firing back up.

He turned to Gina, "How long we got?"

"Two minutes twenty left on the song, ten seconds on the
stingers, then the news is four minutes."

"So, how long we got?"

Gina rolled her eyes, shooting Chuck a look that told
Medina they were screwing. "Well now it's five minutes, fifty
seconds."

"Be ready with something long after," Chuck said. Then, to
Medina, "Let's talk outside, in the sun."

Away from the microphones, Medina thought.

Back down the steps, and out in the sunshine, first thing Chuck said, looking up at the sky, was: "It always seems like a good idea until you do it."

"Almost never. We could sit in your car if it's too hot, blast the AC."

Chuck hesitated a second time. "I don't have it today, it's in the shop."

Medina banked that information and led the way to the Pontiac, sitting in the shade. She turned the key a half step, bringing the radio back on. The newsreader was talking about Sheriff Jed Bashford, and his latest border crusade. They cut to a clip from his speech, Bashford's voice booming out from the speakers.

"He's always got to shout," Chuck said. "You'd think by now he'd know how microphones work."

"Worked with him once," Medina said. "In the Marshal Service. We had to protect him at the courthouse. He was a witness in a trial, and someone had sent in death threats."

"Wouldn't he get secret service for that?"

"Yeah, but we guard the court, the judges and prisoners. And I think he just wanted to throw his weight around, get off on the idea of being able to order us around, just to show he could. So I got the job of guarding him all day, going everywhere with him. Me and another deputy I used to work with."

"And how was he? To be around?"

"Exactly how you'd think."

"Oh, I bet he *loved* you."

Medina could remember exactly how many times she'd had to bite her tongue at the sheriff's comments. His stupid jokes, the way he bullied the people around him, even those with badges and shields. He'd ordered in a steak from Durant's, delivered to the courthouse to keep from needing to go outside, and asked for it to be well done. He'd not offered any tip to the kid who delivered it, Medina handing one over out of her own pocket with a sympathetic smile.

She changed the subject. "You worked here long?"

"Three years. I was in LA for a while, trying to break the market, you know. Get something solid. But we all end up back here eventually." He turned to smile at Medina. "Right?"

She ignored the cue to talk about herself, sticking to the subject. "You always wanted to work in radio?"

"No. Well, I guess. I mean, there was a while there, when I used to watch Kevin Smith movies, when I wanted to own some kind of film rental store. But that was a dumb plan, so, yeah. It was this or comedy, and I don't really like crowds, so this way I can ignore them."

"You didn't watch the movies and think of being a filmmaker?"

He stared at her.

"Did you ever try it? Comedy?"

"Sure. Used to go to the clubs with, uh…" he paused. Didn't say the name, and continued. "I got a decent five minutes on the go at one point. But I could never get loose enough, I was always stiff, like I was just doing bits that I'd rehearsed, it never felt real."

"You used to do announcements at school, I remember that. Try and do funny stuff. Didn't you MC a prom?"

He grinned at the memory, part of him seemed to have never left it. "Yeah. Yeah, that was fun. Then I started doing college radio. You know, the cliché. Now here I am."

Medina had him off guard now, shifting subject again. "You get Gina to drive you in?"

"We that obvious?"

"I was just wondering, did you tell her, when she drove you in, that you let a fugitive with great tits borrow your car?"

Chuck laughed. Not even trying to lie or hide it. He paused to look at the radio, where the news was ending. There was a stinger for the station, then an ad for a local law firm, and a song started to fade in.

"You're good," he said.

"It's my job."

"She's my friend."

"I know. And there's a whole speech I could give. How she's in trouble and bad people are after her, and that she'll be safer if I find her first. And then I'd reassure you, that you're probably safe, because you're a friend from high school, and the bad guys are probably focusing more on her criminal connections. But that can change, the longer she's on the run, the deeper they'll dig, and I'd try and make you worry about that. But..." pausing, she turned off the radio. "Your show is on right now, and you're already wondering if you have time to get back to the desk before the song ends. So, maybe just tell me where she is?"

EIGHTEEN

"This is a bad idea."

Emily Scott looked around the venue. The Maple Bar, a small place on Lime Avenue. It was afternoon in Long Beach and sunlight was a big part of the deal, streaming in through the windows, all open. A large wooden door had been slid open, running the length of the outside wall, opening the place out onto the street, with seats outside.

The bartender, Scott's friend Darrel, was leaning on the bar, wearing sunglasses indoors. "You got a crowd here, man. Twenty people. Twenty-five."

"It's daytime. Comedy doesn't work in the light. People won't laugh, they get self-conscious, too aware of the people around them."

The Maple had started putting on comedy shows in the afternoons a couple months back, Darrel had said. It pulled in crowds. Mostly students and young parents: the bar would let people in with strollers during the day and sometimes the comics would have to deal with crying babies. There was no cover charge, and most of the Maple's money came from the afternoon food specials. Pizzas. Burritos. Tacos. The opening and headline acts got paid from the takings, the open spots worked for exposure.

Scott was watching the crowd now. Listless, whispering to each other, laughing at their own jokes. The seats weren't even arranged to look like a club, facing the acts. They were wooden benches, the customers facing each other, turning to look at the people on the microphone. The stage itself was a spot in the corner, beneath a large television screen, next to the washroom.

Two acts had already been on. The first, an experienced local pro, pulled a few laughs, but went long stretches with nothing but traffic noises and the strain in his voice.

The second act was political, she'd had some good jokes, but the audience didn't laugh so much as agree with her very loudly.

"The one person in life you can't trust," Scott said to Darrel as the set closed, "is someone who comes to a comedy show to clap at jokes."

Now the MC was doing crowd work. Getting people's names and occupations, riffing on the answers, trying to get some extra heat going. Scott would be on in a couple minutes.

"They're not ready," she said. "It's too early. We're creatures of the night. We need dark clubs, shadows. House lights are bad enough, but we might as well be trying to get laughs in the center of the sun."

"You always like this before you go on?"

Scott smiled. "Pretty much, yeah."

"I see why they locked you up."

Scott hated this moment. The wait. The time her brain would start questioning every decision, reacting to things that hadn't happened yet, worrying about the guy on the middle bench, who was primed and ready to heckle.

But Scott had every advantage here. She'd been a pro. She knew how to get laughs, even in a dry room like this. And the crowd were expecting nothing from her. She was going on as a nobody, in the part of the show reserved for new acts and hobbyists. It was almost unfair, to be sneaking up on the crowd like this. Darrel had told her, the night before, you let me, I can put your name on the bill and pay you as a headliner. You're famous, Em. The bank robber comedian.

Scott didn't want her name announced, but she couldn't tell Darrel the real reason why. When she turned up at his door, she said they'd let her out early. She didn't mention the self-appointed nature of the parole. She came up with an excuse about wanting a low profile until she had a strong new twenty minutes. And anyway, it hadn't been a bank.

"Oh yeah," Darrel said. "I thought it was?"

"Credit Union."

"That's not a bank?"

"Different thing. You join a credit union, like a member. It's your money they're using, all shared around, one big pot. A bank has customers not members. It's still your money they use, but they own the pot. I'd figured, with the economy what it was, everyone was using credit unions and they'd have a load of cash on hand, so people could buy cookers, pay their rent, that kind of thing. But they wouldn't have the security of a bank."

"And why you rob the place, again?"

"Seemed like a good idea at the time."

The line usually worked, why would anybody push for the truth when they could get a laugh?

"So cool, man." Darrel sipped on a beer, one of the two he'd got from the refrigerator, offering the other to Scott as they relaxed on the couch in Darrel's apartment. "How'd you do it? Give me the full story."

"Not much to tell." Scott, skipping ahead in her thoughts, leaving out most of the details. "I went in, showed the nice woman my gun, and said, 'Don't panic, I would like to withdraw all of the money you can reach without drawing attention.'"

"She do it?"

"She did."

"How much?"

"She could reach around five thousand dollars. I think probably more, if I'd been willing to threaten her, but that didn't feel right."

"You said you showed her the gun."

"It's more that I let her see it. Tucked into my jeans, you know?" Scott leaned back, mimed opening a jacket, casually, brushing an imagined gun with her hands on the way down to pockets. "I never mentioned it. Never said I was going to use it. Later on, my lawyer used that, tried to argue I hadn't even really tried to rob the place, the cashier misunderstood. I'm a comedian, he said, my line was a joke, but she took it serious and handed me the money."

"That work?"

"What you think? I went into a credit union with a gun. I wasn't a member, and I asked for their money. So then my lawyer tried to use my history, say this was the first time I'd done anything like this, I had no record, no pattern of criminal activity."

"What that do?"

"Nothing. Judge said no criminal has a record on their first job, but most people start off small and get big, I went straight to armed robbery, so I was a danger to the public. I think he'd seen my stand-up act."

"So what changed? They let you out? You not a danger anymore?"

Scott dodged the question with a joke. But thinking back on the robbery had taken her mind right back into that moment. Let her remember how it felt, to walk in there, so calm, no worries. It had been the closest thing she'd ever found to doing stand-up. All the fear was in the anticipation, getting the gun, planning how it would go. But once she walked in the door, she was just in the zone, she was doing the thing, and it was either going to work, or it wasn't.

And now she was back preparing for another trip to the zone, in the bar, on a sunny afternoon. Watching as the MC wrapped up her bit, looking over to let Scott know her time was coming. The laughs were there, she was sure of it. She'd just need to go digging around for them a little, do the heavy lifting to get them warmed up herself, save her really niche stuff for the back half of the set, once she had them.

The MC called out Scott's name, the fake one she'd given, and she headed towards the mic.

No fear now. The jokes worked or they didn't.

Just like robbing a credit union.

NINETEEN

Chuck Thane's Honda Civic was parked out front of an apartment building on East Florida Street, Long Beach. Faded brown brick trimmed with white tile. Three floors, the bottom taken up with white garage doors, the two above filled with balconies outside each apartment. Medina parked up further down the street and watched the car, waiting for any sign of Emily Scott.

After about thirty minutes, another car pulls into the street and parks up behind the Civic. A blue Ford pickup. Medina watched as Darrel Greer got out, recognizing him from the social media accounts she'd looked up after Chuck gave her the name. Darrel locked the pickup and turned to look her way. Medina was used to it. People always needed to scope out the Shelby, the coolest car in any street, and this Pontiac was no different. She'd learned not to worry about it. Let them see you, what they going to do? Most of the time she was wearing sunglasses, and people couldn't see her eyes to know she was watching them back. An innocent person isn't going to think twice, unless they decide to come ask you out. Which happened a couple times, in the middle of a job. Always men. The first guy came right up on her side, tapped the window like he was a cop. The second, a cute blond, she'd given it some thought, liking the way he talked about the Shelby for five minutes before even trying anything else.

Darrel's eyes lingered on the car before he turned and headed up the open staircase to the first floor of the apartment building.

After a few more minutes of no movement, the glass door leading to one of the balconies slid open. Darrel stuck his head out, then ducked back inside. He'd opened it for air, not to step out and smoke.

Medina guessed Scott wasn't up there.

Why would she have been sitting in the heat, not opening the window?

She keyed the ignition and drove down to the end of the road, turning right, then right again into the narrow lane running behind the buildings. Slowing down as she passed the rear of Darrel's place, she took a note of the gate, the back entrance, the pile of trash. There was a back way for Scott to come and go, but she wouldn't be doing that if she felt happy enough parking the car out front. She took the Pontiac down to the end and then back round onto East Florida, pulling in across from the Civic, just close enough that it would be difficult for Scott to pull out in a hurry.

She checked her gun, slipped it back into the holster, and pocketed a taser off the front passenger seat. She patted the cuffs strapped to her belt, and gave serious thought to grabbing the baton from the back seat. But she was pretty sure Darrel was alone up there, and she didn't have any problem with him unless he made one. She got out the car, still feeling strange to be closing the door, it didn't sound like her Shelby, made a whole different noise.

Medina crossed the street and took the stairs slowly up to the next floor. She counted the doors along until she was outside Darrel's place, and knocked like a cop. In the movies there was always that moment, someone calls out, who is it? Already knowing it's not good. Then the character has to make something up, or tell the truth, but the truth always ended in needing to force the door open. Medina couldn't think of one time, in all her years as both a Deputy Marshal and a recovery agent, that anyone had asked who was there before opening the door.

Darrel opened. Looking her up and down, noticing the gun on her hip, then shrugging. "She's not here."

He turned and walked back into the room, leaving the door open for Medina to follow. Medina hesitated, not sure how to play it, before walking in after him.

"You know why I'm here?"

"You're not a cop." He turned, let her see him looking her up and down a second time. "You're something else. But yeah, stranger turns up at my door, packing a gun, when Emi is staying over? I know why you're here."

He waved at the empty sofa, set in the center of the room, facing a television screen paused in the middle of some video game about shooting a bunch of people in a desert. Medina took a step toward the sofa but didn't sit down. She wasn't ready to let her guard down.

"You're sure I'm not a cop?"

Darrel walked through to a small kitchen area off the main room, bent down, opened a refrigerator. "Beer?"

"No thanks."

"I'm a bartender." He came back up holding one for himself, popped the lid on an opener bolted to the counter. "I can read people when they come in. Figure who's a cop, who's a student, who's going to go from zero to stupid in just one drink." Darrel paused to sip, smiling. He was relaxed. Used to talking to strangers. "You're like a PI or a bounty hunter. One of those." He came around this side of the counter to lean back on it, resting one elbow on the surface, holding the beer in his other hand. "She lied to me, didn't she?"

"Depends what she told you."

Medina sat down, sinking into the cushions of the sofa.

Darrel nodded at her, taking the point. *True that.* "Said she cut a deal, let out early for good behavior and promising to leave the state."

"You bought that?"

"I don't know." He sighed, cracked another smile. "Part of being friends with Emi. After a while, it's not what you believe, it's just that she says things and you appreciate the effort, you know? She's got a heart of gold, but shit for brains." He scratched just above his eyebrow. "No, that's not fair. She's smart as hell. I just mean, she has this way, like she makes everyone around her think they owe her, but I I don't think it's ever deliberate or cynical."

"I know what you mean. And she did cut a deal, they were going to let her out early. But she ran before she could hold up her end."

Darrel pulled the beer away long enough to say, "fucking Em." But it was warm. There was no anger or resentment. "We wrote a screenplay together once, a comedy thing. This old guy, a famous bank robber, doing thirty years in prison, breaks out six weeks before he was due to be released."

"Get anywhere with it?"

"Nowhere."

"You're okay with her lying to you?"

"She knows I wouldn't have helped her if she told the truth. I mean, she's a friend, sure. But there's friends and there's friends. I'd lie to the cops for a friend. Not a friend. Well..." His paused, gave enough time for the joke to be obvious. "I'd lie to the cops for anyone. But someone like you comes round, I think Emi knows I'm not going to cover for her without a good story."

"You're not worried I'll get you in trouble, telling me this?"

"What trouble? A friend turns up at my door, tells me a lie, asks for a place to crash. A...which one are you?"

"Bounty hunter."

"A bounty hunter turns up, tells me Emi lied, I co-operate. The thing I did wrong, I didn't know I was doing wrong. Plus," another pause. Medina was getting used to him now, his ways, the same pause before each joke, like he was delivering the monologue on the Tonight Show. "I offered you a beer. You sure you don't want one?"

"I'm good. What's she doing in town?"

"Gigs. That's why I didn't worry too much about her lying, I guess. She turns up, asks me to help find gigs. Point out the local comedy scene, tell her who to be nice to."

"She's performing?"

"Of course." Darrel said it like the most obvious thing in the world. Why wouldn't a wanted felon be hopping up in front of crowds? "Though, to think on it again now, I guess it was obvious. The way she keeps using fake names when she goes up. Said she wanted a low profile because she was building new material, but the one thing about Emi, she never wants a low profile."

"She performing tonight?"

"I know the guy does the booking for the Laugh Factory, downtown."

"You do comedy?"

"No." Darrel finished the beer, went back around for another. He didn't carry himself like a problem drinker, but he put them away fast. "Well, yeah. Not stand-up. I used to do improv and sketches. I'm a writer, that's my thing. Comedy writer."

"Professional?"

"You're never a professional comedy writer. You're a professional everything else. The guy who helps fix other people's shit, the guy who does the coffee run, the guy who's called in at the last minute to fill in on some YouTube panel show. You know, for a while there, I was Emi's big LA connection. The guy she knew that worked at a studio."

"Which one?"

"Warners. Went in to get set up as a screenwriter, ended up manning some mildly unimportant spreadsheets. It got me a pass on the lot, but there's only so many days you can spend your lunch hour watching people cry in Popeyes before you need out."

"You commuted in from here?"

"Yeah, and that was the other mistake. All anybody wants to do, when they find out you travel into Hollywood, is ask what route you took, start comparing notes, like it's a competition."

Medina looked around the room, thinking, living the dream doesn't seem to have payed much. But that got her to thinking about money, and that maybe Scott would have Eddie's stash hidden around here somewhere.

"Where's Emily staying, the sofa?"

Darrel's rueful smile told what was coming next. "No, I take the sofa, she gets the bed."

"That doesn't seem fair."

"Emi is Emi. You just end up...I'm a mug, I guess."

"But her stuff is here?"

Darrel shrugged. "Not much stuff, to be honest. There's the car, clothes. She's got the big bag she takes everywhere with her, like she's a bike messenger, the bag bigger than she is."

"How big is the bag?" Medina holding back from adding, *big enough for a couple million dollars?*

"Like this." Darrel set down his beer to hold his hands out, as wide as his shoulders, "Pretty big. First night she turned up, I asked if she'd got a dead baby in there."

"That a thing people often bring to your door?"

"It's an old joke we had. Everything we carried was the worst thing you could think of on the spot. Like, when I had my guitar case and people would think they were funny by asking what was in it, I'd say something gross, 'Half a pregnant monkey,' Emi would then go up, like, 'we ate the other half.' And I'd have to beat that, or lose, say something like, 'we ate it after we-'"

"Did she tell you what was in it?"

"...had sex with....no, she didn't. Why're you after her? She got a good price?"

That was the first time Medina had given any thought to what the price on Emily's head might be. She needed to look it up on the system. Some bounty hunter she was. What was wrong with her? First finding out Big Wheel was involved, then Treat Tyler, and all those old memories flooding in, and now this.

She wasn't even concentrating on her own words as she said, "I knew her at school."

"Shit, you're, uh, Cassie? Coco?"

"Chloe."

"Chavez?"

"Medina."

"Yes. Yes. We all heard about you. Said she had an ex-girlfriend who was this hot Marshal."

Medina ignored the invitation to flirt. "I was never her girlfriend."

"She told it different."

"One kiss." Medina put her finger up, counting. "One time. And I broke her nose." She stood up. "She's not leaving anything here when she goes out?"

"Nothing to leave."

"Car keys?"

"Takes them with her."

Medina thought it over. If you were two million dollars, where would you hide? This place made sense for Scott. She didn't want people to know she had that kind of cash, and spending it so soon would only draw attention. She was going to have to figure out a way to launder it, if she ever wanted a normal life again. Two million was just about carryable, depending on the denomination and the size of the bag. If you had the option to never let it out of your sight, you'd take it. Medina was sure Scott would be keeping it on her at all times. And the money was only half the game. She needed to get to Scott herself before anyone else. And she knew where she was, right now.

TWENTY

Tyler, looking down into the empty safe, cocked his head in a way that was worse than any cuss word. He turned his attention back to Eddie Wray. "Well, now we got a real problem, don't we?"

Eddie bobbed his head, sitting in the office chair, not meeting Tyler's eyes. "I guess."

"You guess? We're two million light here, and you guess we have a problem? Hey, asshole, look at me when I'm talking to you."

Eddie tilted his head up. Blood running down from his eyebrow, where Tyler had already pistol whipped him twice. "I mean yes, yes we have a problem."

Tyler had been there twenty minutes. Pulling up round back of the Safari, in the spot usually taken by either a pickup truck or Leyton's Toyota. Neither were there. He'd found Eddie inside, cleaning the bar and serving customers. Eddie was stressed, complaining to everyone who'd listen. His night waitress hadn't turned up for her shift. More importantly for Tyler, Leyton was missing, too. Eddie hadn't proved co-operative at first, too busy trying to run his business. Tyler said they needed to talk in the office, Eddie said he couldn't, there was nobody to cover the floor. Tyler hit him a couple times with the gun and said, if pushed, which one of the customers would Eddie trust to man the bar for a while?

In the office, with Eddie sitting down and groaning about his head, Tyler had insisted they open the safe, and now he was all up to speed. That bad feeling in his gut, the one he'd had on the long drive out here, had been right.

The money was gone.

All Tyler was seeing now was that look on Red's face when he turned cold. Wondering, who would be next in line? Who was the man who would walk up and put a bullet in Tyler's head? Did he already know him?

"A girl took it," Eddie was saying now. "This comedian, some girl Leyton booked, and I don't know...."

Tyler, zoning in and out, his mind in too many places. "How'd this girl get the combination to the safe? You giving it out?"

"No, never." Eddie's eyes opened wide, appalled at the idea. "I know the deal, I never mess you guys about."

"What my mom does, she forgets things. Got a list, all her passwords. Every log in, bank detail, user account, whatever. You name it, she got it on this list. I wouldn't mind that, she's old. I tell her, put the list somewhere safe, it's not a problem. She says, with her memory? She'd forget where she put it. So the list is on the fridge, pinned under a magnet with my picture on it." Tyler paused, waited for Eddie to look up again. "You wouldn't have the combination written down somewhere, would you?"

"No way," Eddie said, in a tone that gave the opposite answer.

"Where you put it? A draw? Your desk? It here somewhere?"

"I had one," Eddie waved his hands in small surrender. "I had it written down a while back. Bit of paper I carried round in my wallet, just had my own safe on there at first." He pointed to the one on the right. "I get kept the numbers mixed up, yours and mine, they was so similar. So I wrote yours down, too. Same piece of paper. Then finally the numbers stuck, they just got in my head. Repetition, I guess. I didn't need the paper no more."

"What you do with it?"

"Burned it. Out the back, last winter, when I was burning a bunch of other stuff, papers, old receipts, shit I didn't need."

"Anybody know about it? Know you had it written down?"

"Nu uh. Never told anybody."

"Leyton?"

"Doesn't even know the combination to my own safe. I love the boy, but don't trust him much."

"I see two options here, Eddie. Neither of them good for you. Either you're lying to me about the money, and it's hidden here somewhere, or you're lying about nobody else knowing the combination."

"I swear."

"Okay, option three, somebody saw that paper and stopped it burning. Be straight, did you see it burn? Or was it just in with a bunch of stuff you threw on the fire?"

Eddie looked down at the floor, his voice quiet. "It was in with stuff. A shoebox full of papers. But nobody knew about it, the box was in my trailer and nobody goes in there..."

The way Eddie had ended the sentence, it sounded like a pause, like there was an except coming, but he didn't want to say it.

Tyler nudged him along, "Except?"

"There's a girl, we fool around some. Makes me feel good about myself, you know?"

"She goes in your trailer?"

Eddie nodded.

"What's this girls name?"

"She's my night waitress."

Tyler stood in silence, thinking. He let his hand rest on the gun at his side but didn't draw it. Eddie's eyes flicked up at that movement, seeing the touch.

"Would this be the same night waitress," Tyler said, "that hasn't shown up for her shift?"

Eddied nodded again.

"What's her name?"

"Rose."

"Rose? As in, Leyton's girlfriend?"

Eddie looked up now, more emotion in his face, shock, confusion, maybe a little hurt pride. "No way, she's not, they're not-"

"Man, I'm up here once, twice a month, I'm here for twenty minutes at a time, and I talk to nobody, and even I know those two have been fucking for months. How far is your head buried up your own ass?"

Eddie stared down at his feet, running a hand slowly through his thick hair. Was that a sniffle? Tyler had no time right now for an old man with a broken heart or a bruised ego.

"Okay." Tyler leaned on the desk. "I believe you're telling me the truth here. If you were going to lie, you wouldn't make yourself look and sound so dumb. You get what I'm saying here? You're still alive because I believe you're stupid. Look, the kind of business we're in, we expect to lose some money. My boss plans for you to skim a few thousand, probably for me to skim a few, if I was inclined. But we're not talking some money. We're talking two million dollars, and that's not something I can just let you lose."

Tyler was thinking now. The way shit rolled. If he reported back to Red without the money, he was as good as dead. But there was no lying with Red. That was the one thing Tyler always knew for sure. The man had an inbuilt bullshit detector. He couldn't be bluffed or stalled. Tyler couldn't even try something like, hey, the money is in the wind, but I'll find it. He needed to be up front. If blame was to pass down that way, the shit needed to roll pre-emptively. He'd need to have the fall guy ready. Boss, Eddie lost your money, but I've already killed him for it. Even then, Tyler knew, Red probably wouldn't stop there.

The only reason Eddie was still alive, sitting here now, was because Tyler needed to figure out how to save his own skin, and didn't have the answer yet. Rose sleeping with both Leyton and Eddie, having access to the combination to the safe. Leyton knew about the money. He'd been in on the deal before Eddie, working for Red's organization for five years. He was the one whispered to Tyler about Eddie's casino problem, started this whole thing rolling. Now he was missing, Rose was missing and the two million dollars was missing. There were no coincidences when figures reached seven digits.

"And Leyton books your acts, right?"

Eddie stared up at him, running the stubble of his chin under his top teeth, "Yeah. Leyton sorts it out."

"Leyton booked this comedian."

"Yeah."

"And you think she has the money?"

Eddie nodded the affirmative, but Tyler could already see, in his eyes, he was starting to doubt part of his own story. Thinking about his own nephew now. Leyton, the man with all the connections at the center of the whole thing.

Tyler looked straight into Eddie's eyes. "Her name Emily Scott?"

"I think so, yeah."

Tyler laughed again. He heard the nerves in it now, his own fears. First he loses Scott, the one who can roll on Big Wheel, reveal Red Peters' name. Now Scott gets away with the money Red needs for the big deal he's got going down. He touched the gun again. It felt cool. Inviting. He was thinking now, just do it. Get rid of this old man as a punishment beating. It wouldn't save him, but it would feel good.

Eddie's energy level rose, as if sensing the need to talk his way out. "I'm fixing it though." Hands up, almost begging, the words coming fast. "There was this bounty hunter here last night, I talked to her. Hired her, go after the comedian, bring back the money."

Tyler closed his eyes. Breathed in, out. "Chloe Medina?"

"Yeah, you know her?"

"She knows about the money?"

"Well, I had to tell her, get her to help me, you know."

"You tell her about me?"

Eddie leaned back, waving that thought away. "What can I tell her? I don't even know who you are, really. You never told me anything past your first name. If you've even given me that for real. I tell her the truth, all I know of it. There's an organization use my place as a drop box, there's people come and drop off, collect, and I don't know who they are. And now the money's gone."

Thank the lord for Chloe Fucking Medina.

She was his way out. The angle he'd been needing. Red would remember her, from the problem with the Milk Man and the car warehouse. He'd know the personal connection, Tyler and Medina, send one to stop the other. Tyler could sell this angle, he was sure of it. The money's gone, boss. But I know who has it, and Chloe Medina's going after it, I got to get there first. Perfect. It was the truth, he wouldn't be lying or trying any games. It would buy him some time, get himself back in the old man's good books.

But then came the other thought. Forming so easy it shocked him. Rolling with the change. Find the girl, find the money...if Red's going to be pissed at him either way, why stick around? He'd have two million reasons to go move somewhere warm, out of Red's reach.

He started back to thinking on what he could do to Eddie. What's the cool way to play it. He could pull his star, flash the ID in the old man's face, say something like, now you know who I am, asshole. Then bam.

"I know how you can find her," Eddie said. "She's going after the money, and I know how you can find her, follow her."

TWENTY-ONE

Emily wasn't feeling it. Halfway through the set at the Laugh Factory, doing her strongest material, she just couldn't find the zone. She'd had the same problem earlier, at the Maple Bar. Back then she'd told herself it was the crowd. The sunlight. The laughs had been there, but it had been work, and she'd never felt comfortable.

But this was a place built for comedy. First thing she'd done when she walked in was check the men's room. There was a leak. The plumber hadn't been in yet to fix it. Perfect, it smelled like a comedy club. Looked like one, too. Low lights, a spot with the microphone stand center stage, for you to walk on, grab the mic, move the stand out the way. Telling the audience, *I own this space*.

But she got up there, and started to struggle.

Not for the reaction. The old muscles were still there.

The memory and the skill. When to pause, when to pretend to crack herself up, when to stay in a bit and when to move on. All of that was still there.

But she was *thinking about it*, and that was the problem. Before prison, she'd never thought much of anything on stage. That time, on the mic, had been when she was truly in the moment, when thoughts dropped away and she become one person, one brain, one act. Every other second of her day was spent thinking. Re-living conversations, planning new ones. Questioning decisions. Switching between personalities. What was the old song, about being a million different people each day? It was British, the one the Stones had claimed all the money for. That song was Scott's life. Except when she was on stage. That was her time. No doubts, no questions. No second self, watching and analysing everything she did.

At least, that's how it had always been.

But now, going through the motions in the Laugh Factory, she was watching herself. She was aware of her own voice, in her head, telling her which joke to try next, how to do the job. Not just doing it, but thinking about it first.

Telling herself, okay, now pause. Let the audience see you're expecting a laugh. Have the confidence they'll provide it. Okay, there we go. You have them, you can do whatever you want. Now, go into your pet bit.

"My cat has a heart condition. Has to take a pill every day. It's really put things into perspective. Because, you know, it's quite hard to get good drugs from a doctor these days, but turns out? Real easy to get them from a vet."

Laughs. Not huge, but enough. Scott loved this bit. It was niche, but she didn't care.

"I've started telling the little guy his parents are dead, I want him to get depression so I can get the really good shit."

More laughs. Same level. No real build. The audience was medium cool, the way she called them when they were happy to laugh, but not too much.

"But you know, it's taught me something about health care in this country. Because the bigger the pet you have, the higher the class of drugs they'll give you." Hold it. Wait. Let them breathe. "That's why rich people have so many horses." Huge pop. Way more than she expected. Now, on this joke, the crowd are alive.

The voice in Scott's head, the one she doesn't want to be hearing, saying, okay, now you can have some fun.

"What is it about guys and cars? You know. There's just something. Guys and cars. We sent three guys to the moon, they flew two hundred thousand miles, at a cost of billions. First thing they did? Pulled the car out of the garage and went for a spin."

She slipped easily into the physical part of this bit, where the real laughs were, acting out a couple of young guys riding around in a car, but on the moon. Laying on her dumb guy moves, long swinging arms, moving with her pelvis thrust forward. Something was wrong. Different. Some heckles come out of nowhere, completely catching the comic off guard, others can be seen in advance, like a cloud that rolls in across the room, a certain section of the crowd getting ready to challenge you. Scott could feel the cloud building.

The more she milked the laughter, the more she could feel it.

"*Thief.*" A voice calls out. Scott's eyes dart to the edge of the stage, where she left the bag before coming up here. The cash. Someone started pushing forwards, rushing the stage from the back of the room.

··

Medina parked up on West Shoreline Drive, in front of the Ferris wheel, lit up neon blue now in the evening. The bay behind her, downtown Long Beach straight ahead. She left most of her gear in the car, grabbing two sets of handcuffs and a can of mace, slipping them into her purse. She hesitated before getting out. Something didn't feel right. Ever since she'd left the Shelby. But there was more to it than the car. These thoughts, even sitting here now wondering what the problem was, were new. She didn't like to overthink.

The Laugh Factory was on the corner, next to the wheel. The outside decorated with paintings of comedians made to look like the Oscar statue, each standing in a different pose on the round base. She paid the door charge and stepped in. It was dark inside. She could hear somebody was already up on stage. The audience was laughing. Medina walked down the small hallway from the front, and round a corner. The room opened out ahead of her, with a bar off to one side and the stage straight ahead. The crowd was sat between her and the stage. She could see a bunch of people standing, near the bar. The other comics, waiting their turn to go on. And in the spotlight, controlling the room, was Emily Scott.

Right there.

Emily Scott, the cool girl. Emily Scott, the first girl she kissed.

Emily Scott, convicted for armed robbery, fugitive on the run.

Back here, Medina was in shadow. She stayed where she was, letting the darkness work for her. She watched Scott work. Hearing her voice, seeing the way she moved. She was carrying more miles. Right now she was talking about drugs and animals. Something about going to the vet. And then, right there, the damnedest thing happened. Medina laughed. It was real, and caught her by surprise. She hadn't even really been listening all that much, or thought she hadn't been, but then she was laughing along with the rest of the crowd. Scott was good. Medina relaxed, leaning back against the wall, thinking she could wait, catch the rest of his act. There was a large messenger bag just off the stage. It fit the description Darrel had given. Two million in cash, squeezed into a bag. Nobody knew it was there, right in front of them. That was funny as hell.

Medina caught movement. The other comedians, a few feet away. One of them, a muscular guy, looking too much like a jock to ever really be funny, was whispering to the others. He looked angry. Medina's guard went back up, sensing he could be about to do something stupid. She just didn't know why.

Then Scott made her laugh again. A bit about men flying all the way to the moon just to drive around in car. That was just true. Now she was moving around, one arm crooked like it was resting on a car window, the other out ahead holding the imaginary wheel. She was acting like a guy cruising down the strip, but he was on the moon. The audience was loving this, and Medina had to admit, she wished she could just go along with the show. But she was here for work.

The angry guy bolted forwards. "Thief."

Scott stopped moving, peered in this direction, through the spotlight. Medina knew at this distance all Scott would be making out was shapes. Medina pushed off from the wall and headed after the big guy, though the crowd. She swore under her breath, thinking about the gun in the Pontiac. She hadn't planned on someone else being there to go after the money.

"Joke thief," the guy shouted.

Medina slowed down. Joke thief? If this wasn't about the money, maybe she could just hang back, see how it played out. As long as she didn't let Scott back out of her sight, what's the harm? She stopped moving, already in the middle of the crowd. The angry guy was at the stage now. He made a grab for the mic.

Scott pulled away. "Hey, what the..." Looking around the room, waiting for security, or reality, to step in. "Get off, man."

"You're stealing all of this," the angry guy shouted, grabbed for the mic again. This time he connected, grabbing Scott's hand, starting a tug of war for control of the microphone. They rocked back and forth. The big guy had size advantage, and gravity worked in his favour, pulling Scott forward and down.

"Yo," the big guy had the mic now, shouting into it, turning to address the crowd. "I seen someone do this whole set before, the whole bit. This chick's a fake."

"I'm not." Scott's face flushed red.

Medina knew stealing someone else's material was the worst crime you could commit in comedy. Scott would be chased out of the building if it was true.

"The whole set," the big guy said again. "Same delivery. I saw this girl at the Improv in Tempe. Emily Scott. And she..." the guy paused, looked hard at Scott. Almost like a cartoon, Medina could see the double take, the recognition. When he spoke again, his voice was quiet, embarrassed, maybe. "Shit. Why you using a different name now?"

Scott smiled, letting it spread into a nervous laugh. She was stuck between two choices, Medina knew. Admit who she really was, and risk word getting out, someone in the room knowing about the robbery and conviction, or stick to whatever fake name she'd used, and get attacked for stealing her own jokes.

The houselights flicked on. Someone at the back getting sick of whatever was going on. The audience blinked, started to move in their seats, talk to each other about the drama playing out on stage. The big guy had let go of the mic now, realising who Scott was. Scott, for her part, was looking directly at Medina.

"Chloe?"

"Hey Emily."

Scott blinked. She opened her mouth to laugh, shaking her head. Then moved her hands fast, to cover her nose. Medina smiled at that, put both her hands up, palms out. Peace. Scott pulled her hands away, matched the calming gesture for a second, smiling, shaking her head slowly a couple times.

Then she got that look, the same one Ben Nichol got in the Safari, right before he'd bolted. Medina knew what was about to happen, took a couple steps forward. Too late. Scott jumped off the stage, grabbed the bag, and ran, pushing through the seats to the left of the stage, and then out through a fire door.

Medina chased after her. Out through the door, into the evening air. They were headed towards the Ferris wheel, lit up against the darkening sky, people sat in the bucket seats, watching them from up high. They rounded the fence that surrounded the wheel. Scott hesitated, veered left, towards West Shoreline Drive, then turned sharp to the right, into the large circular forecourt of the Pine shopping precinct. Medina had the can of mace in her hand now.

She got a few feet closer, aimed, and threw the can at Scott's head. Almost a straight shot, with as much power as she could put into it. The can hit her behind the right ear. The impact, or the shock of it, was enough to take Scott over, falling forward into the flower bed at the centre of the court with a high-pitch yelp. Medina was on her in seconds, pulling the bag around on her shoulders, clearing her back, bringing her arms around behind and cuffing them.

"What the hell," Scott whined, like a hurt child.

A security guard was approaching them slowly, from the GAP store. Medina could read his type. It was his job to do this, but he wasn't paid enough to care about doing this. He was already looking for a reason not to. She preferred this kind. The other, the guy who was just desperate to wear a badge and maybe a gun, was always more of a problem. She flashed him her ID.

"Recovery agent," she pointed at Scott, down at her feet. "Fugitive."

The guard said, "Cool," and walked back towards the store.

Medina let Scott sit up, not helping her as she shuffled round onto her back, then eased up into the sitting position in the flower bed. She spit dirt.

"Good to see you," Medina said. "How you doing?"

"What the hell?" Less like a child now, more like a tired, resigned, adult.

Medina unclipped the bag from around Scott's shoulders, pulled her to her feet.

"How long's it been?"

Scott said, quiet, "Could've done with it being five minutes longer."

"Don't worry, it happens to everyone."

Scott tried to turn, not putting enough force into it to be problem. "My bag."

Medina smiled reaching down for it. "I got two million reasons to remember."

She lifted it. The bag was light. Too light.

Scott was staring at her now. "Two million?"

TWENTY-TWO

They stopped at the gas station near a trailer park called *Oracle Springs*. Drey didn't know if this spot had a name. If not, it should just be called Gas Station, since that's pretty much all there was. This, a church, a post office, and a general store that looked like it hadn't been open since she was born, a low building with 'for sale' painted on the side.

She was exhausted. How long had they been awake now? Over twenty-four hours, easy. All she wanted was sleep. Coyote was fading too, which was good news. Whatever anger had been burning him up earlier, it seemed to have faded away now. In spite of what he'd said, they had still headed towards Tucson. They could be there in less than an hour, and she was pretty sure she'd be able to talk him into going to MAB's place for some sleep. Everything else could wait.

They filled up the Toyota. Coyote started to head in to pay up, but Drey put a hand out and said, "Maybe I should handle it this time?"

Coyote smiled. Sleepy. Easy. He said, "Yeah," and handed her some folded notes.

"Where'd you get this?"

"Cash register at the other place."

Now didn't seem like the time to argue the point, but Drey hadn't realized he'd added robbery to murder. Attempted murder, at least, since neither of them knew if the guy had survived. And did it matter? What's a few bank notes in the grand scheme once you've put a bullet in someone?

Inside, she found the clerk on the counter to be young, maybe younger than she was. He was shy, didn't want to meet her eyes as she handed over the money, waited for change. Standing there, she realized Coyote had trusted her to come in, to talk to someone else without raising the alarm or calling for help. And she realized, too, that he was right. She'd not come in here to get away from him, or to do anything other than pay. Where was this all going?

She remembered a conversation they'd had a few months back, both a little stoned, joking around about what they would or wouldn't give alibis for.

"What's your limit?" Coyote had said.

"What you mean?"

"Like, what's the biggest crime you think we'd alibi each other out for? When would we cross the line?"

"Something you want to tell me?"

Coyote, laughing: "I'm not saying I got a trailer full of dead babies, but maybe I got a trailer full of dead babies?"

"Dead babies would probably be the line," Drey had said. "Anything up to that, I got you. But dead babies?"

"What's the word I'm looking for..." He spaced out for a moment. "Shit. It's gone. That was going to be funny."

"I think I'd be cool with theft," Drey had said. "Call me up to say you've stolen something, a car, whatever, I think a friend alibis a friend out over something like that. And I think, if someone came at me, someone tried to attack me, and I shot them in self-defence? I think you'd alibi me out on that."

"If it was self-defence though, why would you need the alibi? Oh wait, you're brown."

"You'd get away with it."

"The minute I commit a crime, I'm going full white, I'm using the shit out of that coding, why not? Hey officer, you can't arrest me, I'm white."

He paused to draw in another toke.

Drey filled the silence. "You pull up at a red light, too, white as fuck."

"Yeah. But I go anywhere on the Rez, though, I'm white as fuck there, too. All of yous, someone from outside says I'm not Indian, you all stick up for me, run 'em off. But when it's just us, bunch of Rez Indians sitting round? You're all like, 'hey white kid, your people done some shit'." He said it dark, letting it look like the joking was done, before cracking a smile. "Serious though, I think you do anything like that, I got your back."

"Anything? There's got to be something you wouldn't cover me for."

Coyote looked to think about it for a while. "Like, anything you do to humans, I'm fine. But don't hurt animals. I see those videos, people stealing dogs and shit? Makes me cry. Shit, I saw one of the Rez dogs the other day, you know the orange one, patchy fur? She had a limp. I cried about that for ten minutes. Wait, I got it. What I was going to say. Back up, you said dead babies was the limit? I wanted to say, you mean plural? Like, is one dead baby fine? Where's the line within the line?"

They'd both laughed at that, the drugs making the joke last. Now, stepping back out into the cold air and walking over to the stolen Toyota, to get back in beside the man with the gun, it didn't feel so funny. She was asking herself for real now, what's the line?

There was an old payphone outside the main building, on a wooden pole, with a small metal hood over the phone. Did anybody still use that? She checked her cell. The battery nearly dead, down to 10 percent and from there it could drop off at any time. She had two bars. Maybe enough for a call. She thought of just calling her mom, crying, hearing her voice and waiting for everything to be okay. But each time she realized, if her mom cared there would have been a call already. Texts. A voicemail.

In their house, half of a run-down duplex, Drey's bedroom had been missing a door for three years. How many shouting matches had she had with her mom over that? How was she supposed to have any space, any privacy? Those first few times she wanted to play with her fingers, starting to think about women, she'd been too scared every time. And all those nights listening to every word of argument between her mom and the asshole boyfriend.

Money, her mom kept saying.

You want a bedroom door, or you want to eat?

You want a bedroom door, or you want clothes?

One time, Drey had shouted back, *you want me to have a bedroom door, or you want to keep buying things for that asshole?*

They hadn't talked for a while after that.

No, if she had a home to go back to, she'd go to it. But she didn't. Crossing back to the Toyota, she saw Coyote was round the back, looking in the trunk, with the light on over his head. He looked up to see her approaching the car, and waved for her to come back to where he was. He stepped aside, pointing at two large bags.

"Check it out."

Drey leaned over and pulled at the first bag, seeing stacks of hundred dollar bills, wrapped in paper bands. Holy crap. She looked at the second one, seeing the same thing. Climbing in to crouch over the bags, she stuck her hands in, pushing down, finding the stacks went on and on.

She leaned back on her haunches. "Shit."

Coyote grinned. "Right?"

"I mean.....shit."

"How much you think is there?"

Drey shook her head, swore a third time, before saying, "I've never seen this much."

"What's the most you've seen?"

"My mom's asshole boyfriend bought a car once, in cash. He came round the house first, put it on the table. I think it was one thousand dollars?"

"This looks more than one thousand dollars."

"I've seen these bags before," Coyote said, pointing. "There's these guys who turn up at the Safari sometimes, I seen them when I was hanging out in the parking lot tailgating with Joe and Deek."

"You didn't invite me."

He shrugged. Looked down at his feet. "You know, those guys."

Joe and Deek were the popular kids. At least, in their circle. They always had the best drugs, the freshest gear. Looked like Coyote had been making new friends behind her back, trying to move up in the world.

Well, fine, they weren't here now, were they?

Coyote continued after an awkward silence. "There's these guys, seen them twice. One time, they came in without bags, left with one each, just like these. The other time, I think they were the same guys, looked the same anyway, they came with bags, left without them."

"There's no way this is legal."

Coyote grinned again. "Means we haven't stolen the car."

"How'd you work that?"

"If this is criminal, there's no way Leyton is going to call the cops, right? Have them track us down, open up the trunk, find this. He won't want the questions. So if he's not going to report it, we haven't stolen it, right?"

Drey thought first, I don't think that's how it works, and second, you still shot someone. But she couldn't take her eyes off the money. Now she was thinking they were in a movie. Each bundle was hundreds. There were hundreds of bundles.

"We're rich," Coyote said. "We should count this."

Drey snapped out of it just enough to see her chance. "Not here. That kid could already be watching us, what if he sees the money? We should go to my mom's asshole ex boyfriend's place. He's round here somewhere, I think I can find it."

"He'll see the money."

"No," she shook her head. "He's gone north, remember? That was the whole thing. Just packed up and left one day, owed some money, I think. Just left my mom, left his trailer, said he was going north where the man couldn't touch him."

"Who's the man?"

"Does it matter?"

"You want to break in?" Excitement in Coyote's voice, getting to play outlaw again.

Drey couldn't shake the feeling they were in different films. The ones she'd seen, this kind of thing didn't end well.

··

"They're moving again," Rose said, staring at the screen.

They'd been slow to set off. First they headed back to Leyton's trailer, got his laptop. But it was a few years old, and Leyton said the battery was shot, it needed to be plugged in to work. He had an adapter that would run off the car battery, but it was in the Toyota. So then they sat in the trailer, loaded up the security app, and watched the blue dot moving west, along Route 53, heading off the reservation. Rose had found an app they could download for their phones, monitor the GPS that way, but then neither of them could find a strong enough connection for the download. They set off without it, on faith, convinced they'd find a connection along the way. The answer came in Holbrook, when a diner at the side of the road offered free wi-fi and coffee refills. They ate chili, drank their body weight in caffeine, and both downloaded the app. By this point, the little blue dot was headed south through the Fort Apache reservation.

The Toyota would have more speed than the truck. Leyton spent at least an hour commenting on this, saying the only way they'd catch up was if the thieves stopped. Rose, calm the whole time, kept pointing out that even car thieves need to take a shit and sleep.

They'd been gaining ground for the past thirty minutes. The dot stopped just north of a spot on the map listed as Oracle Springs. Now it was moving again.

"Tucson," Rose said. "Perfect place to take a dump." She turned to Leyton and smiled. "I told you, we'll get them."

"They've seen it by now," Leyton said, feeling the stress in his gut, mixing with the distant memory of the coffee. "They have to. You drive this far with two million in the trunk, you're going to find it."

"One million, eight hundred thousand." Rose smiled, touched the gun on the bench between them. "If we're going to kill people, I think it's important to be accurate about how much we're doing it for."

TWENTY-THREE

Tyler pulled over to the side of the road just after Holbrook, already an hour into the drive.   The cell signal had been patchy ever since leaving the Safari, and he needed this conversation to be clear. There was no time for miscommunication. Plus, the real reason, it was easier to ask forgiveness than permission. If he'd called Red from the Safari, using Eddie's phone, there's a chance his boss might have told him to wait there while he sent someone else to clean everything up. And that would be the end of it, Tyler finally needing to get his go bag from beneath the bed in his apartment. As it was, he was calling after already starting the chase, making Red's decision for him.

"Hello." Red's voice was friendly, laid back. A little doped up around the edges.

There was the sound of cartoons playing in the background, or one of those superhero movies that Tyler thought of as cartoons. Bunch of animated people fighting. He wondered if his son liked those movies. "You letting the grandkids stay up this late?" Tyler forced the smile into his voice, wanting the conversation to start off on an easy foot.

"They can't sleep," Red said, sounding like the grouchy old grandpa he was at home. "And you know Tessa." That was his wife's name. From the way he said it, he was looking at her, sharing a nod. "She gives them whatever they want. I'm a prisoner in my own damn house. Hang on a minute."

Tyler heard Red wince as he climbed up out of a chair, could picture him now walking slowly over to the stairs, up to his office at the back of the house. "Okay," Red said, with a colder edge now. "Talk."

Tyler reported the whole thing, in the order he'd been practicing for the last hour. Lead with Leyton playing his own uncle, conning him, taking control of the gig bookings.

He talked about Rose, the girl playing with both guys, stealing the combination to Eddie's safe. And then into Leyton bringing Emily Scott into it.

"And now we get to the point," Red cut in. "You going to mention the money?"

"Looks like Scott and Leyton worked together, took it."

"They took my money, and you don't lead with that?"

"I'm already on their tail, boss. Turns out, Eddie got some GPS device installed in the car, pays a subscription so he can see where it is at all times. Given me the log in details, I downloaded the phone app. Eddie's car is in California, I'm on my way there now."

"Leyton and funny bitch working together?" Red cut in. "You didn't see that coming?"

"Didn't know they knew each other, how would I?"

There was a brief pause. Red came back with, "You've been practicing how to say this for the past hour, ah? Thinking if you tell me once you're already on the road, I'm not going to tell you turn around and come back, not going to have someone take your place and bury you out in the desert."

Everything stopped. The world. Tyler's mind. Damn. Nothing got past the old man. Tyler decided to go for a version of honesty. Put the smile back into his voice. "You got me. You talking about the bench. I know how that goes, we both remember it."

Right there, lean on the memory, lean on the fact you were there for Red when he needed you, when the feds were closing in on Milk Man, when Chloe Medina had him tracked down to the big stupid warehouse.

Now push that connection home. "There's more. Eddie panicked, when he found out the money was gone. He hired someone to go after it, figured he could bring it back without us finding out."

A tense response, "Who?"

"Chloe Medina."

The old man cackled. A dry sound. Desert, dust, and age. "Of course. Of course. She was always going to come back some day, wasn't she?"

Tyler was back in that moment now, the warehouse, the shadows. Medina creeping up on Milk Man, ready to take him in. Tyler there under different orders, silence him.

Watching Medina, supposed to be covering her, but knowing if she succeeded, his paydays would be over. He'd always wanted to know which of them was the faster draw. If it came to it, like the old west, which of them was the real Doc Holliday. But in that moment, he'd had to shoot her in the dark, like a coward.

Not. Not like a coward. Like a realist.

She'd always thought the attacker missed. Seen it as a miracle that the bullets missed her vitals and the Shelby's gas tank. Somehow, never crossed her mind, maybe the gunman had been that good. The two best shots of Tyler's life, and he could never claim credit for them.

"So, what I'm not clear on, who is in the car?"

"Eddie's car?" Tyler grimaced, he'd hoped Red would overlook that.

"Yeah, the tracker's in Eddie's car. I'm assuming his nephew would know that, so Leyton wouldn't be dumb enough to steal two million off me, and run away in a tracked car. Who's in it?"

"Chloe. Her car got wrecked by some kids, so Eddie loaned her his Pontiac to go after the money."

The cackle again. "So your second chance at not screwing this up has only come about because of the girl you didn't kill four years ago?"

When Tyler didn't answer, Red continued. "Eddie's got the Bandit car, right? Firebird with the gold trim?"

"I believe so."

"Love that car. Wanted one of my own when I was a kid, but it went against the whole nut farmer look. And Chloe, the girl, she drives the Milk Man's old Shelby, right?"

"She does."

"She let that get wrecked? Now there's a crime. The Feds want me, I never done anything as bad as that."

Tyler took the joke as a good sign. Red easing off. Playing the situation for laughs. He could turn fast, Tyler had seen it enough times, but he didn't sense this was going that way.

"Scott and Leyton ran off together with my money, and you're tracking Chloe, who's tracking them. How does the other girl fit into this, then? You told me her name, the one who played Eddie for a fool?"

"Rose."

"Rose. That's it. She hot?"

Tyler pictured her now. Blonde, tattoos, those looks she could give you, like she knew who you really were, behind all the posing. "Yeah, she is."

"Good for Eddie." The cackle. "At our age, well, I got twenty years on Eddie, but he's past the age, too. At our age, they don't even need to be hot anymore. They just need to be young. A young girl looks at you a certain way, tricks that part of you into feeling young again? You'd give them everything you owned."

"Sure."

"You want to last, in this game, any other, you need to recognize when your ego is becoming your biggest problem. You hearing me?"

Tyler paused. This conversation had turned fast, but in a direction Tyler didn't really understand. He lied, knowing it was a mistake. "Yes."

"No, you don't. Not yet. What I'm saying is, this isn't about you, it's not about Chloe Medina. It's not even about Red Peters. None of the names matter. This is about two million dollars, and I got no time for games, you hearing me now?"

"I am."

"Okay, give it me straight. Leyton, funny bitch, and this Rose, are they all headed off together?"

"No. Or, I don't think so. Emily Scott ran last night, Eddie says she took the money with her. But Leyton and Rose were still around a while after, Leyton fetched Medina. They slipped out this morning."

"Leyton got a car of his own, right? That black one I saw him in, the time he came over to Phoenix, met with you without knowing I was sitting right there, behind him."

"Toyota, yeah."

"If Eddie installed the tracker in his own car, why stop there? Why not put one in Leyton's Toyota, too."

"Shit." Tyler, angry that hasn't occurred to him. He said, "Hang on, I'll check."

He killed the call, loaded the tracker app on the screen. It jumped straight to a map. The blue dot of the Pontiac, moving away from Long Beach, back in this direction.

He flipped away from that screen, into the settings. Right there, he saw the listing for a second vehicle. Pressed the button. A new map loaded. This one showing the dot in Tucson.

He called Red back. Not wanting to, but knowing he couldn't avoid it.

"Yeah?"

"Leyton is in Tucson."

Tyler heard Red's tongue clicking, the sign he was thinking. "Okay. So we got a couple different scenarios here. The kids split the money, they're running in different directions. That's the way most people would play this. Or the way I'd play it, if I was Leyton, I'd tell funny bitch about the money, but tell her less. Keep most of it for myself, let her run with what she thinks is the whole thing. But that's only if Leyton is half as intelligent as me, and I'm not sure he is, seemed like an idiot that time I saw him."

"Yeah."

"So probably, it's a fifty fifty split. But either way, I need people on both. Even if funny bitch only has ten cents, she knows my name, and now Chloe Medina will know it too. First thing she'll ask her, after that warehouse thing. Okay." Red clicking again. "You want to go finish what you started, you go after the Pontiac, track down funny bitch and Chloe, kill them both, bring back whatever money they got, bring it to the farm. Bring the bodies, too. We'll get rid of them the old way."

Tyler reading in the subtext, and maybe your body will be thrown in with them.

"And Leyton?"

"I'll deal with that. Got people in Tucson I can use." Calling them off the bench, Tyler thought. "Send me the details for the tracker." He made a noise. A guttural thinking sound. "California is a problem. Never managed to get anywhere there. Damn well unwelcome, to be honest. But I'll send you some backup for the minute they cross the border. Once they're in Arizona, do them."

After the call ended, Tyler sat in silence for a moment, thinking things over. He hadn't figured out the split for himself. How much of the money was in Tucson, and how much was in California? If he was sure either way, he could go after the biggest number. Like Red said, remove ego, think only of the cash.

To hell with the old man. Red was going to order him dead anyway. He should chase the money and leave the state. Now he knew Red had no power in California, that was an option for a while. Lay low, make a plan. Leave the whole area. Go sit in a big house in Seattle, or something. Vancouver, watch movies being made, sipping cocktails. But each time he tried to think which way to go, he saw Medina, saw the night at the warehouse, and the unanswered questions. Every time since then that she'd refused to have a contest with him.

He flipped the app back to the Pontiac's GPS. The dot pulsed. It seemed to have stopped moving again. Medina stopping for the night, maybe. Getting some rest, ever the student of Reed Palmer.

That was fine. He had coffee. He had uppers in the glove box. Let her stop, let her show weakness. He could be there before she woke up. And whatever money Emily Scott had on her, it was more than Tyler owned right now. He'd make it work.

I'm coming, Chloe. This time, we'll be face to face when I shoot you.

TWENTY-FOUR

Scott was in the front passenger seat, her hands in cuffs. Medina keeping her eyes on the road, navigating the traffic of downtown Long Beach. Neither of them talking about the bag of money on the backseat.

"Nice bar over there," Scott said, pointing. "We could go in, get a couple drinks, catch up." Just talking, like they were old friends, running into each other after years apart.

Medina didn't answer. Her head was full enough of thoughts already. She needed to count the money, try and figure out what was going on. Also, she needed to ask about Big Wheel, get the name. And then what? As soon as Big Wheel found out she was in the game, she became a target.

Chances were, she already was a target. Why would Big Wheel wait for confirmation?

But first, before she did anything, she needed to figure out what she was doing right now. This was the most vulnerable time, in any trace job. She had a fugitive fresh in custody, other people were looking for them, and she'd only slept a total of six hours across the past two days. She could hear Reed Palmer's voice in her head, saying, this is when you start making mistakes.

"How's your brother?"

That pulled Medina out of her head. "What?"

"Sammy, how's he doing?"

"Yeah." She paused a beat. Looking at Scott, then back to the road. "He's fine."

Scott casual, again, still talking like this was a friendly meet up, totally ignoring that she was sitting in handcuffs. The cool girl. "He figured himself out okay?"

"You mean, is he still gay?"

"Well, I mean, has he come out?"

What the hell. Why not.

Medina decided to go with it, a good distraction from all the other thoughts. "He lives in Seattle, sends me postcards. Came out to my folks after he left."

"Postcards?"

"Started as a joke. He said he was going to see the whole world, but settled down in the first place he visited, found a guy he liked and stayed there. So now he sends me a postcard from there, every month, as if he was still travelling."

"That's sweet. And your other brother, I forget his name."

"Gabe."

"Gabe. Yeah. Big guy, scared the shit out of me. What's he doing?"

Medina closed her eyes for a second, and could feel the lids didn't want to go back up. She weighed the options. If she was taking Scott to Reed and the DA, that would be a six hour drive. If she was taking her on to Eddie, that could be ten. Or, say, split the difference, deliver Scott to Reed, then take the money to Eddie. But he'd hired her to go after two million, not two hundred grand. There were still too many questions.

The car swerved. Scott yelped. Medina opened her eyes, pulled hard on the wheel to correct. Damn, that had been close. Okay, new plan. Find a motel here, somewhere secure, where she could bed down for four or five hours, get all she needed, then figure out the rest from there.

"Gabe's a lawyer now," she said, her turn to play it cool, pretending she didn't nearly take them off the road. "Set up his own practice in Phoenix."

"Oh wow, that's cool. That's like, was it your mom?"

"Yeah, she was a lawyer."

Scott turned to look at her, waited a few seconds. "Was?"

"Retired now, down in Florida."

"Oh thank god," Scott smiled, and Medina caught herself matching it. "I thought you were going to say she died, and this was going to be a whole different kind of conversation."

"No, don't worry. Both my parents are still around. Mom took early retirement, headed down to Florida to try writing mystery novels."

She decided the extra detail about pool boys and wrestlers wasn't needed.

"Your dad?"

"Still working, part time. Trying to write a book too. I think they're in a passive-aggressive race to see who can finish a book first."

Scott rubbed her chin, the metal chain rattled again. "I don't remember what he did."

"He's a teacher. Public school."

"Yeah. Yeah. I remember it now. So they're not together?"

Medina shrugged. "Five, six years ago, they just called it quits. Divided everything up."

"You were okay with that?"

She turned to look at Scott again for a few seconds, expecting to lead with none of your business. Instead she shook her head, turned back to the road ahead and said, "I'm too old to be claiming any childhood trauma, they're adults, they can do what they want."

"And have you come out to them?"

Medina look at Scott again. Then back on the road. Then repeated the move.

Looking at her, calm and composed, the cool girl. The one who could still inspire loyalty in Lisa Afobe, even when Afobe hated her guts. The one who could get Chuck Thane to loan her a car after a decade. The one who could get Darryl to drop everything and take in a fugitive. And the one now, getting Chloe to open up like they were having a coffee.

"Yeah," Medina said.

"How they handle it?"

"Dad's fine with it. Asked me for tips on talking to women. Mom, I don't think she really takes it in. Changes the subject, or concentrates on the part where I still like guys, too. Like it's just a fifty/fifty thing, and she can choose option A."

Scott said, "Are we going to talk about it?"

Medina's eyes fell on the bag in the rearview mirror, thinking, here we go.

Scott waited a few more beats, then said, "That time you broke my nose?"

Medina laughed now. Just like back at the club, it came easy, natural. She liked the feeling. "You deserved it."

"I'm not sure I did."

"You kissed me."

"And that's a bad thing?"

"I wasn't ready."

"You asked me to."

The car swerved again as Media whipped her head around to face Scott. "I did not."

"Well, agree to disagree. I just want to clear the air." She held up her cuffed wrists. "Make sure there's no hard feelings before, you know..."

The words trailed off. Nothing else was coming. Medina let that hang there, trying to dare Scott to fill in the silence, elaborate on what she meant. Finally the penny dropped, and she knew what Scott was talking about. If she wasn't so tired, she would've figured it out sooner.

"You think I'm going to kill you?"

"Well," Scott shrugged, went for the callback. "I figured it was a fifty/fifty thing, and you'd chosen option B."

They passed by a motel on Long Beach Boulevard, heading north. It was small and simple, a row of rooms all together, lined up across a small parking lot with only one entrance. There was a church on one side, and a pet grooming place on the other. There was a place a couple hours further on, just across the Arizona border. Medina had been planning to stop there, but maybe she wouldn't make those extra couple hours. She swung the car around, across the opposite lane, and went back, pulling onto the motel's lot.

They sat there for a while, the engine running. She looked at the bag again on the back seat, then turned to Scott. "Why would you think that?"

"You're not a marshal anymore, are you?"

Medina half shook her head, not seeing how that was relevant. "Left four years ago."

"What are you doing now?"

She slipped out her ID and business card, showed Scott both of them. "Recovery agent."

"That's a bounty hunter, right?"

Scott was still being too calm about all of this. Medina was used to fugitives fighting, or running, protesting the whole way back to jail. The quiet ones always unnerved her, there was a fatalism that had set in. Accepting whatever was coming.

"When I ran," Scott said. "I figured the next person I recognized from back home would be coming to kill me."

"Because of what you were going to say to the DA?"

He nodded. "Because I know who Big Wheel is, yeah."

Medina's head felt numb for a second. She opened her mouth, but couldn't speak. Big Wheel was a code name, starting in her office, spreading throughout the other agencies. It wasn't a name the criminal had given himself, or something picked up off the street. There was no reason for anyone outside of law enforcement to know it.

"How do you know that name?"

Scott turned in her seat to look behind them, back to Long Beach Boulevard and the cars racing past. "Can we talk inside?"

Medina looked over at the office, the vacancy sign slit up green in the dark. "One thing I got to ask. If you knew people would be looking for you, coming to kill you, why the hell are you doing gigs?"

Scott looked at her, blinking a couple times. "I'm a comedian, what else am I going to do?"

TWENTY-FIVE

Red Peters stared at the phone long after the call ended. He liked life to be simple. Long ago, he'd realised Occam's Razor was the answer to a good life. Figure out what you want, then look at the easiest way to get it. The higher the stakes, the simpler the decisions.

But Treat Tyler was trying hard to make things complicated.

Eddie Wray, too.

And Leyton.

Everyone lining up take a kick at the project.

Each one thinking they were adding difficulty to the job, but all they were doing was making simple decisions about their own futures.

Red's phone buzzed, a text message. He read the details Tyler sent, loaded up his laptop, and logged into Eddie Wray's GPS tracking service. The one dot in California, the other in Tucson.

Tyler, if he hadn't already been thinking about trying to take the money for himself, he'd be planning on it now. That much was clear. Red never had a problem being straight with the help. If he had two million dollars needing collection, he'd tell them the exact amount, because if anything less than that figure turned up, the help knew they'd pay for it. But now Red had heard it in Tyler's voice, the Deputy US Marshal already knowing he was on borrowed time and starting to think, maybe I don't need to come back with the money? That had been easy enough to handle. The money would be with Leyton. It was obvious. Leyton had set this funny bitch Emily Scott up. But Red watered the seed of Chloe Medina, knowing Tyler would always make the wrong choice. He was obsessed with that girl, all wrapped up in this competition they had, to out cool each other.

The benefit of growing up as a farmer, Red knew, was not caring about appearances. The end goal was money, and food on the table. If you needed to bend down in the dirt, get shit on your hands, crack your fingers, hurt your back, so what? There was no ego in the long game. Nothing personal. Just planning, work and profit. People were useful right up until the moment they weren't. Like horses on the farm. And you did the same thing to both when they stopped working.

Push Tyler's buttons, get him to chase down Medina and the comedian, see if they have any of the cash, then, after Tyler solves that problem, Red can solve the Tyler problem. Easy. Simple.

He dialled a number, waited for the answer.

"Yeah?" Jed Bashford on the other end. Sheriff Jed. Sometimes Idiot Jed. They never said each other's names on the phone, even on these burners, one more line of protection.

"Great speech," Red said, playing to the guys' ego first. He was an old school bully, an egotist, much the same was Tyler. People like that, Red didn't value them, but they were easy to control. "Really, good job. You hit all the right points."

"People are saying it was the beast they ever heard."

"I bet they were," Red grinned. "Lining up for hours after to get your autograph."

"Hours and hours. Never seen anything like it."

"Good work. Listen, I have a problem."

The obvious part staying unsaid, *you need to fix it.*

"What you need?"

"A kid from the drop box has taken some of my money, run down to Tucson. "

"Primo County. New sheriff laid off my guys. But I can send some of ours down there, who cares? People see someone in a deputy uniform, they don't read the badge. What do they need to do?"

"Grab the money, kill the kid. Bring me both."

"How do they find him?"

"There's a GPS tracker on his car, idiot knows it too, and is still running. I'll send you the details."

"I'll deal with it. In fact, the drop box? I'll send McKinley County boys down there. Don't need to pay them extra then, we already cover them to cover those people."

"My boy with the star is an issue, too."

"I always told you. Didn't I tell you?"

"Get me someone to deal with him."

They ended the call without a goodbye. No niceties were needed at this point. There was just the job, the work, the results. The money.

The cash needed to come back. Red didn't over-extend himself often, but getting this next step of his project off the ground had meant going all-in. And if the money was lost, he'd have to make a call he wouldn't like, to his friend with the Russian accent and the blank check book. That call would come with consequences. Obligations. He'd look like an idiot.

He loaded up another file on the computer. One he couldn't help but look at every time. He knew it's not like it was magically going to change, but he couldn't help it. His project, his baby.

Miles of small town and desert, to the south of Phoenix. Land that had once been full of farms, before the water problems started. The press, the few places to run the story, calling it the *water wars*. Conflict between new housing settlements and legacy farms. Generations of people, generations of connections and old-school obligations. People driving themselves out of business. Land going cheap.

Nobody really caring to ask why ten different development companies started buying up the valley. More houses? Who cares. Why would anybody set up the entertainment district way out here? All those buildings for restaurants and shops, sitting in front of a large stretch of dirt. Nothing out there, an hour's drive south of Phoenix, fine, let people build, nobody's going to move there. It's the condo development at Tempe Town Lake all over again. And that large stretch of land running down the middle, between all the new developments, what's that? Room for a new highway maybe? A road to nowhere? Whatever. It's Arizona, man, people like to build.

Keep it simple. Keep it clean.

Phoenix was always a tough nut to crack, even for a nut farmer. It wasn't that the legislature was too honest, it was the opposite, they were too corrupt. The whole city was on the take, and always had been. Every door you opened led to someone with their bank details on a slip of paper, and if you'll do business with everyone, then you're doing everyone's business.

You want to bribe the local councillors? Get in line. And everyone in line expects a cut. What Red did, he found one or two people in each organization with a fragile enough ego that he could play them. Then keep playing them as they rose up to the top. Invest in people, long term. Wait for the investment to pay off.

Nobody really caring to notice that the ten different development companies were each in the same of one of Red's grandchildren.

He traced his finger along the map, the red line he'd drawn from the Gila River right up to Salt River. Let them all miss the point. Let them all think you're a retired farmer.

No ego in the long game. Nothing personal. Planning, execution, and profit.

He closed the laptop and headed downstairs to put his grandchildren to bed.

..

The McKinley Country Sherriff's Department didn't tell Alva Bobelu shit. Not that they knew of. Or maybe better put, not that they thought of. Because they didn't really think about her much at all. Her lieutenant didn't tell her shit either, but that was because he did think about her, and didn't like what he found. He had a fairly narrow interpretation of what the job involved. Anything outside of that box was inconvenience, and he didn't have time for that in his plan. He'd read a self-help book about daily affirmations and setting achievable goals. For the lieutenant these included getting up, not tripping over his own dick, not having too much paperwork to do, then going to bed. He loved his job. Alva Bobelu loved doing hers. This crated tension. Doing her job meant expanding what the lieutenant had to do in his. Unless he ignored her, and let her do pretty much whatever she wanted as long as she left him alone.

Several years ago, back when Bobelu was a part-time civilian assistance officer and teaching at the local school, the Zuni Police Department had signed an agreement with the McKinley County Sherriff's Department, giving ZPD officers the powers and authority of MCSD deputies on reservation land. Investigations. Arrests. Traffic stops.

It solved a whole bunch of budget problems for the MCSD, and freed their deputies up from needing to bother with the reservation except for guaranteed arrests. As part of the deal, ZPD officers got access to the MCSD systems. Their databases, intranet, email, Slack channel, private Facebook groups and radio channels.

This put Bobelu in something of a sweet spot. She had access to everything the Sheriff's Department was doing, and they didn't think about her enough to hide anything. And her lieutenant ignored everything she got up to, giving her free rein to interpret the job her own way, as long as it didn't create paperwork that crossed his desk.

Nobody really gave much thought to the fact Bobelu knew about MCSD sobriety traffic stops on the Rez the day before they happened, and warned people to stay out of trouble. It was how she'd known about the convenience store shooting the minute it happened, even off the reservation land, and why she'd been trying to get to Aidan and Audrey before anybody else. If she could keep them from going into the system through the MCSD, she would.

Which, as an idea, would put her in conflict with her lieutenant again. Because this was the key difference of opinion between them on the nature of their job. She worked to keep the people of the reservation out of trouble. He worked to enforce whatever rules would bolster his pension.

Once a cop, always a cop. Unless you were a teacher first.

The way it worked, nobody cared that she listened in. Nobody gave her any thought. The part that annoyed Bobelu most was how much work they didn't put into hiding their corruption. It wasn't that nobody knew the MCSD was on the take, or that they helped with whatever it was Eddie Wray had going on at the Safari, it was simply that nobody did anything about it. There was no need to hide it. No effort to hide it. Not even as a token gesture.

Which is all, right now, how Alva Bobelu came to be listening in on a conversation between two deputies planning to take an illegal drive down to Primo County in Arizona, not caring that they'd be hundreds of miles out of their jurisdiction, to find Leyton Wray and his girlfriend, Rose.

More accurately, to find their Toyota.

The thing she knew that they didn't, Leyton wasn't in the Toyota. She'd seen him in the pickup. She'd seen him a little while later, heading in that same pickup down the 53, out of state.

So now she had a decision to make. If Leyton wasn't in the Toyota, then who was? Who else had cause to be hundreds of miles away?

Her gut was giving her a pretty clear answer.

So the decision she was faced with was, did she listen to that hunch?

And just how much trouble would she get into if she did?

TWENTY-SIX

"You had no idea about the two million?"

Medina looked down at the money tipped out onto the motel bed. She didn't need to count it, having seen enough cash in the Marshal's Service to know Scott was on the level. One time, in a property seizure for a country singer who'd evaded twelve years' worth of taxes, she'd been part of a team that found twelve million in cash in the en suite bathroom of his Florida mansion. Once you've seen twelve million in cash, everything else becomes easy to count by scale.

There was two hundred grand on the sheets.

Scott held up her cuffed hands, sitting in the plastic chair in the corner. "I swear."

For now, it was fine to just have her hands cuffed together. She'd shown none of the signs of violence, nothing to trip Medina's early warning instincts. But that was another problem with being tired: Medina could be off her game and not realize it. Before they settled in for the night, she'd grab more cuffs from the car, fix Scott to something that couldn't move.

Medina sat on the bed next to the bundles of cash. The minute she touched down on the mattress, she could feel the tiredness welling up. "The two million I could understand. That's a lot of reasons to do something stupid, risk your whole life, go buy a new one. But two hundred grand? How far you think that's going to get you?"

"Well, what's your number?"

"That it would take for me to do something stupid?"

"I bet it's closer to two hundred grand than two million."

Medina started gathering it back up, putting it in the bag. Thinking, Scott doesn't know who she's stolen from. Keep that card back, for the right moment. "This kind of money always belongs to somebody."

Scott leaned back in her seat, looked around the room like there was an audience there, and she was vamping for support. *Check this out, am I right?* "Nobody is that good. Come on, you'd take it. Or maybe you'd take a different amount, but everyone's got a number."

"You're justifying."

"Of course I am. But it's true. Everyone's got a number, what's yours?"

Medina caught herself in the mirror. "I've never thought about it."

"That's not a denial though. Think about it now. Whatever you owe, credit cards, mortgage, loans. How much do other people have over you? I don't mean how much you'd like to win on the lottery. I just mean what vig does life hold over you? Add it all up, think about what you'd need to be clear, just to be clear. Just to wake up every day and not have money be the first thing you think of, or to go to bed and not be worrying about a bill. How much is that worth, in round numbers? Then add on more, keep adding until you don't even think about whether you'd take the bag. The point when it's not even a choice. That's your number."

Medina was doing the math as Scott spoke. The amount left on her mortgage. Two credit cards. A couple loans she'd taken from her mom and never paid back. She caught herself doing it, surprised at how easily she'd slipped into the act.

She pushed it back on Scott. "What was yours?"

"A hundred and twenty." She said it simple, matter-of-fact.

"That's low."

"I live cheap. Figure most people do, when you boil it down. You asked me how far two hundred grand would get me. Come on, how far would it get you? Really?"

Medina pushed it back onto Scott again. "So that extra eighty was just greed?"

"It's what was on the table. I'm just saying, I know you were doing the math just then. You're human. We're all human. If your number was somewhere around eighty thousand, I think we could do a deal here.".

Medina smiled. "You mean, rather than me killing you?"

Scott didn't smile back straight away. The thought was still in there, somewhere. She still had the idea Medina had been sent to kill her. They'd avoided all the real questions so far. Medina got up off the bed and went to the small bathroom, relieving herself before checking the room out for any loose fittings, or a window, any way Scott could turn the situation to her advantage if left alone in there. She caught herself in the mirror again, seeing the tired in her eyes.

She started running the numbers again.

What would I need, just to be clear?

You're justifying.

You're thinking too much again.

The cool girl has you thinking too much.

Scott called out from the living room. "Or even if your number is higher, how many years would eighty take off your mortgage? How many mornings would that be, waking up without money on your mind? What's that worth?"

Medina stepped back out into the room. Scott had moved. She was stretched out on the bed, her hands behind her head. She looked a little different now, adopting a pose. Medina knew she was about to go for a joke.

"We gotta stop meeting like this."

Medina gave a soft smile in response and eased into the plastic chair.

"You don't seem upset about losing a couple million."

Scott held her fingers out behind her head, a shrug with hands. "I haven't. I didn't know about that extra money until you mentioned it. Up until you grabbed me, I was just thinking about being two hundred grand up, I can't be upset about losing money I never gained."

"Leyton told you about the safe?"

Scott nodded. "Yeah. Told me there was three hundred grand, sitting there, and he could arrange for the safe to be open. I'd leave a hundred for him, finder's fee, and grab the rest for myself."

"You didn't get suspicious?"

"Course I did. But he told me three hundred, and when I got there, open safe, three hundred. So I stuck to my end of the deal, didn't give the rest of it much thought."

"Except now, you got a problem. Because someone you don't want to mess with thinks you took two million."

"Eddie?" Scott gave a look, like she already knew Eddie wasn't the answer, but didn't know what Medina was going to say.

"Big Wheel."

Scott went white. She stared down at her long legs for a moment. When she looked up, she was in control again. "Listen, this is going to be a long story and I drank a lot of water before going on stage, can I?"

She nodded to the bathroom.

"Go right ahead," Medina leaned back in the chair, showing she wasn't worried. "Just remember, you already know there are people wanting to kill you, and now you know you stole their money, too. I'm the one person trying to keep you alive, so, don't try anything."

Scott nodded, looking scared.

The reality of the situation breaking through her laid-back act. She shuffled off the bed, waddling forward one butt cheek at a time, until she could plant her feet down and take her own weight, then walked over to the washroom.

"Can I shut the door?"

"You better."

Medina sat staring at the bag, listening to Scott throwing up, flushing the toilet then starting to pee. She wasn't kidding about the water, that noise went on, and on. It stopped. She coughed. The stream started again. Medina heard the chain of the cuffs hit against porcelain, and then a different water sound, the faucet. The toilet flushed again, the door opened, and Scott walked back over to the bed. She held the cuffs out, and Medina thought she was going to ask her to take them off.

"The water on these? From the faucet, I swear."

Medina smiled again. Liking another of her jokes.

"Okay, start talking."

Scott sat down on the end of the bed. Closer to Medina, but it didn't feel like either a threat or a come on. "I guess I'll start at the beginning." Medina braced herself for another joke, something about what happened on the day Scott was born. But she didn't go for it. "It goes back to my brand."

"The stripping comedian."

"Dancing," Scott correcting her, her voice half tease, half pissed. "Anyone can strip. You just stand there and take your clothes off. No, I danced. It was an art. And sometimes I took my clothes off."

"Only sometimes?"

"The whole thing was planned. Like, I mean, people assume it's because I needed the money. Like the dancing was to cover the bills while I tried to make comedy work. But the dancing was part of how I made the comedy work. It was the brand. I got the idea from a porn star over here in the valley."

"An actor," Medina said, mimicking Scott's correction. "Who sometimes takes her clothes off."

Scott ignoring the wise-ass interruption. "She does porn, but she's also a pretty famous nightclub DJ. Does both, and all under the same name, same social media brand, people can book her for one, book her for the other, but they always know who they're getting. And it gives her a thing, a way to stick out."

"And how do you know her?"

"Oh." Scott, breezy. "We used to fuck."

Well, thought Medina, I did ask.

"And I figured that was the way," Scott continued. "I wasn't really getting anywhere with the comedy, even though I was good. And I'd also been a good dancer at college. So I combined them, made that my brand. My way of sticking out. And it worked, my bookings went through the roof. And it was a weird mix. See, guys get weird around female comics. Around male comics, guys get all cocky and talkative and want to show they're funny. Around women comics, it's all that but they're also trying to fuck you. And throw in that I was also a dancer, and guys love to try and show off in front of us."

Scott flashed a smile that said she had been in full control of those interactions. It was a good reminder for Medina. *Watch out for her, she likes to play games.*

"And that's how I got booked for this private party. As both. One set comedy, two sets dancing, and the vague promise I'd throw in a few private dances too if the mood took me."

"What kind of mood is that?"

"One where I want to earn a lot more money. So I get there, and these people, they've hired out a whole nightclub, and there's half a dozen of us, acts. And there was security all over the place. That kind of security."

"Organized crime."

"Yup. But also Sheriff Jed was there."

"Jed Bashford?"

"Yeah."

Medina's brain started to fire connections. They'd always liked Bashford for Big Wheel, but nobody could ever prove it. No investigation into him ever came back showing that he was clean, but he was never dirty enough to motivate an arrest.

"But I do my stuff. Get some laughs, do my moves, get a load of tips. And then I'm at the bar. See, the bar was comped. For everyone. So I was sticking around to enjoy it, and see if I could pick up other bookings. And watching the party without really admitting to myself I was watching the party, because why wouldn't you? How often do you get invited to something like that?"

"Sure."

"And it was getting pretty clear the party wasn't for Jed, he just happened to be there. There was this other guy, older guy, like a grandpa, talked to me a few times between sets, seemed nice enough but I could tell everyone was deferring to him. And then, so I'm at the bar, and this one guy, one of the security guys, starts trying to chat me up. And that's the power, right? The dancer-comedian combo. They try really hard to impress me while trying really hard to treat me like I'm not impressive. And he lets a dumb thing slip. He calls the old guy Big Wheel."

"Big Wheel isn't Sheriff Jed."

"Right, it's this grandpa guy."

"Who was he?"

"I'll get to it. See, what happened after that, this security guy realizes he's screwed up, starts extorting me, threatening me. And knowing what I know now, he had no power. He was scared. He'd made a mistake, and he knew if his bosses found out, they'd hurt him, or worse. So he pushed all that off onto me, twisted it round, got me to stay quiet by scaring me into thinking I was the one who'd screwed up somehow. Because I'd heard something I shouldn't have, not because he'd said something he shouldn't have."

"But you didn't know what Big Wheel even meant at that point."

"I wasn't dealing with the brains of the operation. No. If he'd just breezed onto the next topic, I would have forgotten the whole thing. But he made it into a thing."

"And he was pushing you for money to keep quiet, when really you were paying him for the privilege of keeping him out of trouble."

"Okay, he had a few more braincells than I credit him with. Yeah. Said if I didn't pay up, Big Wheel would kill me."

"What did you do?"

"I robbed a Credit Union, got caught."

"That's the one you went down for?"

"That's the one, yeah. Only one I ever did. I'm in prison. Still no idea what Big Wheel is a reference to, but knowing it's important, and knowing to say nothing about it. Get my head down, try to rehabilitate, try to get my sentence down. And I'm an entertainer, or a performer at least. So I talk the warden into letting me set up these classes and workshops. Acting. Comedy. Improv. The prison started mixing the male and female populations in some of the education and outreach programs, including mine, so I was working with both."

"Someone said something?"

"The classes go great. The warden is talking about using this as a program they can export to other prisons, he's taking credit for it. But it's helping people, you know? Socialising them, helping them to express themselves, building friendships. It's like real therapy. So then I do it a fifth time, and there are some new inmates in the group, people who've only just come in. Week two was all about getting the class to stand up and tell each other stories, for five minutes. Doesn't need to be funny, just needs to be about them. It's to get them confident talking, for me to learn what their point of view is, so I can help find their comedy persona. And it's to show them exactly what five minutes feels like."

"Is that important?"

"Oh yeah. When you're first starting out? It's all about getting a solid five, moving things round, building that set. And learning what five minutes feels like is important, because you can't keep checking your watch when you're up in front of a crowd."

"And making them talk lets you see who they are."

"Right. Some people are naturally funny, some aren't. But everyone can tell a joke, with some guidance, so once I know who I'm dealing with, I can get them to focus in on the version of themselves that will get laughs."

Medina was tempted to ask how Scott would make her funny, what she saw Medina's comedy persona as. But she let that one go.

"Everyone's telling their stories, and this one guy gets up, says he used to work on a farm south of Phoenix, starts telling this story about a criminal called Big Wheel-"

"He used the name, too?"

"Yeah, everyone knows that name. His story is about Big Wheel buying up land between Gila River and Phoenix, says he wants to reroute the river."

"That would never work. No way he'd be allowed to."

"I figured that. But two days later, my guy was stabbed in the shower. Bled to death right there, I'm told nobody called the guard, everyone just watched and waited for him to die. Two days after that, another of my class hung themselves."

"Shit."

Scott nodded, breathing in and out deep before continuing. "Both men. So both over the other side of the prison, different wing to me. I go to the warden, tell my story. I don't say what was said in the class, and I hold back from telling I know who Big Wheel is, but I say I think I'm going to get killed because of the class, and ask for protection."

"What he say?"

"He told me Big Wheel didn't exist, and I had nothing to worry about. Looked me in the eye, told me to go back to my room. That got me scared, I figured now I was next, and he was in on it, so I called in a favour from a girl on my block, had a cell phone, and called my lawyer. Told him the same story, and included that I know who Big Wheel is, said call whoever you need to, the cops, the feds, the FBI, the fucking President, I don't care, but I'm going to be killed in the next thirty minutes. Thirty minutes later, guards come to my room, escort me to solitary. But I'm not there as punishment, I'm being kept safe. And the warden can't touch me, he's clearly had orders. The DA comes to visit me personally, I tell her almost everything, except the name. I tell her I think the warden is in on it, and I want protection. She says, give me the name and we have a deal, I say, give me a deal and you have a name. She goes away, saying she'll think about it."

"I heard there was an attempt on you?"

"Yeah, from a guard, you believe that? The DA started to take things more serious after that, said they weren't ready to sign the deal, but they'd get me out, put me in a safe house, arrange WITSEC, the whole thing."

"If you're getting everything you want, why did you run?"

Scott started to speak, then sighed in frustration. She lifted her hands. "Can we?"

Medina looked at the cuffs. Thought it over. "Until I'm ready to sleep, yeah."

She pulled out the keys, leaned forward to take Scott's hands. Pretending not to feel that old high school rush of blood when they touched. She could feel Scott's eyes on her. The cuffs came loose and Scott rubbed at her wrists, smiled a thank you.

"I felt trapped," she said.

"You were."

"No, I mean..." Scott paused, looked at herself in the mirror. "I started thinking about it. While the DA was listing all the terms, and my lawyer was explaining things to me. It was like the first time I really thought through what was happening. WITSEC? Changing my name? Moving to the middle of nowhere? That's not me."

"It has to be, Emi. That's what you get now. You broke the law, you got information on someone else, now you get to go serve coffee under a new name in North Dakota."

"How will that work? I wasn't joking before. The reason I'm out here doing gigs? I'm a comedian. I'm my own life's work. Getting up on stage, telling jokes. It's the only thing I've ever been good at. Performing. The only time I've ever felt right. Come whatever else happens, I need to be myself. And sitting in the prison, waiting for the marshal to pick me up, I realised that was the one thing I could never do again."

"Let the heat die down, wait a few years, in whatever town they find for you, then start doing some open mics, have some fun."

"You saw what happened back there. I got up under a new name, someone accused me of ripping myself off. I'm too good at being me now, I've put too much work into it. Friend of mine once had a bit about quitting comedy. He'd get up on stage and do this whole thing talking like he was at an AA meeting, but for comedy addicts. He'd be talking about how he's been trying to quit, but can't do it. Then he had this line, he said, quitting comedy is like getting out of prison after fifteen years. The world has changed, and you have no clue what else to do. So you go tell another joke, and they catch you." Scott turned her eyes to Medina now, looking straight into hers. "I gotta be myself."

Medina was back in the warehouse. Creeping through the shadows. Sure that the Milk Man was there. Then she was in the back of the ambulance. And then she was handing her shield over to Reed Palmer, trying hard not to look like she was ready to cry. Trying hard not to let him see that she didn't know who she was anymore.

"I arrested a bank robber once," Medina said. "James Finch, you heard of him?"

"He the one wrote the book? Guy who robbed places unarmed, just walked up to the teller and started telling jokes, relaxing them before asking for money?"

"That's the one. I brought him in. Shot his partner, put the gun on him, he lowered his weapon, surrendered. I visited him during the trial, asked him why he committed robberies, you know what he said?"

"What?"

Medina smiled, "Because he's a criminal."

Scott matched her smile. "Right? See? I get that. At a certain point, you know who you are, you have to be true to that."

Scott scratched her nose, and Medina felt her own starting to itch. The space between them had narrowed during the conversation. She watched Scott's mouth. And now she was in high school again, watching the cool girl move. Watching the cool girl control the boys' attention. Talking to the cool girl.

Telling the cool girl she'd been thinking about kissing her.

God dammit.

Medina leaned back in the seat, putting distance between them again. "Tell me his name."

"Big Wheel? If I tell you, you become a target."

"I'm already a target if I'm standing between them and you. This secret is getting you killed. If it's not a secret anymore, your chances are better."

Scott nodded. "I can give you the name. But there's another question you haven't asked."

Medina blinked. Opened her mouth, closed it. Her tongue going dry, her throat feeling tight. Back in the warehouse again. Back in the moment. Back in the line of fire. Back knowing something she'd really always known, but also only knew for the first time now. Back knowing the reason she couldn't wear a badge anymore.

"The name of the security guy," Medina said, knowing already what Scott was about to tell her. "The one who extorted you."

TWENTY-SEVEN

All things considered, Drey thought they did well only getting lost three times. They came into Tucson through Oro Valley. At least, the names of the retail and residential parks they passed had mentioned the valley. She knew white folks would name anywhere after anything, though, so who knows.

There was a weird haze hanging over Tucson at dusk. Above the buildings, below the sky. It looked like the heat and the electricity somehow mixed to create a cloud.

All the way in, she'd kept saying the address they needed was easy to remember. MAB lived in a trailer on Birdman Avenue, in a part of town called Balboa. That was why it always stuck in her head. Birdman and Balboa, movie and movie. Two film references in one address. They came to Villa Balboa right after all the valley signs. It looked too nice, nothing like the way she remembered. A small subdivision, new houses laid out on a grid, with one entrance, next to the Villa Balboa sign. They drove around for ten minutes, each time they took a turn Coyote would say this it? And she would say no. Frustration creeping into her own voice, which she knew was a bad idea, since it was her job to keep Coyote calm.

On the third circuit of the same streets, they picked up a tail. A short guy in a security uniform driving a golf cart. He flagged them down, Drey instinctively grabbed the gun out of the cup holder before Coyote could get to it, keeping it down out of sight, and out of use.

"You kids aren't from around here," the guard said. A statement, not a question.

He had a manner about him that wasn't aggressive, wasn't pushy. Drey was used to it. It was matter of fact that she didn't belong in the same place as him, so why would he get aggressive about it?

All he's ever needed to do is point it out, and the brown folk will move along. Drey could feel Coyote's mood building again. Like that weird haze sitting over the city, something felt like it was gathering above Coyote's head.

"We're lost," Drey smiled, gave the guard what he was expecting.

Yes sir, this isn't our place.

"What you looking for?"

"Birdman Drive?"

The guards face creased. He'd never heard of it.

Drey tried again, "I'm sure it was in Balboa somewhere."

Now the guard smiled. Look at the little idiot. "You're looking for Balboa Heights," he said, and gave them directions. "Back out onto North Oracle, south past Trader Joe's, keep going down, across West Ina and...."

Drey stopped taking in the information from there. It was an odd thing about being given directions. They really only meant anything if you already knew what they meant. Someone directing to you a place you don't know, in a town you don't know, after a while it's just a list of words.

She could tell Coyote wasn't taking it in either. He wasn't even nodding, or acknowledging the guy, leaving it to Drey to be the human one. She didn't want to ask him to repeat, could already see they were on a countdown to another Coyote blow up. If she could get to MAB's trailer before it happened, she could calm things down. One more wrong turn further down the long road, when Coyote went left after Trader Joe's, and Drey knew the guard had said to go straight, but didn't want to say. Better to roll with it, let Coyote make up his own mind. The third time maybe didn't count, coming before they'd gotten back onto the main road, taking a couple wrong turns trying to double back. Was that a separate time lost, or still part of the first one? Back on North Oracle they passed a cemetery. Drey remembered the guard saying something about that, long after she'd stopped paying attention. She'd heard the mention, thought, well, when we get lost again, we can ask the dead people for directions.

"It's here somewhere," she said.

Two blocks further on, they passed a Mexican diner she recognised. MAB had taken her there for tacos one time.

"Turn here, I think."

Off the main strip and into a small street, running between small houses, beat up double-wides and a couple small businesses. Drey definitely knew where they were now. She remembered the barber shop on the corner, MAB telling her some story about how every guy who ran the place had the same first name, handed over when they retired to the next one. She'd said, you think maybe they just pretend? He'd looked at her like she was crazy.

"Turn right."

Another street. More houses. On the left was a high wire fence, with trailers on the other side, pressed close together into a concrete yard. Just enough space to walk between them.

"There. Turn here. Just here, yeah."

They were in Birdman Drive now. A dead-end street, running to the back of an auto repair shop. On the left was a gate, side entrance to the makeshift trailer park.

"We can't leave the car here," Coyote said. "Someone might steal it."

He stared at her, not blinking, no sense of irony passing his features.

"You mean like we did?"

"Sure but...now I have it."

Drey noticed the I rather than we, but didn't care to push the issue. He wanted the car, he could have it. "Look around, you think anybody coming down here looking for a car to steal?" She nodded to the back. "What we need to worry about are the bags. They come with us. The car is safe here, you got the keys."

Coyote pulled them, held them up, smiling. "Yeah, I do."

Drey nodded, getting out of the car. She opened the back door and grabbed one of the bags. Dropping the gun in the top and lifting the bag out, waiting until Coyote did the same. They walked through the gate, into the narrow walkway between the trailers. Drey counted them off as she went, not remembering exactly where in the yard MAB's trailer was but knowing she'd recognize it. A dog barked inside one of the trailers. Coyote flinched.

The barking continued. Louder, more insistent.

Drey smiled at Coyote, letting him know they were safe. Up ahead now, she could see MAB's trailer.

The battered double-wide, leaning in one corner where one of the legs was bent. She pointed to it.

That's when they heard a door open, somewhere else in the yard, followed by swearing, and the sound of a dog's feet landing on concrete and starting to run. Coyote yelped. If he had the gun, she was sure he'd be pulling it, ready to use. She touched his arm and said to follow her. She ran across the yard to the door of MAB's trailer.

"You got a key?"

She'd never heard Coyote sounding so panicked.

"Don't need."

There was a trick to the door, she just needed to get it right. Pressing her foot against the bottom of the door, applying her weight there, she pulled on the handle, trying to lift the door up at the same time. Now she could hear the growling and barking. Turned to see the dog, a powerful pitbull, large shoulders and red all round its face, charging them down the narrow walkway. Coyote squealed.

Drey tried the door again, this time kicking the bottom, hard, and yanking on the handle. It worked, the door pulled outwards. She stepped inside, grabbed behind her for Coyote. It wasn't necessary, he was already moving, pushing in behind her. They fell forwards, into the trailer. Drey had the presence to know the job wasn't done, the dog was still coming and the door was open. She turned, pushing Coyote off her, and got to her feet. Leaning out into the yard to grab the door handle. The dog was only a few feet away now, and ready to attack. She sucked in breath and pulled, slamming the door just as the pitbull slammed into it on the outside.

It stayed out there for a few seconds, making a rumbling sound as it sniffed at the bottom of the door, then they heard it turn around and walk away, claws clacking on the concrete. In the darkness of the trailer, Drey and Coyote stayed still while they calmed down. Both of them breathing loud.

After a few seconds, Drey said, "Didn't know you're afraid of dogs."

He came back, hurt in his voice, "I'm not scared."

TWENTY-EIGHT

Palmer, answering his cell on the second attempt, said, "Your commitment to calling me out of hours is impressive." Sleep in his voice, making it deeper. He was past that age now, where being up late at night and first thing in the morning would turn even the fittest of men into an old person.

"Hi boss."

"I remember your first day in my office, in Miami, pulling you in, sitting you down, and saying to you, 'the most important thing is sleep.' I remember having the same talk when you transferred into Phoenix, and you stopped me halfway through, finished the speech."

"You sound grouchy, still worried about your grandson?"

"No, that whole problem resolved itself in the *less than a day* since we last spoke about it."

Palmer's sarcasm had two settings. There was the gentle, laconic version you'd get most of the time, when he was enjoying messing with you. Then there was the more aggressive, sulky version you'd get when he was irritated. Medina could feel him pushing into the latter, and decided it was time to get to the point.

"The name Red Peters mean anything to you?"

Silence on the line for a moment, followed by movement. Bed sheets, footsteps, a door opening and closing. "Yeah, it does. What you got?"

Medina knew, from her father, that a teacher never forgets a student. The face might become detached from the name, the years will blur, the parents will fade into nothing. But the kid stays etched into the teacher's memory. The same was true of law enforcement. The names and faces would separate, and the specific details of the case would bury themselves away somewhere deep, but the names and faces of the victims, the suspects and the witnesses were always somewhere at the back of the mind, waiting to be nudged loose by some casual mention.

Medina had felt it happen when Scott mentioned the name Red Peters. She remembered it from somewhere. Some case, or conversation. Maybe even just something she'd read in paperwork. And from Palmer's response, she could tell he was having the same reaction.

Medina met Scott's eyes as she talked. He was sitting on the bed, waiting. "I found our runaway."

Palmer said, "Emily Scott?"

"Uh huh."

"Whatever you do, don't give her chocolate, turns people into assholes."

The joke told her Palmer was edging back into the friendly version of himself, approving of her work, happy to take the call.

"I'll bear that in mind. She's been telling me an interesting story. Good plot, but lacks an ending so far. It stars Red Peters. I know the name, but can't remember the details."

"Same," Palmer said. "Hang on, let me get my laptop, call you back."

He killed the call. Medina sat in silence, resting the cell in her lap. Scott looked nervous. She'd been hesitant about the idea, but Medina convinced her. It might well be that Big Wheel had people on the inside. Certainly somebody had leaked the codename to him, turned it into a joke. But Medina trusted Palmer with her life, and they couldn't do this alone.

It took a little less than five minutes. The cell started to buzz, Medina answered.

"Redmond Peters," Palmer said, his voice telling her he was reading something out of a file. "Retired nut farmer. You remember the water wars?"

"Not the details."

"After another of those big housing developments out in the sticks, the new residents started to complain, said their wells were drying up, turning on the faucet to get dust and mud. The state got involved, there was a whole investigation, turned out the farmers were using up the water. But they'd been there for generations, and the people living in the estates, many of them, were new to the area. It got nasty, there was talk of new laws, licensing the farms, regulating a quota.

Red Peters was one of the ones who retired around then, said they were getting out rather than be regulated."

"Yeah, I remember all that now. What's he been doing since?"

"He runs a convenience store near where his farm used to be. Sold off most of the land to property developers. I stopped in once, passing through, just to put a face to the name."

"So he *was* someone we looked at?"

"He came up when we were looking at Sheriff Jed. Trying to make the case against the slippery bastard. If you recall, we took a long look at Jed's reported interests, around his political campaigns. Red was someone who'd run against him a couple times, for sheriff, as an independent."

"Before he retired?"

"Yeah. Well, once before he retired, and then at the next one, too, which would have been right around the time of all the water shenanigans. Then he retired to his store." He waited a few seconds. "Why?"

"Reed, if I told you I know Emily Scott's secret, and that it could get us all killed, would you want in on it?"

Another pause. "You know those times someone leads up to asking you a question by asking if they can ask you a question?" She could picture the wry smile as he spoke. "I guess I'm already in on it now, so go ahead."

Medina laughed. "Well...yeah. I figure you've already guessed what I'm going to say. But Emi figured out-"

"Emi? You're up to nicknames already?"

"Red Peters is Big Wheel. Sheriff Jed works either for him, or with him. The warden was in his pocket, and so were some of the prison guards. We should assume at this point that Jed's deputies are questionable."

"Okay. Well, we know the DA is on the level, because she's the one with the hard-on to get Emi in here and take her testimony, bring the whole thing down. Anybody else I need to be worried about?"

It was right there, in the way he said it. Asking a specific question without being specific. What about Treat Tyler? Palmer already knowing the truth in the same way Medina had already known it, just neither of them wanting to know it. And again, for a second, she was back in that warehouse. Closing in on the Milk Man. Knowing he was there. Knowing she just needed a few more seconds. Seeing the Shelby. Seeing something in the reflection, a movement, then two shots and she was down. She felt the shots again now, touched her side.

"This needs to stay between us," she said, looking at Scott, who nodded. "The three of us. Four, counting the DA, but nobody else in her office. There's more."

"Of course there is."

"Emi says something about the Gila River. She says Red Peters wants to re-route it, but that's not possible." She paused, expecting an answer from Palmer. When none came, she prompted a reply with, "Right?"

"Who even knows anymore. I take it you haven't listened to the news today?"

"No, why?"

She moved to sit next to Scott on the bed, holding the phone a little away from her ear so they could both hear what was being said.

"Our friend Sheriff Jed." Palmer used every ounce of wry sarcasm he could muster. "Has announced he's going to be running to become Senator Jed. Asshole keeps finding new ways to ruin my party. His platform, which sounded like bluster until about a minute ago, is keep the immigrants out and the water in."

"Meaning what?"

"He went off on a whole tear. You know how he talks, wanders all over the place, says very little. He said that California and Mexico keep stealing our water and we should find a way to keep it here, for the people of this great state."

"Bet that went down well."

"The usual. The crowd cheered, the reporters said he'd gone insane."

"But if he whips people up to that idea, re-routing the Gila doesn't sound too crazy."

"Salt River Project Mark 2."

"And if a retired nut farmer just happens to own all the land that the rerouted river will go through..."

"Yeah. Where are you at right now? I can call the office nearest you, get them to set something up."

Medina stared at Scott again, but she wasn't seeing her. She was seeing Tyler. Seeing the years between then and now. She shook her head, said, "You know me, boss. In the front door."

"And the girl's willing to come in?"

Medina watched Scott's reaction, trying to read her real intent. Was she biding her time? Waiting for a chance to run? Scott, in return, raised her eyebrow, saying nothing, pushing the question back onto Medina.

"We still need to talk about that," Medina said.

Palmer sighed, trying to keep it hidden. "Okay. I'll call the DA." It sounded like he started to hang up, then put the phone back to his ear. "Stay safe, please."

The call ended. Medina and Scott sat in a silence that stretched out. After a while Scott's eyes drifted across to meet hers in the mirror.

"Another time, another place. If none of this were happening..."

"It is happening."

"Only I was thinking. I mean,.." Scott turned from the mirror, met Medina's eyes for real, almost smiled. "We passed a diner on the way here. Twenty-four hours, I think. We could put all of this on pause. I could go a pie and a Coke. Hang out with an old friend for a couple hours?"

TWENTY-NINE

The dot on the screen hadn't moved for over an hour. Tyler, typing the address into Google, found a motel on the edge of Long Beach. Medina was bedded in for the night. Sticking to Reed Palmer's rule. Good girl. Double good, because he was almost there himself. Triple good, in fact. California. Any of Red's backup would have stopped back at the border.

This was going to come down to Tyler and Medina.

And Emily Scott.

The bitch had embarrassed him twice now. She'd not get a third time. And then what? Dump the bodies, have a bag full of cash, go wherever he wanted.

His phone started buzzing, and he was so distracted he answered without looking at who it was.

"Hey there," Reed Palmer's voice filled his ear. Loud, fake friendly. He knew this tone, Reed was hamming up whatever he was about to say. "I know it's late, but I'm sat here, watching my shows, and I think to myself, you haven't spoken to Treat since you sent him on vacation, how's that kid holding up?"

Reed knowing full well that Treat was going to chase down the case on his own time, earn back his reputation. It's what anyone wearing the badge would do. Except Chloe Medina, who turned in the badge and ran away, left Tyler to pick up the pieces.

"Hi, Reed."

"I think I miss the time when everyone used to call me boss. We should bring that back."

Tyler paused. That had never been a thing. Even in the office, everyone called Reed by his first name. Only one person had ever called him boss. Medina.

"Sure thing, boss."

"So how's the holiday going? Seen any good movies? Done some fishing? Tracked down any wanted fugitives?"

Tyler now thinking, okay, he knows, but what does he know?

"I've been thinking of taking up comedy," he said, smiling. "Stand up. I think I'd be okay at it."

"Isn't it traditionally considered an advantage to be funny?"

"This you trying out material of your own?"

"No." The boom went out of Reed's voice. Dropping the act now, getting serious. "I don't find too much to laugh about these days."

"What's on your mind, Reed?"

"One minute, you're already forgetting my new rule?"

"What's on your mind, boss?"

"You ever think about why we wear the badge? I mean really, what it means?"

Tyler didn't have an answer. Too busy trying to get on ahead, figure out where this was going.

Reed continued. "Law and order. We make laws, we need people to enforce them. I guess I've always taken it for granted that people who want to wear the badge are making a promise, to everyone else, to the law."

"Sure."

"But you do the job as long as I have, there's only so long you can really hold onto that thinking without being an idiot. You see all the times people look the other way. All the times people with shields or stars lie to cover for each other. All the times the law is applied differently to different people. And you still believe in the badge, but not so much the people in it."

Here we go, Tyler thought. He Knows.

"Are you okay, boss?"

"The way I see it, no matter what everyone else was doing, I got me a good staff. Four deputies. Okay, one of them's green, and one of them's a PTSD basket case. But I got these two, a man and a woman, these two who really care about the shield, they made that promise to the law. But then one of them quits, hands me the badge, says she can't wear it no more, and I spend four years thinking it's because she thinks she wasn't worthy of wearing it."

"Chloe."

"But I guess I had it all the wrong way round, didn't I? She just got woke up one day, realised the badge wasn't worthy of being worn."

"Hey, listen, boss..."

"Nah, I got a little more to say. Humor me, I'm old. Your runaway, the comedian."

"Emily Scott."

"I know her name, Treat. I said I'm old, not senile. Your fugitive, the comedian. She had a secret, almost cost her life. So now she's told a couple people."

The line was quiet. It felt like Reed was waiting for Tyler to say something, testing his response, so Tyler said, "She told you?"

"If she did, what would happen? The people who want to kill her, where do you think they'd stop? How many people would they kill to keep a secret that isn't a secret anymore? And was it ever really a secret, or just a thing we didn't want to look at? At what point, do you think, everyone just just walks away?"

Was he trying to warn Tyler off here? Telling him to drop it, go back to being straight, pretend this whole thing never happened?

"I guess that would depend," Tyler said, watching himself in the mirror.

"On what?" Reed genuinely sounding curious.

"Well, same as any guy we question, I guess. Depends on why they're doing it. Everybody got a reason for the choices they make."

"It's all just money, end of the day, isn't it?" Reed said. "That's what makes people put on their pants in the morning. Don't matter if they're wearing a badge or a ski mask, they're doing what they're doing for money."

"Money, or debt, maybe. Everyone's got something hanging over them. I figure a lot of people get targeted, don't they? People with debt problems. Drugs. A sick family member, needs expensive treatment."

"I been meaning to ask how you're getting on with your GA meetings, still going?"

"Not as often as I should."

"That's a shame." Not sounding like he meant it.

"Listen, Reed, you want to meet up, get a beer or something, talk about this?"

"Nah. Don't mind me. Ramblings of an old man. One way or another, this problem's going to solve itself."

The line went dead.

Tyler stared through his reflection in the mirror. Not at it, through it. Trying to look into the past. To see the line of choices that led to this moment. Each one of them making some form of sense at the time. Was any one of them the point of no return? Once he'd made the first choice, was he always heading to this point? Or could he have turned a different way at any step along the path?

He was all in now.

They all were.

Just had to roll with it, see where things ended up.

Up ahead he could see the sign for the motel Medina had bedded down at.

He slowed down as he drove by, looking onto the forecourt. The Pontiac was parked at the far end of the row of small rooms, backed up close to the front door. He continued down a couple blocks and pulled off into a side road, stopping beside a closed liquor store. He pulled his spare gun from beneath the dash, and a fresh pair of plastic gloves.

THIRTY

"You didn't tell your boss about the money," Scott said.

Settled into a booth in the diner, on the corner of West Forty-Seventh. Medina with Key lime pie, diet soda and a bag full of money. Scott with coffee, three sugars, and an apple pie. The diner had low lighting, a counter in the middle, booths along both sides. Music turned down enough for people to talk. Some blend of synth and bass, a female vocal. They walked down the two blocks from the motel, Medina trusting Scott to come along without cuffs.

Scott had mentioned three times since coming in that she recognised the place. An episode of The X-Files, or one of those other shows. Not seeming to worry that this description took in every single television show ever made.

Medina set her drink down beside her plate. "Ex-boss."

"You called him boss on the phone."

"I always do, it's just a joke."

"I could hear how you both were, you miss working together."

Medina smiled, liking how easily Scott seemed to read her. "It was a good job. Wore a badge, went after fugitives."

"Sounds like the Old West."

Medina chewed on her pie for a moment, nodded, swallowed. "All I'd ever wanted to be."

"Then why'd you stop?"

"Better pay."

"I bet that line works, doesn't it?" Challenging her, but friendly, not aggressive. "Same as that thing you said in the news that time. 'I like to catch the bad guys.' Sounds cool, shuts people down. What's the real reason?"

Medina looked down at her plate, thinking. Scott could read her too easily. Was she using that? Playing her? Medina sipped the soda through the straw. Wiped her lips. "How about you? Why'd you become a comedian?"

"I like catching the bad guys?" Scott put her palm up. "Sorry. I don't know, you know when I was a kid, I'd look at other people, see them comfortable in their own skin, and think, how do they do that? Like you."

"Me?" Medina's voice was higher than she intended, sounding like a flirt.

"That's why I liked you. You never seemed to panic or worry, always knew what was going on. Someone asked me a question, I'd have to answer as someone else, put on a voice, look for the laugh. You just answered."

"I never knew what to say, so I said as little as possible."

"Well it *looked* cool. For me, I was never being myself, you know? I'd put on those voices, talk in film quotes. Real annoying to be around."

The cool girl talking about not being cool.

Scott continued. "Lisa, my ex, she said to me one time, 'you don't need to try so hard.' Deepest thing anyone ever said to me. Took me a while, but I started to come out on stage. When I was up there, doing my set. First year or so, it was just a glorified memory trick. I'd write my stuff, go out and say it, get laughs. But if someone heckled me, or threw me off, I'd panic, because it wasn't in the script."

"Sure. I think I'd panic, too. Just the thought of it."

Medina had faced down armed fugitives on more than one occasion. She'd stopped two bank robberies. Killed, she thought, three people. But none of that could bring her even close to thinking about going up on stage and doing comedy to a room full of strangers.

Scott flashed her the look. Going up a step now from gentle flirting to the real thing. "No you wouldn't. I can see you, in there, you'd be cool."

The obviousness pulling Medina back out of it, seeing the game being played. "I bet that line works, doesn't it? Telling the woman she'd be a great stand-up. Flatter her, bring her out a little."

"Sometimes." Scott's smile stayed in place as she sipped the coffee, owning up to being caught in the act. "But that fear is the first thing to go, really. The nerves never go, the hour before the show. But the fear of actually being up there and telling jokes? Doesn't bother me."

"Really?"

"The scariest part of riding a bike is not riding the bike. You think about all the things that can go wrong. Falling off, crashing. But when you ride regularly, falling off is just part of the deal. You try to avoid it, but it doesn't scare you, it's a thing that happens. Same deal for me and comedy. I get up there, people laugh or they don't. Sometimes you bomb, you go do another gig."

Scott leaned back into the seat, arm up across the top. Not rushing the food, happy to sit and talk. Medina noticed her calm again. Fear about the situation they were in only seemed to break through in small doses, fading back again afterwards.

Medina wanted to figure her out. "So what changed? You said the first year or so you struggled."

"Never struggled. I was always good. But that first year, I was still playing a role. Get up there, do the script, adopt the persona, get off. But then it changes. You stick with it long enough, it starts to be you up there. You're in the moment. I found I would lose myself in it. Get up there, everything else drops away. I'm not even thinking, really, when it's going well. I'm just doing. I come off stage after a good one, I can tell you loads of things I've noticed about the crowd, details, who laughed at what. But I won't be able to tell you about my thought process, about what I was thinking."

Medina found herself smiling and nodding as Scott talked. This was the same feeling she chased. Not needing to think too much, just doing. "Sounds perfect."

"You know, you can meet a hundred people in LA who'll tell you they're artists. But a stand-up goes into a room, a different room each night, and makes tiny adjustments to their act, to their words, to their cadence, instant decisions every night to tailor the performance to that room, and that moment, and only that moment. The performance is gone after that."

Medina raised her drink for another sip, looking at Scott over the glass. "So, you're saying you're an artist?"

"Probably not, I get the feeling that wouldn't impress you much."

"You read me so well." Telling the truth and hiding at the same time. "You're not how I expected."

"Expected, or remembered?"

"You're not...trying to be funny."

Scott shrugged, easy. "I don't need to try. I can be funny any time I want, but I only need laughs when I'm up on stage. There are a lot of guys the other way, though. Comedians. Most of them are like needy kids, always trying to get a laugh, always looking for compliments. They can't get out of their own heads, always stuck in there, thinking about things."

"Sounds like you don't like comedians all that much."

"You hear the one about the comic who was late for his own funeral?"

"Go on."

"Seven other comedians called up, offering to fill the spot. You know, when you first start out? It's the coolest thing. Most of the reasons to become a comedian are so you can hang around at the back of the room with the other comedians. It's like the best, coolest, most exclusive club. But then you're in the club, and it's all gossip and people pushing for position."

"If you hate it so much, why do you need to do it?"

"It's who I am. It's that thing, I said, that moment when you're up there. That's all I want in life. Not to think, not to analyse, just to do. I've only found that in two places. On stage telling jokes, and robbing a credit union with a gun." Scott looked Medina right in the eyes. "Make any sense?"

When was the moment? That look she'd shared with Ben Nichol, when something in her manner had given her away? That conversation with Eddie, when the job got personal? Or was it when she walked into the comedy club, and found herself laughing at Emily Scott's jokes?

Medina nodded. "Yes."

Scott leaned forward, both elbows on the table. "And you didn't tell your boss about the money."

Medina leaned forward too. Was something going to happen here? It could. She was sure they both felt it. A moment of change. Stop being who she was, become someone else. But if it was going to happen, it needed to be now.

••

Scott was thinking it over, *do I go in closer*? It felt like the moment to do it, try out, slow and easy. But she didn't, she just smiled, stayed where she was. Medina was ignoring the question about the money again. Or maybe, what the problem was, Scott hadn't asked the question.

Twice she'd said you didn't tell your boss about the money. But that's not a question. That's a statement. What was she expecting Medina to do, just say, yes Emi, that's correct, I didn't. What Scott should have done was frame it with a question mark. Why haven't you told your boss about the money?

Now she needed to find a third opportunity, the way to come back to it without being too obvious. And, in truth, she wasn't sure he wanted to. Asking about the money reminded them both of why they were here. And thinking about why they were here took away from the fun of being here. Right now. In this moment. With Chloe Medina.

The cool girl from school.

Everyone has them. The early one. The person who defined your tastes for the first few years, the person who loomed over your first few relationships, helped show you who you were going to be.

Maybe everyone else moved past that.

But Chloe Medina had always been the big *what if* for Emily Scott.

What if the boys hadn't turned around and laughed? What if she'd waited a little longer before making the move?

What if Chloe Medina wanted to take some money and run?

Scott was feeling like the world's biggest hypocrite. Sitting here, preaching about losing yourself, about getting into the place when you don't need to think. But all she was doing was thinking. She was aware of two different versions of herself. She was watching them argue. So, she guessed, he was actually aware of three different versions of herself. The two arguing, and the one watching.

The first voice, the loudest before they got to the diner, was the idiot who'd taken the money. She was saying to get the cuffs off, back at the motel. Find a way. Flirt. Whatever. Get Medina off guard. That's it, now walk outside, on the way to the diner, find a chance to run. Or now, sitting here, the voice was saying, excuse yourself, go to the restroom, find a way to grab the bag.

But the second voice? She was enjoying being here. In the motel, watching Medina talk on the phone, staring at her dark eyes when she was looking away. Sitting here now, talking, like they were...what? On a date? No, this wasn't a date. This was that thing that happens way before that.

This was two adults, hanging out, being themselves, seeing where it could go. Rolling with it.

Except, right now, Scott didn't know who she was. For the first time in years. Was she the woman who took the money, or was she the woman who wanted to hang out with Chloe Medina? Was there a way to be both?

She leaned back, put her hands around the cup, but didn't lift it. "So why'd you really quit being a marshal?"

She watched as Medina moved back too, getting comfortable. Scott could see her thinking about it. Actually see her. Three different Chloes now. The girl she'd known at school, the mysterious one. Then the adult she'd expected. The version she'd kept track of in the media. That news story, after Medina stopped the bank heist, standing on camera with an ice cream, looking cool behind the sunglasses with the shield on her hip. I like catching the bad guys. And now this other version. The one hanging out, talking. Who was this version?

"I got shot," Medina said, touching her side. "On the job."

"God, did it..." Scott paused. Laughed at herself "I was about to ask if it hurt. Getting shot. Like pain is optional in that scenario."

Medina smiled. Nodded along. "That's the first thing everyone asks."

"People are dumb."

"It makes sense. What else are you going to say? There's not really a social acceptable response to I got shot. Not something we're trained to think or say."

"Back up, tell me again."

Medina half smiled, one side of her mouth turning up. The skin between her eyebrows crinkled. But she went along with it, saying again, "I got shot."

"Hey, congratulations on not being dead."

That got a full laugh. The real thing, starting down in the belly somewhere, erupting upwards. "Thanks."

"How'd it happen?"

"Tracking down Big Wheel. We tried to get to him through a dirty lawyer, Clarence Durville, guy everyone called the Milk Man. I'd traced him to a warehouse where he kept a load of cars. I went in with Treat Tyler."

Scott's head was numb for a few second.

Treat Tyler, the guy who'd been security at the mob party, showing off to try and get her into bed. Letting slip the truth about Redmond Peters. Treat Tyler, the marshal who turned up to escort her to the safehouse after the deal she cut with the DA. Treat Tyler, the guy who'd been looking for a chance to just kill Scott, and Scott, for a few moments, seeing him and accepting it, thinking she'd taken the shot at finding a way out and failed. Just go along quiet, let him pull off into whatever side road he wants, it'll be quick. The hating herself for even thinking that. She wouldn't suit being buried in the desert.

"He shot you."

Medina blinked a couple times, looking straight at her. "Yeah. In the dark, crept up on me while I was doing the same to the Milk Man. Then got to play the hero, go after the Milk Man, killed him in a shoot out."

"Did you already know?"

"I don't know. I think so. One of those things, you know it but you don't." Medina was lost in thought for a moment. Scott waited it out, knowing there was more coming. "The way you explain it," Medina said when she was ready. "Losing yourself. That's how I always felt. I was good at my job, never had to think about it. All I'd ever wanted, wear that shield, represent the law, bring people in."

"You get the law thing from your mom?"

She shook her head. "You grow up with a lawyer for a parent, in Phoenix, that's enough to put you off the law for life. She could tell me which innocent people were going down, which guilty people were walking away. Point out the cops who were on the take." Medina paused, like she was listening to the words that had just come out of her own mouth. "You know...maybe I do, now. Different perspective. I think I'd be a good lawyer. Have a conscience about it. Help people, talk their way out of tough spots"

Scott thought about saying *you could put yourself through law school with your cut of the money...*

Instead she said, "I thought about you a lot. Over the years. Saw you in the news."

"I had a slight cheat there. My sister-in-law, Melissa. She works in TV news. Made me look good."

"She did a good job. I used to think, maybe if Chloe met me now, maybe if we met for the first time as adults, not as who we were back then, would we be friends?"

Medina nodded while swallowing a slice of pie then said, "I spoke to Lisa."

A darkness opened up in Scott's gut. Regret. The past, the things she couldn't keep locked away. "I messed her about. A lot. I've always felt crap about that. The math I did, coming up with my number? Some was for me. But some was for Lisa. I don't know how much I owe her, or if she cares, but I liked the idea of putting a number on it, trying to make some of it right."

Medina gave him a look now, the one Scott imagined behind the sunglasses in those photos, playing the cool marshal. "So all told, in the end, your big plan was to give some money to a woman who hates your guts, then retire on whatever you have left in wherever you could find that was safe from Red Peters."

"Now you're starting to see the genius of my plan."

"The problem with your big idea," Medina said, "the problem with your whole 'what's your number' speech, is that life goes on. Unless you die. You have a number right now. So do I. But you go all in to clear that, make a big dumb decision, rob someone, but then what? What's the rest of your life look like? There will be another number. You never stop having a number." She pushed her plate to the edge of the table. "When I told you I'd maybe like to be a lawyer now, I was expecting you to tell me that I could pay my way through law school if I took your bribe."

"I thought about it."

"This whole time we've been sitting here, part of you has been thinking of running away, right?"

"Why did getting shot make you quit?"

"I just didn't feel like wearing a badge anymore."

"I still keep thinking, if I stay, if I do what you want, what the DA wants, I never get to be myself again. I'm giving that up. Go serve that coffee in North Dakota, whatever. Why should we go tell the truth? It's not exactly hard currency anymore, is it?"

Scott knew the moment had passed. If she was ever going to get a second chance at making a move on Chloe Medina, it had just been and gone. Now they were back to being who they were.

For the first time, she allowed her thoughts to expand out from two hundred grand to two million, the rest of the money Leyton had stashed away somewhere.

"Do you think," Scott said. "Let's say I'd gotten the whole two million. Enough money to start a whole new life anywhere on earth. Maybe we met somewhere, as adults, for the first time. No strings. No obligations. Just two people in a bar."

Medina leaned forward. "I didn't tell my boss about the money because I'm trying to keep Eddie out of it. As long as I can. It doesn't need to involve him."

Scott nodded.

Medina continued. "You tried to be someone you're not. And you're paying for it, which sucks. I know. But going and doing what we want, talking to the DA, that's you getting to be yourself. If you run, now?" Medina leaned back again, put her hands up in surrender. "I can't stop you. Or won't, anyway. You can run. Right now. I'll say you surprised me. But then you'll always be running, and you'll never be yourself. You can never be Emily Scott again.

But you stay with me, go do the right thing? You'll always be Emily Scott. Even when we change your name, even when you're pouring that coffee. You'll always be Emily who did the right thing. The stand up girl."

Medina smiled, letting Scott know the joke was at least half intended.

••

Walking back to the motel, the heat of the evening given way to the cool of the night, Medina was feeling herself again. Not dwelling, not doubting. Just *being*.

They were handcuffed together. Scott's right wrist to Medina's left, with the bag of money over Medina's right shoulder and her gun hand free. Medina trusted Scott not to try anything, they seemed to have a bond, an understanding, but she wasn't an amateur. Trust would get you killed.

After a few seconds, Scott said, "What you said back at the diner, I could've walked out, you wouldn't stop me. Did you mean it?"

Medina hadn't been sure of that herself, even as she'd said it. "I don't know."

"I've not got the money you were sent after, so you won't be getting paid for that."

"True."

"Do you really care about the other thing? Red Peters, Big Wheel, getting me to the DA."

"I do."

"Because you got shot?"

Medina touched her side, on reflex. Every time she'd thought of that moment, for the past four years, she'd felt the impact again. But now she noticed it had faded. It didn't seem to hurt. Reed Palmer's second rule, behind getting enough sleep, was never take the job personally. It gets in the way, makes you make dumb choices.

"I would have cared about it before, too." Medina said. "I think things matter if we decide they matter."

"How many people have you shot?"

She was asking two different questions here, Medina knew. "How many have I shot, or how many have I killed?"

"Killed."

"Three."

Medina waiting for the next question.

"How did it feel? In the movies, that's always the thing, they say it changes you."

"Didn't change anything," Medina said, hearing Palmer's voice again. "It was just the job. Only changes you if it's personal."

"That guy, Tyler, it seems personal with him?"

Medina nodded, said, "Yes."

Medina's hand twitched next to her gun at the mention of Tyler. She knew Scott saw it.

Scott nodded at the weapon, "You're expecting to use that."

"I'm expecting Tyler to want me to."

"Like two cowboys."

"Something like that, yeah."

"Everybody wants to be Doc Holliday, nobody wants to die of tuberculosis."

Medina laughed. "You know what his last words were? 'This is funny.' He was in bed, nothing on his feet, and he'd always figured he'd die with his boots on."

"I don't suppose it mattered, in the end." Scott said.

Medina thought back, her first day in the Phoenix office. The guy in the perfect suit, better dressed than everyone else, pacing around the room like a big cat, wanting to talk test scores, case history.

"He's always been worried I'm better than him. Offended by it."

"Guess it didn't help all those times you got in the press. Or did he get the same, and I just didn't notice it?"

Medina slipped her sunglasses on. Feeling ready to go. "The cameras always liked me more."

Another long pause. "Your speech was good. Me doing the right thing, always being able to remember that, always being me. But...what difference does it make, in the grand scheme? Everyone's always known Sheriff Jed is corrupt, and you guys have always known Big Wheel was out there. Me testifying won't make a difference."

Medina stayed quiet. She didn't want to lie.

Their cuffed hands, moving in step together, brushed. Once, twice. Medina stop walking, and Scott came to a halt to match. Medina lifted her cuffed wrist, pulled her key from the pocket on her other side, and unlocked the cuffs.

They both stood there, silent, for something just short of eternity.

"If I run, right now, you're not going to shoot me?"

"No."

"But you're not letting me have the bag."

"No."

"And you want me to testify?" Scott said.

Medina breathed in, let it out, slow. "Yes."

Scott looked down at the ground, hiding whatever emotions were clear on her face. When she looked up again, she was smiling that cool girl smile.

Scott said, "You lied, you know."

"What about?"

"You wanted me to kiss you, back in the day."

"Yeah. I did."

"Have you thought about it, since then?"

"Once or twice."

Scott said, "Felt like there was a moment back there to try again, and maybe I missed it?"

Medina smiled. "Guess we'll never know."

THIRTY-ONE

There was no power in the trailer. Drey didn't know if it was because MAB had fallen behind on payments, or because there was something else she should do.

Like, was she supposed to go plug something in? Turn a switch? No idea. They were sitting at the front, on the cheap cushions either side of the thin plastic table. This was where Drey had slept, the time she'd come down here. The table folding down to meet the benches on either side, lying across them on the cushions, listening to her mom and MAB making all the noises in the bedroom at the other end.

The gas was on. They turned it on to get a little light, but it was still so warm outside, even at this time of night, and with no AC they couldn't keep the flame on for long.

Coyote had already mentioned a couple times they should go back to the car, which had AC and lights. She was coming round to agreeing with him, but didn't want to say. In here, she felt in control of the situation. This wasn't her home, but they were here because she'd said so. If they went back to the Toyota it would feel like handing control back to Coyote.

In here, she could think. In here, they could talk. The darkness was helping. Sitting in their own sweat, talking in low whispers, it was like the real world didn't know where to find them, and they could hide away, regroup.

Across the table, Coyote's face was lit up by the red glow from his joint. The flame would get bigger when he dragged on it, fade a little when it was resting. The bags were in the middle of the trailer, by the toilet door, lost in shadows. Drey wanted to keep walking over to touch them, make sure they were still there. It was irrational, she knew. Unless either she or Coyote made a move, the money was fine.

"He looked really shocked," Coyote said.

Drey knew who he was talking about. He'd said the same thing that morning, a lifetime ago. She waited him out.

"I wonder what I looked like."

"When you did it?"

"Yeah." The red glow bobbed. "Like, he looked shocked. *Is this really happening?* Then he looked right at me. My eyes. We were looking at each other, and I saw this other thing, like him accepting it, just accepting he was on the way out."

"He was still standing up?"

"No, this was after. See, I shot him, and he fell back, against all the stuff he had behind him, you know? The Jim Beam and shit. Condoms, I guess. He hit all of that stuff, and some of it fell, and for a few seconds he put his arms out, like he wanted to catch the stuff that was falling. Then I saw it, his brain telling him he'd been shot, and he looks all surprised." He paused, the red glow grew in strength. Drey could hear him breathing, she could hear emotion in his voice now. "That's when he looked at me. At first it was like he was saying, *you shot me?* He slid down, like went down into a crouch but leaning back, and he was staring at me the whole time. Then he just...he just accepted it."

"You saw him die?"

"I think so. It looked exactly like the movies, and nothing like the movies. That make sense?"

Drey said yes, to keep him talking.

"I don't know how to say it. One minute he was there, looking at me. The next, he was still there, but he wasn't there. And I did it. It was because of me."

His voice was shaky now. Drey heard a sniff.

She said, "Why'd you do it?"

"I don't know. You ever do that thing where you stand on a bridge and think, what if I jumped? Or you pick up a knife in the kitchen and think, what would happen if I stabbed someone?"

"I think everyone does that. I do it on stairs. I think, what would happen now If I just let myself fall? Or by the side of road, a car or a truck coming, I think, I could just step out."

"But you never do."

"No."

"I was just thinking, I wonder what it would be like? Like that, like the stairs, or the car. I was thinking it. How would it feel to shoot someone? Then, next thing, I've shot someone. I don't even remember deciding to do it. It was a second, two seconds, I was thinking about it, I'd done it." Another deep breath, this one not accompanied with herbal remedy. "That's all I'm going to be now, isn't it? There's no way back. I can't undo it. I'm just going to be a kid who shot someone."

Drey wanted to feel for him. Right there, in that moment, she wanted to comfort him, tell her best friend that they'd find a way. But all that was running through her mind was, *yes, and I'll always be the brown kid who helped you. I did nothing wrong* here. Okay, I pointed a gun at that bounty hunter with the hot eyes. Okay, I helped steal a car. But did I? I sat in it. Coyote can pass. Not even pass. Face it. He's white. If he goes somewhere new, where nobody knows him, he can do whatever wants. But Drey? There wasn't anywhere she could go that people wouldn't know what she was, just from looking.

I just want to go home.

I really, really, want to go home.

I want to see my mom.

That was it. That was all she really needed. Talk to her. See her. Fix things. She knew it wasn't her mom's fault they were both always angry. There was no money. Wake up worrying about debt for long enough, you just start shouting. Just a bedroom door, that would ease things. Maybe a new toilet. More food.

Money.

Just money.

And then *the* money. How was she not thinking about the cash? It was sitting right there. Could they take it back? If she could talk Coyote into turning back home, putting the car and the money back where they found it. What's the worst trouble they'd be in then? Just pretend most of today hadn't happened. Well, Coyote would still be in trouble, but maybe Drey could get out...

She stared at the shadows covering the bags.

"We should count it."

Coyote sniffed a couple times. He stubbed out the red light. "Yeah." He paused. "How though? It's dark."

"We'll figure it out."

..

They began closing in fast once the blue dot stopped moving. Somewhere in Tucson, the map saying Balboa Heights. Rose was behind the wheel now. They'd swapped a few hours back, after a couple state troopers seemed to take a long look at them. Leyton had felt their eyes on him, not liking the feeling that one mistake could cost him. He'd said, before we start dealing with city cops, we should have the white girl driving.

Down through Tucson, past expensive-looking subdivisions, then steak houses, chain restaurants, gas stations, a couple banks. Leyton looked at one of the addresses, on the sign next to an open air shopping mall, it was 6000 North Oracle Road. The numbers always impressed him. Growing up on the reservation, he was amazed every time he saw how big the numbers could get on long roads into a city. That many people living in one place. They passed a new development, houses and a two-storey apartment building, red brick, black metal. It looked good. That was his dream. With his share of the money. Him and Rose splitting it fifty/fifty, netting him around eight hundred grand. That wouldn't buy much of a life these days, but he could buy something nice, in one of these big developments, somewhere far away, where his uncle wouldn't find him. There was a huge mall on the left, with a parking lot that seemed to go on for miles. Then, beyond that, everything started to look older, cheaper, more run down. On the right was a graveyard that went on for longer than the mall parking lot. The businesses were down now from chain restaurants to car washes and beauty salons. The blue dot was nearby. The highway forked right, but North Oracle Road continued on straight, they stayed on. A Mexican diner came up on the left, Leyton felt his stomach growl, remembered how long ago the burgers had been.

Rose, keeping one eye on the tracker app, turned left, then right. They drove by a small trailer park, the other side of a wire fence. It looked more like someone had converted their yard, or a parking lot, the trailers pressed in tight together. They drove on, until Rose realized they'd missed a turning or something, gone right past the Toyota. She turned in the seat to look behind them, seeing no traffic, and hit reverse, taking them straight back until they were level with the blue dot.

"There it is," Leyton said, spotting it through Rose's side window.

The Toyota was parked up in a small side street, more like a dirt lane. Rose killed the engine where they were, not worrying about another car coming along, and they both got out, walked over to the Toyota. It was locked.

"Car thieves already doing a better job than Bosco," Leyton said.

He pulled out his spare set of keys and opened it up. The bags were gone.

"Shit."

"Shit is all you've got right now?" Rose seemed angry for the first time, the emotion breaking out through the zen-like calm she'd held since this morning. "You lost our money, and all you can say is shit."

"I didn't lose it."

"Then who did? Who left it in his car, then loaned his car to an idiot kid who doesn't understand how locks work?"

"What was I supposed to do? Huh? What? You didn't include any of what happened in your *master plan*. There being a bounty hunter in the Safari, Eddie getting the idea to hire her, me needing to keep Bosco up to go fetch this bitch, where the hell were you when all this was going on? You didn't think, maybe, you should check in with me before I went to Phoenix, see where the money was, offer to move it?"

"I trusted you."

"And I didn't do..." He stopped. Their voices were getting louder. This wasn't helping. "How come you're angry now? You've been the calm one all day."

"Now it feels real," she said, her shoulders dropping, voice cracking. "Now it feels like we've lost it."

Leyton was the opposite. Nothing about this had felt real at any point, and now it just kept getting crazier. The whole thing had felt surreal from the moment she raised it. Laying in bed, after another great session, and she goes up on one elbow to say, "hey, remember that money you told me about?"

He'd paused, asking the question but knowing the answer. "What money?"

"Your uncle's safe. Or the other one, next to it."

"Yeah."

"Whose is it? The money?"

"I don't know, really."

"You don't know what it's for?"

"Whatever deals they got going on." Leyton shrugged, not wanting to stay on this subject. He didn't like where his mind went whenever he thought about it, but he would bet Rose's mind was there now.

"So it doesn't exist, really," Rose said. "If it existed, they'd be transferring it digitally, wouldn't they?"

"I guess."

"Money that exists, you never see. It's all numbers in a computer." Rose's fingers started to trace their way down Leyton's body, beneath the covers. "Money that you see, like the stuff in Eddie's safe, that doesn't exist."

"...Yeah."

Her voice dropped down low around the same time she took him in her hand. "So, if it doesn't exist, and we don't know who owns it, why can't we have it?"

Nothing had felt real since that moment. Leyton playing out a role, a cool movie guy, part of a scam. And now it only felt like they'd gone up a gear, into a different kind of story.

He looked around, wanting something to grab onto, something else to think about. "They're here somewhere," he said. "We just gotta find them."

"How?" Rose threw her arms out either side, exasperation in her voice. "How we going to do that? Do you know who they are? Do you know where they live? We just going to knock on every door, say, excuse me, did you steal my Toyota, and can we have our money back please? How many nos do you think we'll get through before we get to the *no* from the person who means *yes*?" She stood there, shaking her head, biting her lip, before adding. "They could be watching us right now, we wouldn't even know."

Leyton held up his keys. "We can wait in the car. They'll come back for it, and when they do, we got them."

Rose looked back to the road, chewing her lip again, before nodding. "I'll move the truck down the block. If they haven't seen us yet, don't want to draw attention."

••

Tyler, flashing his badge at the old man on the check-in desk, had shown him a picture of Emily Scott and said, "which room is she in?"

The guy shrugged, paying even less notice to Tyler's plastic gloves than he had the marshal star. "I don't know."

"You didn't see her?"

The guy pointed to a large green sign in the window, taking up the bottom half. Self-service check-in details. A QR code, website and instructions. "People use that."

"So why are you here?"

Another shrug. "Got to be somewhere."

"A Pontiac pulls up in front of you, two women get out, you're saying you paid no attention at all to which room they walked to?"

"They're not here."

"I'm telling you," Tyler pointed to the Pontiac, "they are."

The guy got huffy. Looked up at Tyler like this was the most pointless thing he'd been asked to do all day. Tyler thinking about how, if he wasn't trying to control his impulse control problem and had already resolved to only kill two more people, he could happily shoot the fuck out of this idiot.

"No, I mean they're not here." He said. "They walked off a while ago," pointing out onto the street, "went that way."

"So how about you tell me which room they're going to be coming back to, and give me a key, so I can go do my fucking job?"

The guy huffed, handing over an electronic key card and saying, "six."

Tyler took the card without saying thanks and headed out, across the forecourt, and let himself into room 6. He looked around. No sign of the money. He tossed the room, lightly at first, then more seriously. Ripping covers back, moving furniture. No dice. Either the money was in the car, or Medina was carrying it with her.

Stepping back out into the night air he looked inside the car, the front seats, the back. Nothing. It wouldn't be difficult to pop the trunk, but he'd rather not do anything yet that might tip Medina off when she came back. There would be time to search the car for real afterwards.

He settled into the plastic seat by the mirror in room 6, with the door shut and the lights off. He started running scenarios in his mind. What he wanted, the full-on old-school draw. Facing each other. He wanted to see Medina's eyes when she went down, the moment she knew he was better.

But could he make that happen? Emily Scott would be there, and that was a problem. If she shot Emily first to cut it down to just him and Medina, Medina would have time to draw and shoot. But if he challenged Medina, put the gun on both of them while he said what he wanted, play on the ego she pretended not to have...

Maybe that could work.

..

Leyton eased into the seat. He needed to move it back, whoever had been driving, they were a lot shorter than him. He wiggled around a little, getting comfortable. He said hello to the car, called it baby. Then he remembered the drugs he'd left in the glove box and leaned across to check. Gone. Something else he'd need to take out on whoever came back to pick up the Toyota.

He watched in the rearview as Rose climbed into the truck, started the engine, and headed south, out of sight. They'd agreed she'd take it down the block and round, to the other side of the trailer park. Close enough they could get to it in a hurry if needed. He leaned across to check the box again, thinking, there's a bunch of papers in there, maybe he'd missed a bag. No luck.

As he came back up, he saw the blue strobing lights. A cop car pulling up behind. Or, no, as he looked in the mirror, Sheriff's Department. Why would they come all the way down here just to... That was when he took the extra look, saw the logo, saw the patch on the shirt of the deputy approaching, gun drawn. McKinley County. They were way out of bounds here.

These were Sheriff Jed's men. Big Wheel's men. Leyton knew they'd done some of the pickups from the Safari, not caring who saw them.

"Hands up." The deputy, short and strong, shaved head, pointed the gun at Leyton in the open doorway. "Now."

This was Big Wheel, for sure. But how had they tracked...

He looked at the steering wheel, the dashboard. The Toyota. They tracked the Toyota. Uncle Eddie gave him up. Well, what else did he expect? He'd stolen two million dollars.

Rose's voice popped in his head.

One million, eight hundred thousand. It's important to be accurate.

Rose. Could he try saying to the deputy, it wasn't me, it was Rose?

If he didn't put his hands up, they'd shoot him, nobody would care. He didn't have his gun. Rose, she still had it. If he played nice, played along, maybe another chance would come. But he was walking away from two million dollars.

Leyton played for more thinking time, put on a confused expression. "What?"

"You heard me. Hands up."

Big Wheel thinks we have the money, he thought. He'll have me tortured to get it. And I don't have it. They won't believe me. I wouldn't believe me. They'll cause a lot of pain on the way to not believing me. Was it worth playing for time if staying alive meant what would happen once the deputies got him back to their home turf?

He lunged for the glovebox, as if going for a gun. He heard the shot. Didn't hear anything after that.

..

Rose drove down the block, turned left, then left again. She passed the car repair shop, a square concrete building, like a large brick dropped at the side of the road and painted. That would be the thing they could see the back of from the Toyota. She slowed down and pulled to the kerb. Next to the repair shop were two squat adobe houses, one painted green, the other left to be a faded brown. There was a large gap between them. Rose inched the truck forward and saw the gap was a dirt road, leading back to the same kind of wire fence they'd seen over the other side, this time with a large, and open, gate. The real entrance to the trailer park.

She turned onto the dirt track and drove through the gateway, seeing a small patch of concrete full of cars and trucks. She pulled in behind a VW that was up on bricks with no wheels, knowing she wasn't blocking anyone in, and killed the ignition.

From here, maybe they would stand a better chance of finding...

She saw the lights. Blue and flashing. Already knowing what it meant. She turned off the engine, killing the lights, and grabbed the gun from the seat beside her. She opened the car door and started to ease down to the ground, hoping not to step on anything, make a noise. Even from here, she could hear the muffled sound of talking, one of the voices coming in that commanding tone, the one that told you to get out of a car, or open the door, or to stop flashing your tits.

Then she heard the gunshots. Two of them. And the blue lights stopped flashing.

Rose froze, half out of the truck. She could feel her heart beating. Feel the pulse in her wrists and the blood in her neck. Mostly, she felt sick. She pulled herself back into the truck, holding her breath, and pulled the door shut, leaving it slightly ajar rather than risking any noise as it closed. She lay down across the seat, making herself as small as she could, and closed her eyes, finding a very fast, and very desperate, form of religion.

••

Medina and Scott hadn't said much since the cuffs came off. There didn't seem to be much to say. Both happy in their own thoughts for a time. They reached the motel and rounded the corner into the forecourt.

Medina's heart skipped for a second when she saw the Shelby missing, before cursing herself. She relied on that car so much, being without it was like losing a limb.

But now, with her emotions heightened by that mini drama, her gut was telling her something else. Medina, six feet from the door now, not passing by the window yet, taking Scott's hand. Scott hesitating, turning to look at her face, seeing the hand as a warning gesture rather than affection. Scott starting to speak, but Medina giving her a *shush* gesture.

Just feeling it. Something wrong.

The same hesitation she'd felt in the car warehouse, the one that made her pause a step, made the bullets hit her a little further over, missing vitals.

She turned to look across at the reception building, the lights from inside spilling out into the darkness around it. The old guy in the window, making eye contact with her, shaking his head slowly. She looked at the Pontiac, parked ten feet away, but framed square in sight of the window from her room. A great idea usually, but now something that felt dangerous.

She took out her cell, dialled Treat Tyler.

Did she see the faint glow of a screen lighting up in the room's window, or was it just her imagination messing with her?

"Hi Chloe." She could hear the mean smile in his voice.

"Treat."

"You still catching bad guys?"

"You still a bad guy?"

A quiet laugh. "Know how long we've been playing that game?"

"Since the day we met."

"You coming in the office with your coolest walk."

That was not the way Medina remembered it. Walking into the office five minutes late on her first day, feeling all eyes on her. Feeling Treat Tyler's eyes especially, that look, telling her they had started the countdown timer to him making a pass at her. "Just my normal walk, Treat."

Treat still talking about the past, rewriting it to make himself the hero. "You transferred in at Reed's request. Everybody knowing it means you're his star pupil. Didn't matter how good the rest of us were."

"Just good at my job, that's all."

"Were you, though? Which one of us put the Milk Man down?"

"The job wasn't to put him down, the job was to bring him in."

"But then he shot you."

"Had to sneak up on me to do it."

Medina stared at the door. Standing in front of it now, a few feet back. She could feel his eyes on the other side, staring back, trying to see through the wood. Was he standing up or sitting down? Waiting for her, either way.

"The way he picked those shots," Tyler said. "I'm not so sure. Think he had you beat."

"That's probably the way he tells it to himself after the fact. Wants to think he aimed it the way it came out, good enough to choose where I got hit."

"You think?"

"I moved at the last second, is the thing. I saw him, or part of him, reflected by the Shelby. I was moving by the time he pulled the trigger, so no way he was aiming for those exact shots. He wanted to kill me, just wasn't good enough."

"You think?"

"You still want the competition, Treat? Use the shot timer on your phone, pick a wall, see which of us can draw and shoot fastest."

"Why use the app?" Treat paused. Maybe trying to fight back the edge to his voice. "We could just do it the old fashioned way."

"Tell me where you are," Medina said. "I'll come running."

"In through the front door, just like always."

Medina, still staring at the door, but her mind somewhere else now. On the walk back, with Scott saying *it seems personal with him.*

Like a couple cowboys.

Something like that.

I don't suppose it mattered, in the end.

••

Drey wasn't sure why she'd woken up. She thought her eyes opened a few seconds before the dog started barking, but in her sleepy state she couldn't be sure of that. If it hadn't been the dog, what was it? She also thought the room had been lit up, shining blue, like they were in a club or something. She was in complete darkness now, blinking, waiting to get used to the shadows again.

"Did you hear that?" Coyote, down on the floor.

They'd abandoned the idea of counting the money in the dark. After a conversation that took an hour, constantly going off topic then drifting back again, they'd agreed to wait until daylight. They'd also failed to figure out how to fold the table down into a bed. Coyote had taken his cushions and settled down in the dark, somewhere near the bags. Drey pulled her legs up close on the bench seat, closed her eyes, thinking it would be difficult to sleep, and was gone in seconds. Until now.

"What was it?"

The trailer rocked a little, she saw shadows move, a solid shape taking form as Coyote climbed to his feet. "Shooting."

Drey turned, pulling back the curtain. The dog was still barking. Lights were on in some of the other trailers, she could see people looking out, nobody getting out. The dog's owner was shouting at it to shut up. There were no sounds of its claws on the concrete, Drey guessing it was still indoors. She rose, walking over to the door, and eased it open. Coyote followed. They stepped down outside, and moved slowly between the trailers. The lights were going off, one by one.

In the walkway they'd used before, the path between the trailers, they could see the gate at the end, and the Toyota. Two men in deputy uniforms were lifting someone out of the front seat. Drey almost gasped, recognising Leyton, blood all down the side of his face, his eyes open, but not alive.

The deputies put Leyton's body in the back, then stood having a quiet conversation. One of them pulled out a cell, making a call. Drey was rooted to the spot, wanting to get closer, wanting to run far away, but unable to do either. Behind her, she could feel Coyote going through the same emotions.

"Yeah..." she heard the deputy on the phone say. "No, just the guy. There's nothing in the....no. Yeah."

He turned around, looking in their direction. Drey stepped back, bumping into Coyote, further back into the shadows. The deputies eyes passed right over them, not registering anything.

"Trailer park," he said into the phone. "But nobody want to know...yeah. No, we're cool. Want us to...Yeah, right. Okay."

He ended the call and turned to his partner, saying something Drey didn't catch, but she was sure he'd used the word daylight. His partner walked out of view, but she heard a car door shut. The deputy climbed into the driver's seat of the Toyota. Another engine started, followed by the sound of a car pulling away, then the Toyota backed out of view and Drey heard the two vehicles moving off into the distance.

Her mind was trying to figure everything out as they moved back to the trailer. Why would the law switch their lights off? Why would they move the body and drive away? Why would they even be talking about coming back in daylight? What was Leyton doing...it was Leyton's Toyota, he'd come for the money but now...

For the first time since all of this started, Drey felt like she knew something. Had a grip on what was happening.

Back inside the trailer she put the stove on for some light, and whispered to Coyote, aware ears would be on high alert in the park: "We can get away with this."

"With what?"

"The money. They just killed Leyton looking for it. It's his car." She felt confidence filling her words. She was right and, finally, she was in control. "They don't know who we are. They're coming back to search the park."

"So if we're not here when they come..."

She nodded. "Right."

Her eyes flicked to the bags. Coyote's did the same. Then she watched as his gaze moved, settling on the gun, still sitting on the table where she'd left it. He was closer. He didn't make a move, but their eyes met again, and she could read his thoughts, knew what had crossed his mind. And in that moment, finally, the new version of Drey thought, you don't owe this guy a fucking thing.

She turned her back on him, took the two small steps from the stove to the bags, and picked one up. Just one. She straightened up, facing the door, not wanting to turn and see whether her best friend had picked up the gun.

"I'm leaving," she said.

Drey waited a few second, giving him time to speak. When he didn't, she reached forwards, gripped the handle, turned it, and left.

··

Tyler still held the cell to his ear. The call was connected, but nobody had said anything for over a minute. He could feel the side of his face getting warm, the phone hot in his hand.

She was right outside, he could feel it. Feel her, getting ready to come on in, knowing what would happen next.

He'd been waiting a long time for this.

His gun on the table in front of him. Ready to go with whatever version she wanted. She came in with the gun in hand he'd pick it up, put her down. She came in with the gun still at her side they could play the game, prove what needed to be proved.

That voice though, back of his mind, what if she *is* faster than you?

No, not possible.

But Chloe wouldn't run. He knew her too well. She was itching to solve this question, too. Dying to know which of them was best.

The noise in his ear went dead, followed by two beeps. She'd disconnected the call. He braced himself. Looking at the outline of the door in the darkness. The Pontiac visible through the window, to the left of the door, The shadows out there not moving.

Come on.

Come on.

His right eye felt funny. Ready to pop. A fizzing feeling at the back of his brain.

Come on.

Then he knew it. She'd gone. He just knew it. Felt it, the same way he'd felt her standing in front of the door. He jumped up, grabbed the gun, was at the door in seconds, opening it, through it, outside. Nobody.

The car was still there, but Chloe Medina and Emily Scott were gone. He ran down to the end, to the road, and looked around. No sign of them. Which way had they gone?

Shit.

THIRTY-TWO

The Greyhound depot, Drey remembered, was down past the university. One time she'd come down with her mom to see MAB and they'd caught the coach all the way here, only to find he was off somewhere else. They'd walked up from the depot to the trailer park and then back down again, an hour each way.

Her mom passed the whole thing off by blaming herself, saying she'd got the dates mixed up, or the times, or some other mistake. All on her. Drey had known the truth, but didn't say it. How do you tell your mom she's dating an asshole?

Drey would like to tell her now. Like to tell her anything. Like to be talking to her.

She'd like to be doing basically anything else.

Well, almost anything, because she had a bag full of money, and would want that factored into the scenario.

Two or three times on the walk down she started to second guess herself, saying out loud, "you're lost. This isn't the way." But she stayed on the same route, heading straight down, block after block, waiting for things to get familiar.

And along the way, she was sure she was about to get caught. The cops from the trailer park, or someone else. Step by step, just waiting for the shout, or the sound of an engine, or anything. The streets were quiet. Nobody stepping foot outside in the heat. Drey wondering if some of it was the buildings. It felt hotter here than back home, did having so many people packed into a city make it warmer? Did all the extra electricity give off heat?

Finally reaching the depot, she found it closed. Not opening for another couple hours, when the first coach service would start. She could get a bus to Gallup, and from there it would be easy enough to get down to the Rez.

And then, what?

Just go back home, like none of this happened?

Who knew she'd been involved, really?

She had all this cash, but knew that didn't mean anything. Cash is cash. But real money is in banks. Real money moved around in computers. This stuff was crisp, like brand new, never used. Drey couldn't think of ever seeing money quite like this. Fresh in the world, not passed through years of pockets and wallets and cash registers.

This definitely wasn't something she could pay into a bank. They'd ask too many questions. Maybe if she buried it in the dirt, left it there to age a little, dug it back up in a couple years? Or what was that other thing, the way she'd read about criminal gangs doing it...*money laundering*.

Drey had no idea how that worked, but it was what people did to make money like this turn into money like everyone else had.

But she'd figure it out. Somehow, she just knew. The same way she'd known to pick up the bag and walk out. The old Drey would come up with reasons to put the bag down and walk away from it. Let it be someone else's problem. But this new Drey, she held on tight to the handles, knowing she'd figure this shit out. This was going to be her own, specific, problem.

The depot door was locked. Sometimes they'd be left open for people who were late or early for a ride. Drey looked in at the air conditioned space, swore under her breath, and went looking for a quiet spot of shade to wait. She was sitting under the overhanging roof of the next building when one of the McKinley County sheriffs drove by.

··

Rose eased up off the seat. Her skin made a smacking sound as it came away from the leather, slick with sweat. No air conditioning without turning the key, she'd just been lying there, baking. She hadn't slept. Hadn't moved. There were moments she hadn't been sure she was breathing. Just listening, boots walking across concrete, trailer doors being knocked on, opened, muted conversations, doors being closed again.

Now it was getting hotter. The sun not up yet, but getting ready to start the climb. Time to make a decision.

Somewhere way down in the questions she was asking herself was how the hell this had all happened. She didn't ask it too much, because the answer was obvious.

Really all that mattered was, what are you going to do about it?

Those guys, the deputies, they had to be after the money. And they didn't get it. No way they could find something that Rose and Leyton didn't have. They got the car and Leyton's...Leyton's...They got the car and Leyton. They would know the money was here somewhere. What time would they be back? She wiped sweat off her forehead, looked at the sky. The light was coming on fast. She guess they'd be back soon, a dawn raid, going door to door pretending to be official business.

Time to get moving, be far away when they came back.

But where to?

Well, there was always home. Real home. But Shitsville, North Carolina was less appealing to her now than when she first ran away. And she was pretty sure the people there had good memories. Long enough to remember the girl who stole from her boss and ran. Maybe she could just head back to the reservation? People liked her there. And she had Eddie's truck. She could just pull out in front of the Safari like nothing had happened. Say, what? I went for a drive out into the desert, have I missed something? Deny any knowledge of whatever else had gone down.

Leyton did what?
With your money?
Why would he...

She could see it working. Eddie was easy to fool. He wanted to be fooled, that was the start. You can only trick someone who is willing to be tricked. She could picture him, angry at first, then listening to her as she played dumb. *What? Me? You thought I could do something like that?* Then push it back on him, making him need to apologise. How could you? I'm hurt, Eddiebear. Is this really what you think of me?

It would work. For sure. Probably get a pay rise out of him. With Leyton gone, he was going to need someone to help him run the place. Okay, it wasn't her cut of one million, eight hundred thousand. As much of that as she was planning to get from Leyton. Which, face it, was going to be all of it, one way or another. But she'd be back working at the Safari, with more influence than before, and something else would come along eventually.

And if it didn't work, well, she had the gun.

Or did she? Where was it? She looked down on the floor. Nothing. It had to be in here somewhere, she remembered. Leyton hadn't taken it. Rose had a made a point of keeping control of the weapon, planning for the time she'd need it. But now....where the hell?

She became aware of the lump beneath her on the seat. She was sat on the gun. She turned, easing herself up, to slip her hand beneath her hand and grab it, barrel-first. She pulled it free and swapped round to grip the handle. It was warm, incubated by her on the seat. She smiled at the thought of that, like a hen keeping eggs safe.

••

Drey stayed low, pressed down against the wall, squatting on her haunches. There were two guys sitting in the front of the deputy car. They were parked in the corner of the Greyhound lot, watching the door. One of them got out and walked over, trying the door, rapping on the glass, waiting long enough to be sure nobody was answering before heading back to the car.

The two of them talking now, laughing, but keeping their eyes on the depot.

Drey didn't move. This spot she'd picked, under a square bit of roof sticking out over the front of a car showroom, had her hidden in shadow. But the horizon was starting to change color now, going grey from black, touches of red. The light would be moving soon and the shadows would change. And in the meantime, the deputies' car was facing her, she was in their peripheral vision even if they didn't know it yet, and any move might give her away.

What were they doing down here?

Had they tracked her? Had something given her away?

No, she figured this was just a good educated guess. Either they'd found Coyote and he'd given her up, or they'd found nothing and, knowing they'd already found the car, figured the coach station was the most likely place she'd head.

A *plan* was the thing.

Any time now, if one could announce itself, that would be great. A second car approached. Coming in from the same direction Drey had walked, pulling onto the parking lot. Dark, unmarked, but some shade of law. They came to a stop a few

spaces over from the deputies, and two men got out wearing
ICE jackets. The deputies got out to talk to them, shaking
hands, laughing about something. They were all standing side-
on to Drey now, facing each other. One of the ICE guys turned
her way in passing, smiling. His eyes passed across where Drey
was crouching. He didn't register, or didn't seem to, anyway.
But his smile faded. Was it just because of whatever had just
been said, or had some part of his brain registered the young girl
with the bag of money? Was it now just a matter of how many
seconds it took for his mind to filter that down?

A third car came along now. A battered old VW Bug. It
drove past the depot at a steady speed, the other side of the
block, kept on going. All four men turned to look, keeping their
eyes on the car until it was out of sight. Drey took the chance,
lifted the bag and walked to her left, in the opposite direction to
where the men were looking. She didn't run, not wanting to
make enough of a jerky move that they would notice her. Slow
and steady, trying to be natural, trying to be part of the
landscape. At the end of the building she turned left again,
around the corner. Before she stepped out of view, she stole one
glance back over her shoulder. Three of the men were touching
their ears, listening to something. The fourth, the one who had
maybe seen her before, made eye contact with her now.

Shit.

Drey sucked in a breath, looked down the street, and ran.

End of the block, movement to her left, a car down the
street coming this way. The VW Bug. The car accelerated, as
much as something in that condition could, and pulled up
beside her as a rattling, humming, mess of metal.

Officer Bobelu leaned across and opened the passenger
door, "You want to get in, or keep running?"

••

Rose, sitting up in the seat now, caught movement up ahead,
beneath the nearest trailer. She cursed. She'd stayed down out of
sight until all the noises stopped, until whoever was searching the
area seemed to have stopped. But now, someone was right in front
of her, climbing up from beneath the trailer, still just a dark shape
in the morning shadows. Rose ducked down, hoping whoever it
was hadn't seen her yet. She stayed low, listening as someone
walked nearby, and it sounded like they were trying car doors.

The steps came this way. She lifted the gun, aiming it at the door seconds before it opened.

The dim light filled the truck. She looked up and blinked, recognizing the kid standing there. She hesitated, not pulling the trigger. It was the redhead off the reservation. The one everyone said was weird.

He jumped back as he saw her, startled, saying, "shit."

Rose saw him going for a gun he had tucked into the front of his jeans. She sat up, raised her own weapon, pointing it at him and shaking her head. She followed his other arm down, seeing it was holding a bag. One the two bags she'd given Leyton to take the money. Her money.

She said: "don't move."

He was still going for his gun, slowly. "I know you."

"Don't move."

"Seen you, you dance at the Safari."

"I look like I dance?"

His hand stopped moving. The kid looked like he was taking her serious now, reading her tone, and the gun facing him.

Rose said: "drop the bag."

"I drop it, gotta come out here to pick it up."

"Don't get smart."

"I'm just saying," he lifted the bag, "I could put it in the back behind you, or on the hood, then you don't gotta reach too far for it."

Rose leaned forward, pressing the gun closer. She could hear the tension in her own voice as she said, "Drop. The. Bag."

"There's people here, in the trailers, getting up for work, you want a scene?"

That struck a nerve. He was right. There were people all around here. It was just dumb luck that nobody had come out yet to get in any of the cars, there would be witnesses here any second.

Seeming to read her pause, he added: "The others, the people looking for this bag, I'm sure they'll be back in a minute, trying again. You want us both standing here when that happens?"

Rose turned to look at the trailers and realized her mistake a split second too late. The kid swung the bag up at her. She pulled the trigger without aiming.

Her hand jolted back and her wrist stung, feeling like the time she broke it in junior high, and she dropped the gun. The bag hit her full in the face, and she fell backwards onto the seat. Now, somewhere that was both a million miles away and right in her ears, above a ringing sound, she could hear a dog barking.

The bag pulled back out of her face, swinging down, still gripped by the kid. The momentum almost dragged him backwards, but now he was holding his own gun, aimed at her, point blank. His mouth moved. A few seconds later she heard the words.

"Get out."

She sighed. Nodded, got out of the truck. She wasn't sure whether he'd told her to put her hands up, or whether she was just doing it because that's what people did, but she put them up all the same. His mouth moved again. The voice came quicker this time.

"Go sit over there."

She walked slowly over to the place he'd pointed to, a rusty old oil drum, and sat down, gripping her wrist, thinking she'd legit injured it. The kid got into the van. She heard the engine turn over, there was no delay now. He said something else. She looked up, still feeling dazed.

He repeated himself. "Which way is Mexico?"

Uh, what? Rose had no idea. She pointed in the direction she thought to be south. He nodded, said thanks, and reversed the truck away out through the gate. Rose sat there, not moving, almost not thinking, like she was an audience member, as the kid pulled out onto the road, and headed south, out of sight, taking her money with him.

After a few more seconds she breathed out.

"Well, shit."

..

Officer Bobelu didn't say anything for a while. Both of them sitting in silence while she took a few turns around the local streets, checking her mirror. The ICE car cut across behind them at a junction, about half a mile back, but didn't slow down or stop.

Drey said, "Did they see us?"

Bobelu shook her head, "I don't know."

She turned the car down a narrow track running behind a restaurant, parking up behind an overflowing dumpster that hid them from sight.

"We'll wait them out," Bobelu said. "Trafffic'll pick up soon, then we're just another car."

Drey looked her over. She looked tired, especially in profile, showing lines around her eyes that Drey hadn't noticed before. The older woman was out of uniform, dressed in a battered old leather jacket and jeans.

Drey said: "How'd you find me?"

Bobelu tapped a radio on the dash, and this was the first time Drey concentrated on it, realized it was on, but turned down low. Bobelu picked it up and pressed a button, raising the volume.

Voices, talking. "Lost her."

"We don't even..."

Then a crackle. Somebody else on the line. "...another report of shots fired by the trailers."

"They're just talking on the radio like that?"

Bobelu tipped her head forward, like half a nod. "They don't need to be subtle."

They both fell silent again as they heard a car driving by, slow, as if looking down the alley. A few more seconds of silence. They hadn't been spotted.

"Been looking for you," Bobelu said.

"Yeah."

"Do I want to ask what's in the bag?"

Drey shrugged.

"Right." Bobelu laughed to herself. "Right."

"Am I under arrest?"

It was Bobelu's turn to stay silent.

They heard more cars now.

One. Two. Three. Different speeds. Morning traffic.

Bobelu said, "Where's Coyote?"

"I got away from him."

After another slow nod, Bobelu said: "That's good."

Drey tried again "You arresting me?"

Bobelu smiled. "You done something wrong?"

Drey didn't know how to answer. She opened her mouth, closed it again. Thinking, neither the old or new version of her had this part figured out.

Bobelu keyed the ignition but didn't move the car. "If you could be anywhere in the world right now, if nothing else had happened and you could just be wherever you felt safest, where would you be?"

Drey didn't hesitate. "At home."

Bobelu added, in a way Drey didn't understand straight away: "Took my uniform off before coming down here, didn't realize how heavy it was." Almost talking to herself. Then, turning to look at Drey. "Let's say I'm going to ask you if you know anything about the whereabouts of Aidan Coyote Coady, and you say you don't. Then I ask if you know anything about a shooting in Gallup, early yesterday, and you say you don't." She paused, holding eye contact with Drey. "You hearing me?"

"Yeah."

"Then I ask why you've run away from home, and you tell me you made a mistake, had a bad day, and just want to go home to your mom. Do you think that's all how the conversation would go?"

Drey nodded. "Yeah."

"Your mom does love you, you know. It just..." Bobelu sighed, looked in her mirror, put the car in gear before backing up and then driving forwards, out of the lane. "It just looks different when you have no money."

"Yeah."

"It looks like not being around much, because of the second or third job. Or letting things around the house stay broken because food is getting expensive. Sometimes it looks like not talking to you, because she knows you feel disappointed in her, and she's scared of that conversation, and doesn't want to tell you how shitty life can be."

"Yeah."

Bobelu gave Drey a very old-person smile. "You know, I think the world needs teachers more that it needs cops."

THIRTY-THREE

Medina, sitting on the hood of Chuck Thane's Honda Civic, sipped from her coffee. She was parked up outside Darrel Greer's place, enjoying the early morning sunshine. It felt different here, so close to the coast. Less like an oven. Scott was in the apartment, showering and saying goodbye to Greer. Hopefully apologizing for the latest time she'd upended someone's life.

Coming back to Greer's place had been the best move. Medina couldn't see a way Tyler knew about it yet. She was betting he'd tracked the Pontiac, not her. Leaving it at the motel and running a couple blocks down, they'd actually passed Tyler's Dodge, parked up beside a liquor store. Medina and Scott hid out a few buildings down, in the shadows, and watched until they saw Tyler running down to the car, looking around with more than a hint of desperation in his eyes, then tearing off at high speed in the direction of the 405.

"You did the right thing," Scott said.

"Yeah."

"I mean, for a minute there, I thought you were actually going to walk through the door."

"It would've been embarrassing to be killed by someone who makes as many bad decisions as him."

"You'd never live it down."

At Greer's, they'd taken it in turns to sleep.

Or to rest, at least. Scott didn't get much sleep. Medina went out like a light as soon as her head hit the pillow, her mind at ease for the first time in a long time.

Now, morning. Medina waited outside with a coffee enjoying the early sun while Scott said her goodbyes. There was a call Medina needed to make that she didn't want Scott to hear.

Reed Palmer picked up straight away, he'd been waiting for her.

"You on the move yet?"

"Not yet," she looked up at the apartment window. "Emi's picking up a few things."

"She's still *Emi,* huh?"

Medina smiled. "Emily Scott is picking up a few things."

"You've not got eyes on her?"

"She's in a friend's apartment, I've got the only exit covered."

Medina didn't pause to ask herself why she lied.

Scott could go out the back way. But she trusted Scott wasn't going to do that, and it had felt easier to lie to Palmer rather than start talking about trust. She didn't want to dwell on whatever it said about them.

"She's going to come?"

"Yeah," Medina said, deciding not to add, *because I asked her to.*

"If she decided not to, I don't think either of us could blame her."

She said *yeah* again, same distracted tone, before adding. "Been thinking about that. Are we doing the right thing here?"

Palmer didn't answer. That told her more than if he had.

She followed up with: "You get much sleep, Boss?"

"No. I was up most the night, making calls at first. Then I couldn't go to bed. Couldn't switch off, so I just sat up, thinking."

"Want to share them?"

Finally she could hear him smile. "Last time I told you what you already know, you said I was mansplaining."

"I walk Emi in through the front, old school, we get her to testify, she reports everything she knows on Red Peters and Sheriff Jed and, what? We're not cutting to the montage of the whole system coming down. Whole time we were working on the Big Wheel case, we all knew Jed was dirty, he was just wasn't dirty enough for anyone to care."

"With your friend, we have some proof. An eye witness. Without her, we just have what we have now. Rumors. Don't ask me to tell you it's all going to be okay, and that Scott's testimony will bring everybody down. But if she doesn't come, it can't happen."

"We need to at least guarantee she'll be safe."

"On it. Some of the calls I made last night. Pulled in a few markers from old offices. I've got deputies coming in from Boston and Miami, handpicked for the detail. You get Scott here, we'll walk her in together, stay with her, then get her out of state straight away and into WITSEC. The DA's onboard with that. You just need to get Scott to us. Or tell me where you are, we'll come to you."

"Tyler's looking for me."

"Yeah." A soft sound, not quite a sigh. "I figured. Talked to him last night."

"Can you pull him in?"

"On what? Right now, you've got a thing you haven't said, I've got a thing I haven't said, Emi has a thing she needs to say, and we don't have proof of anything. Once we're all sworn in and on the record, we'll take him down."

Medina smiled now, changing gears. "She's Emi to you, now, too?"

"Maybe I'm just rooting for the kid, is all. We all like an underdog story."

"Tyler's going to try and stop us. And we have no idea who else is on Big Wheel's payroll between here and the court."

"Listen, give me five minutes, I could get a trace on Tyler's cell, get some of my friends out to wherever he is, stop him."

"That just wastes time. If he's still here, then we'd be waiting six hours for your friends to get here, then we get back to you, suddenly it's night and we've wasted a day. Or he's waiting along the interstate, by the time your friends get to him I could've been halfway to you. He doesn't know what I'm driving. Nobody does."

Scott came down the steps, carrying her messenger bag plus some clothes wrapped in a bundle. Medina nodded, letting her know it was okay to come over. The sensitive part was done.

"We're ready," Medina said to Palmer, before pulling the phone away to check the time on the screen. "Six hours."

Scott put the bundle down on the hood. She unfolded it to show two parcels, shaped like house bricks, wrapped in Christmas paper. Medina knew what was inside, it was just a question of how much.

"Still an unanswered question," Scott said. "Looks like you have two jobs now. Get me to the court alive, and get the money back to Eddie Wray. But..." she smiled at Medina, showing the cool girl was back. "Leyton has most of it. This is chicken feed. And why would you risk your life to do the right thing, and then just go and hand money back to a criminal?"

After neither of the felt the need to answer that question, Scott tapped the first bundle and said: "Can you make sure Lisa Afobe gets this?"

"And the other one?"

Scott met her eyes, held them. "What other one?"

Another time, another place. If none of this was happening.

I don't suppose it mattered, in the end.

Medina slipped her sunglasses on. "Get in."

THIRTY-FOUR

Breakfast for Red was always something to do with fish. His wife, Gloria, took charge of it. Ten years ago the doctor had started giving him the bad news. Cholesterol. Blood sugar. Bad liver. All the usual crap, he knew. All the stuff they'd been saying for years, and they said it to every man his age no matter what. But then he'd made the mistake of letting Gloria come to one appointment and suddenly all he was allowed to do was eat fish, nuts and fruit. Green tea instead of coffee. Maybe a steak once a week if he was lucky. Maybe.

Heading out to the old family shop had once been just about business. A good personal space to carry out meetings, stay on site and keep up the nut farmer front. But now it had become about food, too. On the drive there he could grab a cheese burger. A bag of chips. Soda. Oh, man, he didn't realise how much he would miss soda until Gloria removed it from his life. And, why? Just because some quack says so. Fine, they could afford a different quack. It's not like he needed to worry about his teeth, he'd been wearing dentures since 2001. When one pair got old and stained, he swapped them out for a new set. Better than teeth. He'd come round to thinking everybody should have dentures, at all ages. Body parts you can just use up and replace. His main plan, live long enough to see the day when heart surgery is as simple as swapping out a toupee, then get a new heart every few years.

But for right here, right now, he was eating some warm fish thing, on something that looked like bread, but was cold and hard. He'd put some salt on when Gloria wasn't looking, and the small act of rebellion brightened his morning no end.

He was reading the news on his tablet. All the news, from all the sides. He liked to check in here, every morning, in this huge house, before heading out in his hybrid car, to the garage he owned south of Phoenix, changing to the beat-up old pickup, and driving out to the shop, to talk to the struggling families. The people, as he saw it, who didn't have his smarts to get out, or up. He could play a role for them, and they'd buy it, just like everyone else was going to buy everything, and he got to go home every night to fresh silk sheets and an air-conditioned swimming pool.

After the news, he turned to emails and phone messages. Changing in his mind now, from the life he'd built here with Gloria, to the things he'd done to build it. Seven emails from his lawyer, Andrew Case, all routed through a server in a country that didn't extradite people or information to the States. Plans and backup plans. If this, what then. If the comedian testifies, do the Feds have a case? If he dies on the way to court, how exposed are we? If he dies after testifying, does that change anything?

Red was careful. Always. Other people's egos could be massaged just as easily as bank statements and financial records. Even easier, in most cases. Idiot Jed was on the hook for most things, unless the old man had been clever enough to keep tapes of conversations. And even if he had, Case could throw up enough objections, writs and counter claims to keep most of the tapes off the table.

If it came to it, fine, let the Feds try and build a case. Jed goes down. Tyler goes down. Half the law officials in the state go down. The mayor of Phoenix was actually clean, but her staff were dirty enough that she'd go down. Red could just step back, behind his thousand-dollar-an-hour lawyer, and wait it all out.

Angel Creek would still continue. Diverting the Gila, run it up through the valley through land Red's grandchildren owned without knowing it, and cutting out the Indian Reservation. Connect up with the basin at Tempe Town Lake. Control the water supply in a desert state, write the rules. Things would just take a little longer. That long game. Plant the crop, nurture the crop, harvest the crop, repeat.

The only problem he really had was the money. That damned money. Literally. The people who'd been subsidizing the expansion of his union, the people who'd sent two million in clean, untraceable, cash, to pay for the last step of the plan.

Losing their money was the one thing he hadn't planned for. The one call he didn't want to make.

This, right here, was the worst time. Waiting to hear back.

Two of Jed's men were on their way to the shop with the Toyota and Leyton's body. They'd pulled the trigger too soon, wasted the chance to talk to him, find out where he'd put it. Now Red was waiting for the other team to finish sweeping the trailer park, doing whatever they needed to do, find that fucking money.

His cell rang. He almost jumped. The number was one of Jed's burner lines.

"Morning. Good news?"

"It's gone."

"How?"

"They've gone all through. Every door. Nothing."

"How did they do it?"

"We roped in a couple ICE guys we got, went door to door. If someone was home, we showed 'em a form one of the guys made up, saying it was an emergency check, illegals in the neighborhood. If nobody was home, we bust in, tossed the place."

"How's that going to look when they come home?"

"Who cares? What they going to do? Call the cops? They'll say what happened, if anyone else in the park talks they'll say it was sheriffs and ICE. The cops call the Primo County department, they'll say no, they had nobody out there. They maybe call ICE, but they know to keep quiet. You know what I was thinking? We need to get you some bounty hunters on staff. Recovery agents, you know? Once a fugitive has signed their bond paperwork, a bounty hunter owns their ass. Basically waived all constitutional rights. All you'd need to do, for anyone you want to go after, is make up the right paperwork, and the law is on your side."

Red sat there, thinking about one specific bounty hunter causing him all kinds of trouble, but said: "You only think of this now?"

Feeling the anger build. Knowing, really, this was on him. He could blame Eddie. He could blame Tyler. But who was the one to make the decisions on bringing those guys in? Ultimately, it was all down to Red. He'd left one hole in the operation, taken one part for granted.

He couldn't fire himself, though.

He said to Jed: "You got eyes on my boy with the star?"

"You mean Treat Tyler? Got a trooper on the lookout, sticks out a mile in the car, he won't be a problem."

He stopped short of giving the order.

Wait. *You mean Treat Tyler?* That was off. Why, now, was Jed feeling the need to get specific and clarify Red was talking about Tyler? A Deputy US Marshal?

Thinking back to his lawyer's emails now.

Has Jed started recording the call? They both already knew what the order would be. Kill Tyler. Kill Emily Scott. Kill Chloe Medina. Anyone with them. But if Jed pushed Red into giving that instruction clearly, with no wiggle room, on a taped call...

Suddenly everyone was covering their own ass.

Red hung up. He stared at the fish on the plate in front of him. The green tea. He held his breath as anger surged up, managing to keep calm enough to not throw his phone, tablet or laptop across the room. It was time to change the guard. It would be a shame to lose Jed right when he was making the move to Senator. Red would need to find someone else to push the agenda. But if he was going back a few steps, he may as well commit to it, build a new team.

He needed to call his lawyer.

And then, the one he really hated to think about, he needed to talk to his friends with the Russian accents and two-million-dollar hole in their finances.

THIRTY-FIVE

Tyler blinked once, twice, and found himself in a ditch at the side of I-10. His Dodge had rolled to a stop in front of the sign for Exit 19 for Quartzsite, missing the metal support strut by a couple of feet. He rubbed his eyes, drew in a deep breath.

He didn't want to admit it, but Reed Palmer was right.

Without sleep, you did dumb shit.

How long had he been out? Was it sliding off the road that woke him up, or the state trooper tapping on the window of the front passenger seat? Tyler too groggy to really think, why not the driver's side? He pressed the button to lower the window and waited, running his tongue over his teeth, willing his breath to freshen.

"You okay there?" The trooper was tall, young and lean, wearing his hat on an angle, enjoying having it. He looked back the way he'd come, towards the road. "You have an accident here?"

Tyler smiled. "I'm going for my wallet." Reached into his pocket, pulled out his ID and flashed the shield at the trooper. "Been working late, you know how it is. Tracking a felon. Got a lead in California, but you know, I just hit the wall back there." He grinned. "Poor choice of words. I just had one of those moments, you know where you realise how tired you are? And these roads, man. Just hours of roads, nowhere to stop. I figured I'd pull over before I did something stupid."

The trooper had visibly relaxed during the story. Tyler had this theory: that all law enforcement - cops, deputies, troopers, whatever - they all really wanted to be marshals. One mention of a felon, dressed up to sound like a cool story, and the trooper was on his side.

"I got some coffee in my car, if you want?"

"Oh hey, that would be great."

Tyler got out of the car, leaned against the side waiting while the trooper went back to his own car, coming back with a flask. Rather than handing it over where Tyler was standing, the trooper nodded, walked round to the Dodge's passenger door.

"Mind if I sit?"

"Be my guest."

Tyler eased back down into his seat, taking the offered drink.

"You're not wrong," the trooper said. "I tell you that. Out here? Just nothing. For hours. Gets to the point, you're almost excited if something goes wrong, break up the boredom. Or you know, you start thinking, maybe I'll pull over the next car I see, just to have someone to talk to."

"You ever done that?"

"Let's say no." The trooper gave a look that said the opposite.

Up close, Tyler could see he was older. Lines around his eyes and mouth.

"Sure," Tyler grinned. The coffee tasted like shit. He said: "This is good, thanks."

"So what's your perp done?"

Perp. This guy with a badge, still managing to sound like he watches too many cop shows. "Armed robbery, held up a Credit Union with a gun."

"Serious stuff." The trooper watched a couple cars go by, looking like he was poised to attack if they did anything wrong. "That's a marshal thing?"

"Also escaped from custody. Managed to get away from the Sheriff's Department, got away with the service revolver, too."

The trooper snorted. "I trained up a bunch of Jed's boys. You know sometimes they don't have the resources, get us to do it for them? I trained a bunch, don't hold out much hope."

"Yeah," Tyler nodded.

Still too tired. Still not thinking right. Not picking up on the Trooper's hidden message about Jed's boys until the Glock was already raised and pointing at him.

Tyler smiled. Thinking of the bench. "Red sent you."

"Don't know for no Red," the trooper said. "But I guess we both see the Big Wheel turning."

"You know, I gave him that name? Or he gave it himself, really. We were talking, I told him I was part of a joint agency task force to figure out who he was, and that we couldn't agree on a codename for him. He said, call me Big Wheel, like the song. I threw that name in at the next task force meeting and, there we go, it stuck."

"It's a good song."

"I hate it."

The trooper nodded a few times too many without speaking, then said: "Well. I guess we got to get this wrapped up. Don't you move, now." He swapped the gun into his left hand to allow for him to reach out and pull the door closed with his right. "This is a nice car, marshal. Real shame what we gotta do here."

"Where you dumping me?"

"Orders haven't been what you might call specific on that front. Just wherever suits. Would you happen to have the title and registration in the dash? Car'll make a nice payment."

"If you can get the blood out."

"How hard can it be?"

Tyler looked down at his feet. "This is funny."

"What's that?"

Tyler drew his spare piece from the door compartment. The trooper didn't even see it coming, three rounds at close range. Gut. Chest. Neck. Tyler grabbed the Glock from the trooper's hand, then sat there, ears ringing, watching as the guy's eyes went out.

Okay.

New plan needed.

THIRTY-SIX

Closing in on Phoenix now, going by the Buckeye airport, Medina couldn't allow herself to relax. She'd noticed the same state trooper car twice. Once, they'd passed it about two miles after Quartzsite, heading the other way, then again it had come up close behind them twenty minutes later and been happy to sit there, at the same speed. There was a town car, too, hanging back, been there for the past thirty minutes.

There was no way she planned to die in this car.

"I saw this film once," Scott said. "Clint Eastwood. He's a cop, taking a witness from Vegas to Arizona so she can testify against other crooked cops."

"Gauntlet." It was one of the movies Medina watched with her dad. "Sandra Locke is the woman, she's a sex worker, got some dangerous information."

"Right."

"I remember a scene, Eastwood finds out bookies are taking bets on whether he can get her there alive, it's up at something like seventy to one. And Eastwood's meant to be this really broken down, alcoholic cop. Except he looked too good, like he'd just walked off a photoshoot."

"His friend in it, the guy who played his partner, was in the Batman movies..."

"Pat Hingle."

"Right, Hingle. He should have been Eastwood's character."

"Perfect," Medina nodded. "Yeah. The last guy you'd think of, the perfect guy for the part. That's the thing with any of those roles, it should be the out of shape guy, or the one you'd least expect, but they always cast the leading man."

"They get on a motorbike, without helmets, and they're chased across the desert by the mob, or the cops, or both. And the bad guys are in a helicopter, with machine guns, and they're shooting at Clint and, what was her name?"

"Sandra Locke."

"Locke. Right. They're shooting at them, and keep missing. Then Eastwood steals a bus, a big Greyhound one, and they drive that straight into Phoenix. The whole police department lines up to shoot the bus."

"Only realistic part of the movie," Medina said. "People saw a bus in Phoenix and tried to shoot it."

Scott turned to her, smiling, "Hey, I'm the one does the jokes."

"Please, ma'am, continue."

Medina was feeling good. She couldn't describe it. The same, but different. She'd changed, but stayed the same. A better version, now with added jokes.

"Main thing I remember," Scott continued, "is that whole scene with the bus. Eastwood and Locke crouched down, hiding behind a metal plate or something as they drive it down the street, right through the city. And there must be over a thousand guns in that scene. Pistols, rifles, machine guns. Everyone shooting the bus. And all I could think, the whole time, is why is nobody shooting the tires?"

"Turns into a fantasy."

"Yeah. Well, I can't imagine why I'm thinking about this film now."

"No idea." Medina checked the cars in the mirror again. "Sounds like you're trying to write a new joke."

"That would be too niche for a club set. But I guess…I am starting to think that way again, looking for the ridiculous things in every situation, write new jokes."

"A whole new set?"

"Maybe." Scott paused, checking her own side mirror. "You noticed the trooper?"

"I wasn't going to mention it."

Behind them, the trooper picked up a little speed to come in closer behind them, dropping into the same lane. There was a turn up ahead that would take them off the freeway. Medina drifted into that lane. Her sunglasses gave her cover to keep checking the trooper's reactions in the rear view without him seeing her eyes. The trooper waited a few hundred yards, then drifted across. Medina waited until the last second then cut back into the previous lane, to stay on the freeway. The trooper didn't react in time and had to take the turn. She was confident he'd be back, but that gave them a few minutes.

Up ahead, on the left, huge mountains. Ahead of them, it just looked like flat desert.

"This bit is crazy," Scott said, pointing ahead. "There's a city, right there, but we can't see it. Looks like there's nothing. Then, couple more miles, boom, city."

Medina's phone buzzed on the dash. It was Reed Palmer. She told Scott to put it on speaker and then called out, "Hey Boss."

His voice sounded more distant on this setting. "Nice trick."

"The trooper?"

"That town car back there, one of my guys, following you in."

"Any sign of Tyler?"

"Traced his cell, found an empty trooper's car and maybe some blood by the side of the road, we haven't tested it. We found his cell a few feet away, so I guess he figured that part out."

"What's the plan?"

"I'm at the courthouse, ours, not the Maricopa."

"401 West Washington."

"Right. Cleared out everyone I don't trust. We got the DA, a clerk, the judge, right here in the office keeping together. And I got five guys out front, the ones I said were coming in from out of state."

"The way ahead of me clear?"

"Why I called. We got word there's a gathering of deputies, Sheriff's Department, not ours, in a parking lot up by the Denny's at Goodyear. Like they're tailgating, having a party. We can roll out and meet you, give you cover, but you'll need to slow down for that, be on them any minute."

"Don't worry about us," Medina said, mostly meaning it. "Just get ready at your end, we're on our way in."

"Chloe, you sure?"

"Yeah, trust me." She nodded for Scott to hang up, then nodded a second time. "Send the text, say Goodyear, too."

Scott slipped through to the messenger, added the new information, and pressed send. This was where Chloe's long shot needed to come in. Behind them, the town car pulled up close enough for the driver to nod a greeting, letting them know he was there.

Chloe thought about the route ahead. The Denny's was two exits further on. She signalled to take the next exit, looking in the mirror to make sure their escort had noticed, then headed down the off-ramp and turned south down North Bullard Avenue. She took a left onto Van Buren, and immediately realized her mistake. This route took them past the Goodyear courthouse. Two Sheriff's Department cars were parked out front, and both of them pulled out to follow her. She saw the town car had dropped back, putting enough distance between them to not be obvious. The deputies were between them. She eased down on the accelerator. Not speeding, but hanging around. At the next junction, which would connect to the Denny's exit, she headed straight over with no sign of any further surprises. It was two streets further on, near the next freeway exit, that they saw the line of cars. Troopers and Sheriff's Department, blocking the way.

Medina pulled the Civic to a stop, leaving the engine running. The two deputies that had been tailing them since the courthouse stopped a hundred yards back, one in each lane, blocking their retreat. The town car pulled round in the road, to be side on.

Up ahead, a deputy walked out in front of the roadblock, and called out something Medina couldn't make out, but was going to be some variation on surrender or come out with your hands up. Other deputies were leaning on the hoods of their cars, pointing guns this way.

"Here we go," Scott said, her voice full of nerves that she was failing to hide. "Am I Thelma, or Louise?"

Medina turned to him, flashed a calm smile. "As long as they don't think to shoot the wheels, we'll be fine."

The lead deputy took a couple steps forward, resting his hand on the holster at his side. In the mirror, Medina saw the two tailing deputies starting to pace forwards, guns drawn. On instinct she touched the Kimber strapped to her side, but had no intentions of pulling it.

She saw the lead deputy and paused mid-stride and look up. His motion coming before the sound, as a chopper moved in overhead. A van pulled in behind the town car, with a news media logo painted on the side. A woman got out the passenger seat and opened the back, letting a camera man get down out the back. The chopper had a different logo, another channel.

Perfect, the long shot had worked.

"You were right," Scott said.

"Never in doubt."

She switched on the radio, already tuned to a local station, and heard, "...where a retired US Marshal is said to be trying to bring in a witness who will testify against Sheriff Jed Bashford, we're seeing reports from reporters at the scene that the sheriff's deputies have formed a blockade to stop the...."

Up ahead, the lead deputy had walked back to the line of cars, where some kind of conference was taking place, and she could see some of them covering their faces, trying to stay out of the camera's view. After a few more heated exchanges, the deputies all got back in their cars, started the engines and started to move out of the way, forming a line at each side of the road.

Medina eased forward on the pedal, driving along West Van Buren, with the chopper following her overhead. Some of the deputies got out of there, heading off in different directions to get out of the news. A few, probably those most loyal to Jed and Big Wheel, followed on along behind, forming a procession. In the passenger seat, Scott was counting off the avenue numbers as they went by, the numbers getting lower as they closed in on their destination.

They passed by houses and small businesses, then into the built-up part of the city, the buildings rising up around them. Medina turned right at Seventh Avenue, seeing another small gathering of deputies waiting at the corner, probably the last line of defence for the original plan. Down to West Jefferson and then left, she headed down one block.

"You're going round the front?"

She nodded. "Always."

Left, and left again. She pulled the car to a stop in front of the large, modern courthouse, reflecting the white light from the early afternoon sun. The chopper was still overhead. Two news teams were waiting in front of the court, and the trucks that had followed them were pulling in around the Honda.

Medina said to Scott, "Glasses and hat."

Scott bent down into the footwell in front of her, pulling out a cheap pair of sunglasses and a baseball cap they'd bought from a gas station before leaving Long Beach. Not much of a disguise, but enough that her face wouldn't be plastered all over the news, giving her more of a chance of a normal life in whatever town WITSEC dumped her.

Four people, three men and two women, in suitably bland suits, walked towards the car from the courthouse. Medina would recognize marshals anywhere. Reed Palmer pushed through them to lead the way, brushing off questions from the media.

It was the first time Medina had seen Reed in close to a year. He still had his height, and his broad shoulders, but his belly was starting to sag forwards, giving him the look of being dragged forwards by his belt. He walked like John Wayne now, looking to be carrying age in his knees.

Chloe nodded to Scott and moved to open her door.

"Wait." Scott put a hand out.

They stared at each other for a moment, leaving things unsaid, before both smiling and getting out of the Honda.

Palmer's team surrounded Scott, forming a barrier between her and the news cameras that were now pushing in close, looking to get more material for the story. The team walked Scott towards the courthouse. Palmer waited, letting his team move off, taking the news cameras with them.

He touched Medina's arm affectionately and leaned in to talk beside her ear. "In the news again, huh?"

"The cameras love me."

He walked away, laughing.

Medina looked up the street. The few remaining deputies had formed a line, coming the wrong way down Washington Street. She recognized the one who had been walking towards them back at the roadblock. They didn't seem to care about being on camera. She stepped out into the road, knowing the cameras would be on her, enjoying the feeling as she marched out into the middle and turned to face the deputies, letting them see her hand down at her side, the gun on her hip.

They reversed up, turned, and headed away up Washington Street. Reporters closed in around Medina, shouting questions, jostling for place. She nodded at them, smiled, and headed up to the courthouse.

••

The whole thing took four hours. Medina sat on the sofa in Reed's office, watching as people came and went, scuttling between the conference room and whatever else they needed to do, or walked around outside making hushed phone calls. The energy in the building was weird. Frenetic at first, then tense. There was a break halfway through, and Reed brought her some fried chicken and a Coke, talked her through what had happened so far, then they all went back in.

Finally she heard movement. Bustle. All the chairs moving at once. Armed men came in from the elevator, and then she saw them come back out of the meeting room on either side of Emily Scott. They walked her over to the elevator, stepped inside, and pressed the button.

Medina stood up to watch Scott go. Their eyes met before the door slid shut, and she smiled.

Reed came in carrying two coffees, handing one to Medina.

"Got bourbon in my draw," he said. "Sure I can't get you to start drinking?"

She almost said yes.

"All done." Reed settled into his chair, rocked a couple times looking up at family pictures on his wall. "Emi's already being processed into WITSEC." He paused, looking at Medina, either waiting for a response or giving her time to think, then added. "She really stood up."

"You thought about going for the joke there, didn't you?"

He held up his thumb and forefinger, a couple inches apart. "Came that close."

Medina's phone buzzed. She looked at the screen. It was Eddie Wray. This would be a conversation best not carried out in front of Reed. She pressed to answer and said, "hold on" motioned at Reed to say she needed to take it, and headed out into the hall.

"You get your car back?"

"Question is," Treat Tyler replied, "Will you get yours?"

THIRTY-SEVEN

Several hours after leaving Tucson, with a few diversions taken along the way to root out any tails, Drey and Bobelu turned onto Cedar Street and came to a stop outside Drey's home.

Drey and Bobelu looked at each other. Bobelu nodded, and Drey mumbled a thank you. She got out of the car, and tried to close the door quietly, but by the time she turned round she could already see her mom waiting for her in the driveway.

Drey Bowekaty walked over to hug her mom, with a bag full of money.

THIRTY-EIGHT

It was full dark by the time Medina pulled up outside Eddie's Safari in the Honda. A handful of cars out front, music coming from inside. The drive over had been an odd one. It was almost like trying to remember a dream. Medina was aware she'd been thinking about things on the way here, but couldn't remember what any of them were. She couldn't see Tyler's Dodge, or her Shelby.

She paused to touch the gun strapped to her hip, then took the steps up to the front door. Her first thought after stepping inside was that the place hadn't changed at all since the last time she was here. Her second thought was that of course it hadn't, the last time was only two nights ago. Less than that, really. It felt longer.

There were half a dozen people in there, drinking and talking, split into three groups. Eddie was sitting on a stool at the bar, watching her. Tyler was sat next to him. He nodded when their eyes met. She headed over to them, slowly, thinking, how does he want to play this? Have it out right here?

Tyler was sitting on the same stool Ben Nichol had been using, back when this all started and she'd walked in to arrest a wanted counterfeiter. Now she was back, looking at the same spot, summoned to play a game with a crooked marshal.

Tyler's shoulder moved, his arm coming off the bar, and she could see he was holding a Glock. It had been pressed to Eddie's back, but out of sight from anyone else. He straightened his legs and stood up, prodding Eddie to do the same. He whispered something to Eddie that Medina didn't catch, then nodded towards the private door at the back. Eddie went first, walking on ahead. Medina didn't move until he pointed the gun at her, trying to force the issue and let everyone else see the weapon, but nobody looked up. When he gestured with the Glock a second time, she walked after Eddie. Tyler fell into step behind her.

They walked down the narrow private hallway, past the door to Eddie's office, and then out through a rear exit, down some metal steps onto a large concrete yard, a bungalow on one side, a trailer on the other, and both the Dodge and the Shelby in the middle, with a beautiful moonlit butte in the distance behind them.

There was something off about the Dodge. The passenger-side window, which was closest to them, was cloudy, covered with something. It looked like someone was slumped inside, and Medina realized what she was seeing was blood. She walked over to the Shelby, ran her hand across the hood. It was still damaged, she hadn't been away long enough for Eddie's guy to fix it. She looked along the body, to the two bullet holes near the gas tank.

"She really is something, isn't she?" Tyler was talking too loud. She'd noticed that on the phone. Like his ears were ringing or something. "I look forward to driving her."

Medina turned to face him. There was a good distance between them. She could almost hear a film director shouting action, the scene starting. Eddie was backing away slowly, off to the side, towards the bungalow. He shared a look with Medina and mouthed that he was sorry.

He grinned. It was more of a leer. "Good to see you're still catching bad guys."

Medina didn't reply, not caring about the game anymore.

With a touch of disappointment in his voice, Tyler filled the silence. "I heard what you did, on the news. Neat idea. Really went old school, huh? Get the cameras on you, get your name right in the middle of the story again. You think any of this will do anything?"

Medina shrugged. "It was the right thing."

She was aware of herself. Watching the scene play out, almost out of body. She was aware of how calm she felt. Almost cold blooded. Sure of what came next.

Tyler snorted. "Bullshit. That's all it is. All of it. You know what? All you done, you signed that comedians death warrant. Wherever she goes, Red'll find her. And Red? You think this will stop him? He's got lawyers charge more per hour than the government, they'll tie you all up in tape, and he'll walk away, and then what? You already know. The media will forget. The people won't care. Six months down the line, someone walks up behind you in the street, or follows you into the ladies room at a public place, puts a bullet in you, walks away. Everyone will know who ordered it, and nobody will do a damn thing about it."

"That what he's got planned for you?" Medina smiled, tilted her head. "That why you're unravelling like this?"

"Unravelling?" Tyler's voice rose. "You think that's what this is? Bitch, this is my win. You always known it was coming to this, one way or another. Face to face. I put a couple bullets in you, I take your Shelby as payment for my troubles, plus whatever the old man here has in his safe, then I'm away."

"You really want to do this?"

"You know it."

"This can go another way."

"You want to go into your whole story. How does it go, you warned that bank robber three times, wanted it to go another way. What's the line you use on people, there was three of them and you won, and whatever I'm thinking, I can't beat that math?"

Medina didn't reply. She breathed in and out. She watched herself.

The moon slipped behind a cloud. Everything around her became shadows, dark shapes and distant desert noises. She saw the shape that had been Tyler move slightly, shift his stance, squaring his shoulders. When the moonlight came back, she saw he was ready, arms out at his side, right hand hovering a few inches from his holster. Media planted her feet, put her hands down at her side, and breathed.

Tyler was fast.

His hand was on the gun before Medina's eyes even registered the tell-tale shoulder movement. He had the Glock up out of the holster, bringing it up ready to go, when Medina's two shots hit him in the chest. She saw surprise in his face for a few seconds before he fell backwards onto the hard concrete.

Medina walked over and kicked the gun away from his limp hand. Kneeling down, she took his hand in hers and squeezed it. He looked up at her, his mouth tried to form a word, but nothing was quite working right.

"At least you got your boots on," Medina said.

The moon slipped behind another cloud. This time, when the light came back, Treat Tyler was dead.

Medina straightened up.

Eddie came running over. He was muttering something that sounded like, *oh my god, oh my god, oh my god.*

Medina said, "You okay?"

"Am I okay? You...he..." He paused, waved his arms around. "Who's gonna clean this up?"

"I imagine that will be you."

He took half a step back, putting a hand on his chest, trying to look affronted.

Medina shook her head, cutting off his protests. "You got balls of steel, Eddie. And you're willing to let people think you're the idiot in all this. That's clever."

"What?"

"I didn't figure out until just now. Seeing Tyler sitting in the same spot as Ben Nichol. Nichol the counterfeiter."

"He is?"

"Let's say, sake of argument, a guy's been given a bad deal, found himself in a debt he can't pay, his bar's been stolen by the mob, used as a drop box for dirty money. He contacts a counterfeiter, someone on the run, maybe has a reason to need a place to lay low. He says, the bar owner, he says, you help me, I help you."

"I'm sure that's not-"

"They make a deal. See, the bar owner, he has two million in dark money sitting in a safe, ready to be picked up by his bosses. But are they going to check it? Would they know the difference between the real stuff and the counterfeit? How hard would it be to swap them over?"

Eddie stared at her, not saying a word.

She continued. "Perfect plan. And two million would be enough for all kinds of things. Maybe this guy wants to get his racino dream back on track, or maybe he has a whole new dream. And he's going to get away with it, because he's let everyone think he's the fool, let everyone talk down to him, crap on him. But then," she smiled, "his idiot nephew messes everything up, steals the counterfeit money after his uncle had swapped it over, so now all the attention is back on the cash."

"I don't think you could prove any of that."

"Eddie, I don't think I want to. But don't treat me like an idiot, okay?" She turned to look at Tyler one last time, then back at Eddie. "Pay me my share. In real money. Get rid of the bodies and the Dodge. And you still owe me the repair on my Shelby, then we're even." He smiled, started to say okay, but she raised her hand. One more thing. "Fix the bullet holes, too."

THIRTY-NINE

Treat Tyler hadn't been wrong, as far as that went. Chloe Medina was news for two days; the court case was news for a week. In that time, Sheriff Jed Bashford disappeared, and his entire staff was suspended without pay by Maricopa County. The name Redmond Peters barely came up at all. He got passing mentions when the story first broke, but who really cared about some broken down old nut farmer when there was a corrupt sheriff to talk about?

There was no talk of plans to divert a river. Nothing to suggest that was either progressing or being stopped. Details like that just weren't sexy enough.

The DA's office went with the most provable case. They already had a large file on Jed Bashford and the testimony, plus further information they got after leaning on a bunch of his deputies, gave them all they needed. They would prosecute with extreme force if they ever found him.

Medina doubted they would.

Either he'd planned ahead and gotten out of dodge, crossed the border into Mexico or used mob connections to set up a new life somewhere north, or Red Peters got to him and he was on the wrong side of the desert.

Medina gave Lisa Afobe half the money Eddie had given her. The rest was in a box beneath her bed, beside the brick of counterfeit bills Emi had given her in Long Beach. Medina hadn't touched any of it yet. Hadn't admitted to herself that she was going to. But she did find herself regularly looking up the costs of law school, and college catch-up courses, doing the sums in her head of how close that box of cash could get her to a whole new version of herself.

It felt good.

And she didn't even pretend not to have dreamed about the new sign she could make for herself and her brother, setting up their own law practice.

Eddie delivered the Shelby two weeks after the incident at the Safari, all clean, all fixed. Medina took her out for a long run, getting up into top speed and enjoying herself. She drove all the way out to that diner in Long Beach, had a coffee and a pie, then turned round and came back.

Shot got a news alert on her phone as she reached the outskirts of Phoenix on the way back in. Red Peters had been found dead. Shot. She pulled over to read more. The headline said it was a gangland style murder. But the story itself mentioned he'd been shot in the face. Whoever had done it, they'd wanted it to be face to face, not in the back of the head, which was the usual execution.

Back in her apartment, she put the television on and started scrolling through the streaming services for something dumb to watch, maybe fall asleep to. Her phone buzzed again. This time it was a text message from Reed Palmer, asking if she wanted to meet for a drink.

··

They met at Carly's Bistro on East Roosevelt. The place looked too hip for someone like Reed Palmer. A bar serving toasted sandwiches, with local art for sale on the walls. But it was far enough away from the courthouse, the jail, and the police station.

There weren't any good dive bars near those buildings anyway. It was some great cruel joke of the universe, put the courthouse, the police, the jail and half a dozen security firms, all within two blocks of each other, in a part of town that was all warehouses and office buildings. No good bars, no quiet spots to go and talk.

Reed was already there when Medina walked in. Settled at a dark brown lacquered table in the corner, by the men's room. He had a beer in front of him, with a few inches taken off the top, and a glass of Coke set in front of a vacant chair for Medina.

He looked up and smiled as Medina approached, pointed at the vacant seat.

"Hey Boss."

He smiled slowly. "Chloe."

There was something to his expression, she couldn't place it straight away.

He said, "How're you doing?"

"I got a couple other bondsmen trying to offer me gigs, I think they want the chick on the TV working for them."

"You thinking about it?"

"I'm thinking my options over. I like the idea of law school. A whole new start."

"You'd be a great lawyer."

Medina nodded while sipping the drink. "How about you?"

Reed leaned back. "Been thinking about a lot of things, you know? Watching you leave. I never got why, until this all happened, then I got all of it."

He sighed, leaned over to the side and pulled out a Marshal's Service badge, tossed it on the table between them. Medina opened her mouth to say she didn't want it, but then realised it was his.

He continued. "It's been eating at me, didn't sit right. So I did something about it."

Getting to it now. Saying the thing without saying the thing.

Medina waited a beat. "How you feeling about it?"

He met her eyes. "Pretty good."

Medina could read that emotion she'd seen in his face now. Relief. He'd taken a weight off his shoulders. "If you think you did the right thing, then I guess you did."

"That simple?"

"That simple." She nodded at the shield. "And that?"

He didn't answer straight away, and when he did, he dodged the question. "We've about stopped looking for Treat. It's causing some problems. We called his wife, you remember Jasmine?"

"She was nice."

"Yeah. Turns out she hasn't spoken to him in over a year, cut off contact completely when he missed two of his son's birthdays in a row. So he's not out there. The DA wants to talk to him, and I've gone on record with what I know. But until he turns up..." He met her eyes again. "He's not going to, is he?"

Saying the other thing without saying it.

"No."

"Waste of a good car."

Medina smiled. She thought about the Dodge, now the proud possession of Eddie Wray. Last she'd heard, the blood had cleaned out quite nicely, but Eddie still kept seeing the dead guy out the corner of his eye when he drove it.

"And that's the way you're looking at it?" Reed said, sounding lost in thought. "If you think you did the right thing, you did."

"I figure we should live to three rules."

"Go on."

"Find a thing you love doing. That's the first one. Put in the work to get good at it, that's the second. The third is the hard part. Start taking your meaning from doing the thing, not from what you hope to get at the end of doing it."

Reed laughed. "You're a walking fortune cookie."

"Live in the moment, Grasshopper, and be who you are."

Reed reached out, tapped his finger on the badge. "This is who I am."

"It's always suited you."

He pulled it back across the table towards him, leaned to the side, and clipped it back on his belt. They sat in silence for a moment, letting the sounds of other people's half-heard conversations fill the space between them.

"Treat's causing me one other problem," Reed said after a while. "Staffing. I've finally convinced them to send me a replacement, told them Treat's AWOL and we should consider he's quit. Under the circumstances, I think that's the least we should consider him. But there's paperwork, due process. We can't sack him for what we know, because we haven't given him a chance to be investigated, go through a disciplinary process. HR are scared he could turn up, come back to work like nothing happened, then sue us for unfair dismissal when we don't let him in. Or he comes in, says he was having a mental health thing and we didn't support him. So he's officially suspended on full pay until the people in HR can make a decision, and that pay is still coming out of my office budget. But they've agreed to send me two new recruits, and we're going to move the budget around a little, figure out a way."

"He's still being an asshole, even now."

"Yeah. One of the new kids reminds me of you."

"Don't let her give you any shit."

He squinted, leaned forward. "Just the right amount."

Draining the beer he said, "Thanks for coming out."

"Any time, Boss."

He chuckled, looking and sounding like an old man now. "I still can't get anyone else to call me that." He pulled an envelope out from his jacket. "This came to the office. Envelope's addressed to me, but I think you'd want to see what's inside."

He stood up and put his hand on her shoulder affectionally before walking on out.

Medina looked at the envelope. Reed's name, and the office address at the court. She turned it over, seeing the flap where Reed had messily torn it open. She reached in and pulled out a postcard.

It had a picture of a lake, under red print advertising Champaign Illinois.

She flipped it over. The address part on the right said, 'Chloe Medina, Arizona.'

On the right was a small, neat, handwritten message. There was the address of a bar and grill on West Church Street. Along with the line, *It might not be Minnesota, but they have an open mic every Tuesday. I think you'd like it.*

Medina smiled and read the message a couple more times.

BONUS CONTENT

Chloe Medina was first mentioned in print in the following story, Half Inch, part of the 2019 anthology Trouble & Strife from Down & Out Books.

HALF INCH

How would you do it?" Megan said, letting him see the smile.

Jimmy Finch met her eyes, "This place?"

She bent down and sucked iced latte up through the straw, "Uh huh."

Jimmy took a look around the diner, pretending like he hadn't already done it.

The diner was wide, split into two sections, with the kitchen through a hatch at the back, behind the counter. The cash register was in the center of the room, on a wooden stand, like a lectern. There were eight customers, including Jimmy and Megan. Three couples, and two people on their own.

Nobody was reading a newspaper. That was the biggest change from when Jimmy started out. There would always be a couple people reading newspapers. Now it's all cell phones. Everyone has a camera, and a way to call the cops.

Well, there's only two servers working. One for that side, one for this side. They keep meeting in the middle, at the register, to talk. They've looked over our way a bunch of times, so they think we're on a date."

Really?" Megan turned now to look at them, seeing them standing together. Her voice rose, just a little. "That's what they think?"

Sure. Young attractive woman like you, flirting with an older guy like me."

I'm not flirting."

The problem here is, their attention is already on us. I mean, they've been aware of us since we came in, they've talked about us a bunch. If I was to try anything in here, they'd notice me sooner than anyone else, more likely to stop it. Plus, they'd remember me to the cops, describe me, you. We'd get caught too easy."

Okay," Megan's tone was colder now, the playfulness gone. Obviously, I don't mean how would you do it right now, in this meeting. But if this was one of your jobs, you walk in for the first time, how would you do it?"

Jimmy leaned back in his seat, looked Megan up and down. This Hollywood producer with an option out on his story. No, not producer. He couldn't remember what. She'd told him her job title a bunch of times, and it had the word producer in it, but he wasn't sure she had any actual responsibility.

You're looking for the ending to the movie."

Megan leaned forward, Of course I am, we got nothing right now."

Jimmy put his hand on the manuscript between them, his autobiography, Pinch: The Story of the Joke bandit. Optioned before publication. I robbed 237 places. At least one in every state. All but one of them unarmed, walking out with money without ever pointing a gun. Only served time for one of them, you can't find a story?"

It's not the story that's the problem, it's the ending. Every writer we get on this tanks, tells us the same thing, there's no ending. Your book gives us you, but that's not enough. We know your past, we know the jobs you did, we know the prison stuff, but then you get out and...what? Where do we roll credits?"

You want me to pull another job."

It would give us an ending."

But I've gone straight, so you're stuck."

Maybe you don't need to actually do the job, maybe you're just thinking about it. That could be the scene. Yeah, I can see it." She shuffled into the middle of the booth, directly across from him, putting her hands up on either side of her face, making an imaginary camera lens. You're in a diner, like this one, or a different one. We make it look just typical of all the places you robbed earlier in the film."

This place is pretty typical."

Right, so you're sitting here, and we've had the build-up of you going straight. How you've come out of prison a changed man, but we also show that you're tempted, that you can't just switch off who you are. Then someone says to you, how would you do it?"

Who?"

In the scene? I don't know. Doesn't matter yet, we'll think of somebody."

So it could be in the middle of a date?"

We are not on a date."

No, but in the movie."

So this person, okay, let's say it's a date. Maybe, what's the name of that woman on your last job, the one made you carry the gun?"

Lisa."

So, maybe it's Lisa."

She's dead."

Sure, but she doesn't need to be. Not for the story. It could be the two of you talking. That's how we frame it. That's how we frame the whole thing, we start on this scene, the two of you meeting up after years apart, start talking, then we flash back into your life, and we show that Lisa's always been the temptation, right? Then at the end, we cut back to this scene, and maybe she doesn't say how would you do it, maybe it's more like she says, so, are you ready? Then we close in on your face, like this." She moves her hands in closer. Let the audience see you thinking about it, just long enough, then cut to black."

That's your idea for the ending?"

I think it could be pretty cool, arty like, you know? People love that."

They don't actually see me doing the job, though?"

Don't need to. They know you're going to. Or maybe some think you don't. They can decide for themselves, like that spinning top thing in the dream movie."

I hated that."

Point is, we've given them an ending to the story."

Why can't this be the ending? Just sitting here talking, on a date."

We're not-"

Or the real ending. You've got the book. Can't we just end where the book does?"

You walking out of prison? Terrible ending. What's the structure there? What's the punch? What are we asking the audience to take away?"

I'm not asking them to take anything away, that's the truth of it, that's where my story ends."

Unless..." Megan was back into pitch mode again. Unless we see you walking out, you've just had some exchange with the warden where he says, see you soon and you say no, you're done, you're going straight. Then we see you walk out, right, and.....we hear a car coming....and then we see Lisa pull up in front of you. She smiles, just smiles, but we know what it means, and then we see you smile, fade to black. Or better, cut to black. Instant."

Feels a bit too much like a crime movie."

We're making a crime movie."

They're always fake. You're just making the same thing over and over. If that's all you wanted to do, why not just go do that, you didn't need my book."

No, we wanted your book, we wanted you, your story. That's what the viewer wants, too. Real life, you know?

But you want to change it."

Movies have certain rules, like a language, a different language. We need to hit certain beats, because that's what people expect."

Like this thing you've got for Lisa. 'She represents the temptation'." Jimmy made air quotes. Like I need temptation. Or the last writer you hooked me up with, said he wanted to get to the heart of my story, and I said, well, here's the book. And he goes, no, I want to know why you did it, why you decided to rob those places."

Megan looked down at her notes on the table, and Jimmy guessed that was the next item on the agenda.

You need to make some big scene in the movie about me being tempted, or something that makes me commit the crime, you want me to rationalise it. You want to know why I robbed places?"

Megan's face lit up.   Yeah."

Because I'm a criminal, and good at it. Lisa didn't tempt me into anything. It was a job. She knew I didn't use guns, but offered me more money, and I said yes. That's not temptation, it's a job offer."

So money was the temptation."

Is money the temptation for what you do? We need to try and figure out the deep motivation for why you're in this job."

I love working on movies."

There you go. We both like what we do."

What you did. Now that you're straight. What are you planning to do? Maybe we can work that into the movie, like a redemption arc?"

Jimmy wasn't paying attention. He was busy watching a new customer. Small and wiry, wearing an army castoff jacket. One of those German ones with the flag still on the sleeve. He'd been seated over this side, a few booths over. Jimmy had watched as the guy scoped the place out, the same way he did.

••

This guy was *impossible.*

Megan Quinn wanted to call her boss, just say,   We can't do this, let's make a different movie." But she couldn't. You didn't get to run your own movie that way. She figured, get good information from Jimmy Finch, get good story, and she could make this into her ticket.

But now he wasn't even paying attention.

 Hello?"

Jimmy's eyes shifted back to her. He didn't apologise.

Megan was like, really?

So rude. So sure of himself. Just sitting there, not interested in explaining himself, not interested in telling his story. Who Does that? Who doesn't want to talk about themselves?

Megan looked down at her notes. The list of issues given to her by the writer and studio. All the things they needed to fix to make the book into a film. A couple of the notes had come from the publisher, too. Over a coffee the day before, his editor has said,   hey, we're having the same issues, maybe if you can get him to talk, we can change the book."

340 pages, and nowhere did he explain himself, nowhere did he give any kind of justification. And that ending? What

was that? The guy just walks out of prison and smells fresh air and that's it?

Okay," Megan said, swirling the straw around in her now-empty glass. Lets' talk about the jokes."

You want to hear them?"

No, I've read the book."

They're not all in there, I got a bunch you won't have heard."

Jimmy, I don't want to hear the jokes, I want to know why you told them."

Jimmy cocks his head, like he's never heard that question before. He looks like a confused puppy for a second. This guy in his late fifties, gray hair. In good shape for his age, but nowhere near as much as his self-confidence suggested.

Who doesn't want to hear jokes?"

This was good, this was her way in. I would think, people being robbed don't want to hear jokes. Cashier's don't want to hear them. Server's don't want to hear them."

Again with his confused look. Megan could tell now he was doing it for show. They're the exact people who need them. You got to put people at ease if you're robbing them, make them relax, let them know things are okay, they don't need to do anything rash."

Megan looked down at her notes, why not guns?

Okay, but tell me how that started? I mean, most people would just use a gun. You walk into places, up the register, and start telling a joke. Why not just point a gun, or pretend you're pointing a gun?"

I don't like guns."

Megan felt the frustration rise again, her voice rising. There has to be more to it."

Why? Why you need more than that, I don't like guns, so I don't use them. I like jokes, so I tell them. You walk in, you spot the person most amenable, and you start talking to them, engage with them. Nice and friendly. You're telling them a joke, and while you do it, you hand them the sign that says, this is a robbery, give me all the money in the drawer.' You're still telling them the joke, so they're off balance, their brains going in two different ways. But everybody likes jokes, so they're still relaxed, deep down."

You said find the person most amenable, how do you know?"

It's just a sense, you have it or you don't."

Jimmy's eyes drift again. He keeps looking at something over her shoulder.

Megan isn't used to this kind of behaviour. In these meetings, everyone wants to focus on her, to answer her, to work with her and be important.

Maybe the jokes are the way? Maybe it's in his childhood? He skips over that in the book.

Okay, so let's talk about the jokes then, you like them so much. When did that start? Was it maybe a defence mechanism at school? We could frame it that way, show you using humor to get out of trouble, as a kid, you know?"

Jimmy rolled his eyes, looked at her again. You want to make a crime movie, but you don't want to make a movie about criminals."

But at school..."

I tell jokes because I like them. Because I loved watching Johnny Carson, and I figured being him was the best thing in the world."

Why not try being a comedian?"

I wanted to make money."

Megan made a couple notes on the page. That was a good line. It wasn't much, this angle, but maybe they could use it. Show him as a frustrated comic, build up that way. She could see it, now she was thinking it. Early scenes, watching Carson. Maybe a flashback.

Yeah, it could work.

She looked at the next question.

So, this Marshal who arrested you..."

Jimmy's eyes opened up, Deputy US Marshal Chloe Medina."

Was that a smile? It was.

His focus was full on her now.

Megan tapped the notes, bingo. Yeah. Tell me about her."

She didn't shoot me." He paused, leaned back in the seat. I mean, she could've shot me. She shot Lisa. But she didn't shoot me."

Why do you think that was?"

You should ask her."

We've tried, Megan thought. They'd tried to do a deal with Medina already, use her name, put her in the story. She refused both, they were going to have to change the name if they used the scene in the film. Someone else who didn't want to be in a movie. What was wrong with the world?

Tell me what happened."

Jimmy shrugged. Not much too it. We've gone in the bank. I hated doing banks, but Lisa had this idea. And she's got me packing, and I hated packing. But it's all working, this trick she had, knew the exact time the manager was opening this small safe they had behind the desk, like a drop box they put money before taking it all out the back? Lisa knew the exact time of day they opened it, and we'd got bags full of cash. We come out, and there's this Marshal standing there on the steps, just watching us."

You knew what she was?"

Well, you could tell she was something. Some kind of law."

And she pulls a gun?"

She's got her hand on the gun. On her hip. Which, by the way? Hottest thing I've ever seen. I mean, I don't like guns, but she made it work. And she identifies herself, says Deputy US Marshal Chloe Medina, don't do anything stupid. But then Lisa does something stupid."

She tries to shoot her."

Well, I guess. Her hand twitched. Lisa's gun was down at her side, we'd both lowered them as we came out the bank, thinking we didn't need them. Lisa's hand twitched. Not even an inch, really, and Chloe shot her. She drew so fast."

Chloe.

Megan was right. Jimmy had a thing for this Marshal.

Then she looks at me, just looks at me, cocks an eyebrow, and I drop the gun. So yeah, she could've shot me, and she didn't."

The one time you got caught."

The one time."

Love story between a criminal and a Marshal," Megan said, circling Medina's name in the notes. There's a story there."

Jimmy didn't answer. He was gone again, focusing on something behind her.

She turned to look. A small guy in an army surplus jacket was standing at the register, pointing a gun at the two servers. He looked twitchy, nervous.

The gunman called out, Nobody move."

Jimmy leaned forward. That's not how I would do it."

••

The kid in the jacket looked scared. His gun pointing one way, then another.

All the money," he was saying. All of it."

The oldest of the two servers, the middle aged woman with red hair, said, Where you want us to put it?"

He didn't have a bag. Hadn't thought that far ahead.

Jimmy figured the kid hadn't even intended to rob the place. Just came in, maybe for a coffee, maybe to get off the street. But the gun in his pocket had made a stupid decision, and there was no way this ended well.

Jimmy slid out of the booth. He saw Mega turn to him, panicked, mouthing for him to stop. The kid spun halfway round, towards him. Jimmy looked at all the other customers, none of them sure what to do next, nobody having any idea what to do when a gun shows up.

Freeze," the kid's voice going up a level. Stop effing moving."

Effing? Jimmy put his hands out, palms up, and smiled. I got you, I'm staying right here."

Get back," the kid took a few steps towards him.

Jimmy watched the thoughts pass across the servers faces, was this their chance to do something?

What I'm thinking," Jimmy said. Is that everybody should keep still."

I already said that," the kid was whiny now. But somebody didn't listen."

I just want to help, give you some on the job training."

The kid pointed the gun square at Jimmy's face.

I'm Jimmy Finch. You don't know me? Jimmy the Pinch? Nothing?"

Uh..." A shrug. No."

Jimmy took a small step forward. 237 robberies, only caught one time. My date over there," he twitched his head, indicating Megan behind him. Is a Hollywood producer, going to make a movie based on me. So I'm basically an expert at what you're doing."

Okay."

How do you think you're doing right now?"

Uh..." The kid looked at the two servers. They both shrugged. He turned back. Okay?"

I gotta be honest. This is not going well."

A flush of anger welled up in the kids face, but Jimmy read it for what it was, embarrassment. No, man, I'm doing okay."

You're scared, that's okay. You didn't plan on this, did you? Came in for some pancakes, maybe a coffee, a burger. You've had a bad day, right?"

The kid nodded.

Jimmy continued. You know, when I was a kid, I liked two things. Johnny Carson and westerns. I decided, when I grew up, I was going to rob a bank in every state, get famous." Jimmy gambled on another step forward. You know how many banks I've robbed?"

Like, two hundred, something, you said."

The kid turned for approval from the servers, not confident in his answer.

One," Jimmy said. Just one. See, when I looked at it, I figured, there's no real money in robbing a bank. It's too difficult. If you carry a gun, you got more chance of being shot. And there's not as much cash in banks as people think, they got sick of being robbed. What I did, I started hitting places like this. Fast businesses, where people paid in cash, and there was no real security. But you know the problem with that?"

There was real doubt in the kids eyes now, but his finger was still on the trigger, he could pull at any second.

The problem is, everyone is security now. Walk in a place like this, everyone's got a cell phone, everyone's walking around with surveillance devices. You've just pulled an armed robbery, with no mask, and I'm guessing no getaway plan."

The kid looked round at the other customers now, at the phones they had on the tables in front of them.

Jimmy said, What you have here, is a mistake you made. And you can't un-make it. The cops are gonna come, and you're going to do time. But what you can do, is not make an even bigger mistake." Jimmy looked directly at the gun now. You can put that down."

The gun hand wavered. The eyes behind it, young, confused, really wanted permission to lower the weapon. Jimmy could see it. The anger. The pride. The kid needed to relax.

What's your name?"

Uh...Ed."

What's your full name? Come on, we're all friends here."

Foley. Ed Foley."

Ed, you ever hear the one about the three dwarves?"

Ed turned to the servers as if to ask, is he for real?

They both shrugged, don't ask us.

See, there are these three dwarves outside the head office for the Guinness Book of Records. Never met each other before, just turned up at the same time. They're asking each other why they're there. I mean, might be the same thing, right? That would be awkward. So the first dwarf says, I'm here to get tested. I think I have the smallest hands in the world'. And the other two are like, well...okay. Good luck. It's an achievement, I guess? So he goes in. Thirty minutes later, he comes out. All happy. He's in. Number one. Smallest hands in the world. Brilliant. Then the second one says, I'm getting tested too. I think I have the smallest feet in the world.' Okay, they say. Well....good luck. He goes in. Thirty minutes later, he comes out. Jumping around, happy. He's in. Smallest feet in the world. Fantastic. So then they ask the third guy. He pauses, he's nervous. He says, I'm here to get tested. I think I have the smallest....uh....you know." Jimmy made a show of looking down at his crotch. 'I think I have the smallest....thing.' And the others, I mean, they want to be supportive, so they go, great, well good luck. So he goes in. Comes out five minutes later. He's all angry, like really shaking. And he looks at them, and he says Who the fuck is Ed Foley?'"

There was a pause. Just long enough for Jimmy to doubt his play. Then Ed started to laugh. One of those that rumbles up, starting like indigestion sounds in the gut, before fighting up the throat. He shook his head and smiled, then laughed again.

He held the gun out, and Jimmy took it.

Sirens were approaching, still a little way off.

Jimmy turned to look over at Megan. There's your ending."

ABOUT JAY STRINGER

Jay Stringer was born in 1980, and he's not dead yet.

His crime fiction has been nominated for both Anthony and Derringer awards, and shortlisted for the McIlvanney Prize.

His stand-up comedy has been laughed at by at least three people. Jay is English by birth and Scottish by legend; born in the Black Country and claiming Glasgow as his hometown for the last 17 years.

Jay is dyslexic, and came to the written word as a second language, via comic books, music, and comedy. Jay won a gold medal in the Antwerp Olympics of 1920. He did not compete in the Helsinki Olympics of 1952, that was some other guy.

DID YOU LIKE THE COVER DESIGN AND TYPESETTING OF THIS BOOK?

Jay is a freelance artist available for hire to do either or both. Check out

www.jaystringerbooks.com for more details, or email Jay at

jay@jaystringerbooks.com